The Beta's Betrayal

Book three.
The final book in
The Alpha's War Series

S. E Dymek

Warning: book contains scenes of sexual content, violence, adult content, and foul language. Some scenes may be triggers to some and are not appropriate for all ages. Thank you for reading- S.E Dymek

Dedication

To Aaralyn, Ivy, and Caiden. My biggest inspirations for everything I do. To my husband, Aaron, who is my biggest support.

Acknowledgements

I'd like to thank my parents, close family, and all my inner, dearest friends who listened to me babble about ideas and were willing to read them. I love you all. Thank you to all my readers!

About the Author

S.E Dymek is an upcoming author who has published **The Star Saga:** Including The Morning Star, The Evening Star, and The North Star available with Barnes and Noble, Amazon, Kindle, and other book selling sites. She is also published on several ebook platforms. She has a passion for writing romance novels including paranormal romance novels and fantasy. All of her works include twists and turns, keeping her readers on their toes. She is a mother of three and loving wife. When she is not writing; she is working as a veterinary technician. Born and raised in Rhode Island, she has found her second home in Texas.

Chapter One
It begins

*H*er screams echoed down the hall. Matt threw his hands behind his head as he paced. He glanced over to Lilly who was rocking in the chair. He gritted his teeth and knew her thoughts mimicked his.

"She's gonna be ok." Logan said, grabbing the back of Lilly's chair to make her stop rocking.

"She will be fine." Dante said his tone is not as strong as Logan's.

"I can't listen to that anymore. Let me know when she's ok." Lilly said getting up and rushing out of the hospital door.

Matt glanced at Logan confused before following Lilly out. Dante rubbed Sarah's shoulder feeling her need for comfort. They were all waiting and they were all scared.

"Lilly!" Matt called after her.

Lilly stopped short, not saying anything. Her back facing Matt as he felt her overwhelming feeling of fear.

" She's strong, she's going to get through this. She's -

"Matt, I'm pregnant. I don't know if I can do that." Lilly blurted out.

"Really." Matt said trying to mask the happiness in his voice because she was scared.

Lilly nodded her hand going to her stomach. Matt came over and placed his hand on top of hers.

"How far along?" Matt whispered.

"I don't know. Not far. I was late two days ago and took a test."

"I love you." Matt blurted out, then his stomach twisted tightly. They had not said it yet, I love you was such a big confession to Lilly.

Lilly laughed at the worry that flashed across his face. She couldn't help but reach out and touch it, hoping to wipe the worry away.

"I love you too but what if, what if I'm not strong enough." Lilly whispered.

"You are. You are the strongest person I know. We will figure this out." Matt said his hand captured the back of her neck as he leaned his forehead against hers.

"I'm strong but am I strong enough to birth a wolf…look at Nora. Do you hear her pain? She's half wolf." Lilly whispered as another yell came out from the hospital.

"We will figure this out." Matt said, trying not to let fear come through his voice.

He was scared and part of him kind of hoped that the baby would be just a hunter so maybe Lilly would be safe.

"Ahhh!" Nora yelled through gritted teeth as she pushed.

"You're doing great Luna. She's almost here. Few more. Few more, you got this." Abby said, holding her leg.

"It hurts." Nora whispered, wanting to give up.

"I know Luna, but we almost got her. Big push." Abby said as she glanced at Wyatt, she saw the worry in his eyes and she was trying her best to not to show it as well.

Nora clenched her jaw, balling her hands into fists as she pushed as hard as she could. She felt like she was ripping and tearing. She fell back against the bed.

"I can't. She's stuck. Something is wrong." Nora said breathlessly

"Wyatt." Jace said his voice needing answers as he tangled his fingers with Nora.

"I can see her head, Luna. We need one more big push you can do this." Wyatt said, glancing at Jace.

"You save her no matter what." Jace sent Wyatt *through a mind link.*

"I can't sit up. I need to sit up." Nora said, trying to pull herself upwards.

Jace climbs in the bed within seconds. Sitting behind her and bracing her. His hands wrapped around her arms. Nora sat up straighter and leaned into him. Having him close she felt the rush of calmness he always brought her. She took a deep breath in and pushed as hard as she could.

"Here she comes. Keep going Luna." Abby said, encouraging her.

Loud cries erupted into the room as Nora felt the pain subside.

"Baby girl!" Abby announced as Wyatt began cleaning her off.

"Alpha, do you want to cut the cord?" Wyatt asked with a smile on his face.

"It's ok. I'm going to stay right here." Jace said watching Nora carefully, he didn't want to move from her.

"Is she ok?" Nora asked, her voice sounding weak as she leaned further back into Jace.

"Happy, healthy and beautiful." Wyatt said, holding her up to show Nora.

"She's beautiful. My little Mallory." Nora whispered.

"Like her mother." Jace said, kissing the top of Nora's head.

"Luna, do you want to hold her?" Wyatt said, wrapping the little girl in a blanket.

There was silence. Wyatt eyes shot over to Nora and then Jace felt her go completely lifeless.

"Nora!" Jace yelled, scooting back and looking down at her.

Abby ran to the side of bed with a stethoscope. She pressed it into her chest.

"Heart stopped. Alpha, I need to lay her flat." Abby announced.

"Alpha, you need to move and hold your child." Wyatt said quickly.

Wyatt said, grabbing Jace with one arm and tugging him off the bed. Jace's feet hit the floor and his baby was placed in his arms. Abby began compressions as Wyatt ran to get drugs.

"Alpha I'm going to need you to place that oxygen on her face and hold the mask to it." Abby said in huffs as she continued to work Nora's chest.

Jace nodded, grabbing the oxygen mask and placing it over Nora's mouth. Each compression Nora moved up and down in the bed. A loud crack echoed in the room as Nora's ribs broke from how hard Abby was pressing. Jace looked at Abby when the sounds happened. Abby ignored the look and kept going. Wyatt rushed back into the room with bottles of injectable drugs in his arms, one already drawn up.

"Abby pause." Wyatt announced as he placed a long thin needle on the end of the syringe.

"Alpha move, hold the oxygen in place still." Wyatt said coming for Nora's chest as Abby paused compressions.

Jace cradled the baby in one arm close to Nora as he watched Wyatt about to plunge a needle into Nora's chest in hopes to start her heart. The infant in his arms moved towards Nora almost as if reaching for her. As Wyatt drew the needle above his head about to slam it into Nora's chest a light erupted in the room blinding them all, as the infant touched Nora's skin. The light dimmed, Nora jolted up right gasping, knocking Wyatt off of her.

"Nora!" Jace yelled as she looked around bewildered.

"Jace…the baby." Nora asked, panicking.

"She's right here." Jace said, looking down in his arms.

The little bundle of jet black hair and ice blue eyes was glowing slightly still from the light.

"She's ok. She's ok." Jace said looking from the baby to Nora.

"Ok. Ok." Nora said, sitting back in the bed.

"Luna, I need to check your vitals." Abby said, coming to her side quickly.

"Nora you-"

"I know I died again." Nora said quietly.

Jace looked at her confused as if he was wondering how she knew.

"Close calls keep happening." Nora laughed.

"What just happened?" Wyatt asked, getting up off the ground.

"Mallory, she saved me." Nora said, reaching over and taking a hold of the little one's hands.

"Vitals are all normal." Abby said to Wyatt as he watched Mallory reach for her mother.

"Is she like you?" Jace whispered.

"I don't know but I…I am no longer like me. I lost my powers. I don't know if they went into her or if it's because I did fully die this time." Nora said quietly.

"Nora, you do not know that." Jace said, seeing the small glimpse of sadness.

"Jace I can feel it. It's gone but that's ok, look at her. Look at what we have. It's so much more and so much better than powers." Nora said, reaching out to hold the baby.

---

*H*e watched him move. He had no idea that he was there. He had spent his whole life in hiding. Waiting for his moment. He watched the guard shift in his stance. He narrowed his eyes at him. The guard was so relaxed nothing was making him on alert. That had been their whole life. Easy, peaceful…. effortless. He could feel the rage and anger boil in him. He crouched lower to the ground, his body feeling numb as he began making his way towards him. His stomach twisted with excitement and anticipation. His heart pounded in his chest. The man was looking at the sky.

He threw his arm around his mouth covering it. His warm breath rapidly came out of his nose as he crushed his hand to it. His blade ran across his throat, slicing like butter, his skin pulling apart against his blade. Warm blood poured out of the wound, like a waterfall coating his forearm. He held onto the man a moment longer before letting his body collapse into the ground. He stared down at the lifeless body. His jaw clenching, the rush that went through him, made him feel alive. The adrenaline coursing through him made him want to do it again and again. He looked around and no one else was there. Why would there be? They have lived like there were no threats for so long. That was changing now. He grinned, his eyes flashing gray as his wolf pushed forward.

"Well I guess we're starting this now?" A voice came from behind the brush.

"Now's better than never." He growled back.

"It would have been nice to let me know. Heads up maybe?" He shrugged like nothing mattered.

"I am your Alpha, why should I give you a heads up, Ronan." He said looking down at his blade, his hand still tingling.

"Being your Beta maybe? You just declared war? A war they don't even know exists. But what do I know Alpha Knox," Ronan shrugged.

"I haven't declared war yet but it's coming. They should know the big bad wolf is here and it's coming for everything they have." He grinned, kicking the body of the fallen guard.

He watched the body roll down the hill further into Cross River's territory.

"Red Woods will be ours once more and then all the packs." Knox grinned looking out.

"*M*allory Renee Lynn!" Nora screamed rounding the corner of the hall.

"Mallory!" She yelled, becoming frustrated.

The council had gathered and she wanted her daughter to start participating. She was an adult now and needed to start acting like one. Nora clenched her jaw.

"Find her?" Nora mind linked Jace.

"Give her time." Jace linked back, his voice comforting.

"She has less than twenty minutes." Nora said, annoyed.

"Nora..you know why she hates this." Jace sent back his voice patient.

"She shouldn't. She is not weak regardless of how she thinks." Nora said a tinge of hurt in her voice thinking of her daughter.

"She'll be here." Jace sent back quietly.

"Adam." Nora mind linked Dante's oldest son.

"On it Luna. I've got her." Adam sent back a small smile in his voice.

"Thank you." Nora sent, relieved.

---

*H*e watched her trying to be as quiet as possible as he approached her. She was sitting with her back to him. The long grass formed a wall around her. Her long raven colored hair down around her blowing in the wind. Her knees pulled up to her chest as her arms wrapped around them. She was inches from the edge of their territory and her eyes were focused on the woods, as if she was debating a grand escape. He heard her groan to herself as she pressed her forehead to her knees.

He knew the minute she snuck out. The minute she left. He had been following her to make sure she was ok and to make sure she was safe. He knew that every day that went by she was beating herself up more and more.

"What are you doing out here?" His soft voice came from behind her.

"I could be asking you the same thing? Or maybe why it took you so long to catch up?" Mallory didn't even raise her head to look in his direction.

He smirked sitting down on the ground next to her. He nudged her lightly with his arm.

She groaned, leaning into him. Her head going to rest on his shoulder.

"Shouldn't you be by your father's side? It's nearly time." Mallory asked, making a small face.

"Shouldn't you be your mother and father's side ..princess?" Adam smirked.

"No and don't call me that. I have been yelling at you since we were kids." Mallory growled at him.

"Ah I know but it suits you." Adam nudged her again.

"There are lots of words that would suit me-""

"Stop." Adam said sternly.

"It's true and you know it. They know it. So why bother? Why bother going to the meeting at all? I see the way they look at me. Every time they come. I am not going to sit there and let them stare at me like some pitiful wonder." Mallory said as her head snapped up and her fist went to her side.

"No one looks at you like that." Adam growled at the idea of her thinking that was insane.

"Really? The daughter of Nora and Jace, no wolf, powerless and ordinary. Before it was a wonder and waiting. Now it will be a pity." Mallory said her eyes narrowed.

"Mal-"

"Adam you know it…just leave me here." Mallory said going to turn from him.

"What and you'll just become..a wildflower?" Adam smirked, reaching out and grabbing her arm and pulling her back to him.

"Adam!" Mallory yelled as she fell backwards into his lap, her hair spreading over it as she looked up at his face.

"Mallory, you can't hide out here in the long grass anymore like some child." Adam said his thumb brushing her cheek.

"No, because you found me." Mallory grumbled, her hand caught his.

"And I always will." Adam laughed.

"You know what really sucks…it's knowing I took her powers..She lost them because of me but I don't even have them so it was all for nothing." Mallor said slowly sitting up.

"How can you even be my friend knowing that?" Mallory added, squinting her ice blue eyes at him.

"Mallory you are not weak, you didn't cause your mother to lose her powers. No one understood her powers. It might have been the cycle of it. She didn't need them anymore. The wolf, hunter, and human world formed together and was at peace. You can't blame yourself. You are their greatest blessing." Adam said, trying to reach out and grab her hand again.

"Mallory, we do not know what the future holds for any of us. The moon Goddess has a plan." Adam sighed seeing her move away.

"I don't understand how you can have so much faith." Mallory grumbled getting to her feet nearly head butting him as she did.

"Well someone has to balance you." Adam chuckled standing as well.

"Shut up." Mallory said, sticking her tongue out at him.

Adam smirked and stepped towards her. She was about to say something but then saw the look in his eyes.

"Adam no." Mallory said her eyes were getting big as she stepped back.

He stepped towards her his eyes glowing, his wolf just under the surface.

"Adam. We are not children anymore. I am not playing this game." Mallory said, placing her hands on her hips.

"One." Adam grinned, taking another step towards her. He could see her wanting to give in.

"No. I am not playing." Mallory said, crossing her arms across her chest.

"Two." Adam took a step forward towards her, almost in slow motion as his voice dropped even lower.

"Adam-

"Three." Adam dared her, his smirk turning into a grin.

"I. No! I'm not!....Damn it!" Mallory laughed and took off running.

Her hair flying out behind her as her eyes locked on the woods across the field. She knew she couldn't outrun a wolf but she was going to try. She was fast, unbelievably fast for just a human.

"Four!! Run Mallory!" Adam's taunting voice echoed behind her, his laughter following behind her.

She was so close to the woods, heart pounding in her chest. Her mind pushed herself to run harder and faster. She was going to win this time. If she could just get to the woods.

"Five!" Adam yelled excitedly.

"You better move faster than that Princess!!" Adam taunted her from the long grass.

She didn't pay attention to his taunting; she was focused on the one tree that seemed to be calling her. She heard him starting to shift. She must have been a good ways away from him for him to decide to shift.

"Cheater!" She yelled over her shoulder starting to get a little breathless.

A howl rose up behind her in response as she made it to the woods. She grinned ducking into the forest. She knew it better than Adam, better than Adam's wolf Owen. She could get away from him. She was going to prove she didn't need to be a wolf.

Chapter Two
Gathering

Nora bit her lip as she strangled her pinky finger in her hand. She glanced at the clock, the council members and a small amount of their pack's were filtering into the grand hall. After a quick meet and greet, the council members would go to the office and discuss issues and plans for the future. Where was her daughter? She was in the back office pacing the floor.

"If you break your finger I am going to be upset and if you dare chew off your bottom lip I am going to be very..very.. Sad." Jace whispered into her ear coming up behind her and wrapping his arms around her waist as he pulled her into him.

"Where is our daughter?" Nora sighed, closing her eyes and letting Jace's presence comfort her, even though her stomach was twisting inside of her.

"She will be back. She might have her mother's stubbornness and flight risk attitude but she holds her father's responsibility in her." Jace smirked.

"Ohhh so all her bad behavior is my fault and nothing to do with you?" Nora laughed, turning in his arms.

"You're a lot to handle." Jace grinned.

"Oh…so you're incapable of….handling me." Nora smirked, her eyes sparkling with mischief.

Jace's grip tightened on her hips, his fingers applied a small amount of pressure as he growled next to her ear knowing what she was implying.

"Maybe I should find someone…capable of handling…a lot." Nora smirked.

Jace spun her into his chest backing her up into the wall as he did; she let out a small squeak of surprise, followed by a giggle.

"Take it back." Jace said, pinning her to the wall, a lock of his now salt and pepper hair fell down into his face, as his ice blue eyes narrowed in on her.

"Make me." Nora said, biting her lower lip.

Jace grinned accepting the challenge. His hand slipped under her shirt. The touch of his skin against her skin sent instant chills through her. She leaned into his touch. His mouth went to the side of her neck. His teeth grazed her mark. A small whimper escaped her mouth as she looped her fingers into his belt loops pulling him closer to her.

"Ahem." A voice came from the doorway.

Jace ignored the voice and let his hand travel down her hips, burying his face into her neck.

"Jace." Nora whispered her voice trying to find strength.

Jace growled his mouth vibrating from it, teasing her skin as his mouth moved down her shoulder pulling her shirt to the side.

"Alpha…it's time." Dante said again.

"Hey what's the hold …up" Matt said walking into the room and then shaking his head.

"Jace!" Nora said more firmly and he grumbled moving away from her.

"Later." Jace promised her hand to capture her chin and run his thumb over her lower lip before releasing her.

"How have you two managed to live this long?" Jace asked, narrowing his eyes at them.

"Good looks…charming personality?" Matt smirked.

Jace growled at him going to go towards him. Nora laughed, grabbing Jace's hand and stopping him from going after Matt.

"You would miss him if you killed him." Nora said, patting Jace's hand.

"For a second." Jace grumbled.

"Ouch." Matt laughed.

"But in all seriousness, Alpha, Luna. The hall is full." Matt smiled.

"Dante, has Adam brought Mallory back yet?" Nora asked her gaze, switching over to him.

"He will, they'll be back in time for the important piece." Dante said, reassuring her.

"Ok let's do this boys." Nora smiled at them, slipping out from behind Jace and walking to the doors.

She could hear him searching for her. She sunk back against the tree she was hiding behind. She was debating climbing it. She watched the dark brown ears perk up and he smelt the air. She knew he was zoning in on her. She pushed back into the woods, her eyes locking with Owen. He spotted her. She shuffled backwards as he went in for the lunge. She moved backwards still looking at him, her foot pressing into the soft soil. The earth began slipping out from underneath her. She quickly began to lose her footing and she tumbled backwards. Owen's eyes flashed concern as he tried to reach her in time. Her hand reached out for him as she fell down.

The ground scraped against her skin as she began rolling down the small hill. A root sticking out of the ground grabbed a hold of her shirt and made her pause for a second. She winced as she felt it tear into her skin. She tried to reach up and grab ahold of it but it slipped through her fingers and she continued to roll.

"Mallory!!" Adam's voice shouted from the top of the hill, it was all a blur.

Mallory hit the bottom of the hill, the wind getting knocked out of her. She felt a burning pain spread through her chest as her lungs begged for air. She squeezed her eyes shut trying to move. She rolled over on her side hoping that it would work. She dug her fingers into the rich soil, her eyes tearing up as she was drowning without water. She pulled herself on to her knees. Her vision going foggy, the world soundless. She tried to suck in air and nothing was working. She was going to die from rolling down a hill.

"Mallory!" Adam crashed to his knees in front of her, his hands going to her shoulders.

Mallory grabbed ahold of his forearms, squeezing them. Her eyes filled with tears as she panicked.

"Mal you gotta breathe, take a breath in. Come on!" Adam orders her, shaking her arm fiercely.

As if he shook air back into her, she inhaled in one giant gasp. She breathed deeply like it was her first time ever breathing air.

"Oh god that hurts!" Mallory said as she exhaled her.

"Shit, let me see." Adam said going to lift up her shirt.

Mallory didn't fight him, she clung to his shoulder as she focused on breathing. He rolled up her shirt slowly trying to be careful. Her ribs and sides were already purple and covered in blood blisters. Mallory felt something warm drip down from her forward and run down her cheek.

"We got to get you back." Adam said, looking at her face and noticing the blood.

"You hit your head too. Shit Mallory." Adam said, looking through her hair, trying to find the source of the blood.

"Adam." Mallory whispered her eyes looking past him, there was something just behind him at the bottom of the hill.

"You got a small gash, it's not bad." Adam said, looking at it.

"Adam!" Mallory said firmly, trying to get his attention.

"Mallory we gotta go come on." Adam said ignoring her to focus on needing to get her back.

"Adam! Stop, what the hell is that!" Mallory said, grabbing a hold of his hand and pointing behind him.

Adam stiffened up, the smell of blood hitting him. It wasn't Mallory's blood. This was too much blood for it to be just coming from her head wound.

"Stay here." Adam ordered, all of his senses heightening, Owen pushing forwards as he moved away from Mallory.

Mallory shakingly got to her feet trying to see what Adam was looking at. He kneeled down over something. She heard him swear under his breath before getting to his feet. He turned back to face her, his hands soaked in red.

"There's been a breach." He whispered his eyes scanning around them as he held his blood stained finger up to his lip, telling her she needed to be quiet.

"Breach?" Mallory whispered, walking around him trying to see.

Then she saw it, one of her father's men, his head nearly decapitated from his body, slumped down into the ground. His body was covered in mud. He rolled too. She thought, her eyes looking back up at the hill. She scanned her surroundings. Her eyes looked across the grassy field. There was someone staring at her from across the way. They were too far from her to know but for some reason she knew his eyes were a deep red brown. She found herself captivated for a moment before the person moved back into the forest.

"Adam." She whispered, her eyes locked on something in the distance.

She spun looking at him, his eyes glossed over. She knew he was sending a mind link out. She crossed to him and grabbed his hand. His eyes came back into focus.

"We need to go now. There's someone across the field." Mallory whispered.

"What?" His head snapped towards the clearing, trying to see what she saw.

"Adam now." Mallory said moving towards the hill, she knew she was slower than wolves and now even slower injured.

"Adam, what if it's a trap? We need to move." Mallory said, digging her the toes of her shoes into the dirt trying to begin climbing.

Adam clenched his jaw, she was right and he couldn't let her climb up the hill injured and alone. He moved to her looking over his shoulder, his eyes set on the woods across the field as he began helping her climb.

Chapter Three
Panic

"Allies and friends, I am so pleased to see us all gather together. It has been twenty years. Twenty years of peace and working together. Cross River welcomes you all to eat, drink and be merry." Jace's lip curled up as he said the last sentence.

"The council members will proceed into discussions as the rest of you all enjoy yourself." Nora spoke after Jace with the same smile resting on her lips.

Her eyes looked out over the crowd. Asher leaned down and placed a kiss on the top of Hannah's head. Nora smiled bigger. She was so happy when the girl had stumbled onto Red Woods lands. She was a rogue hungry, frightened, and lost. She was now an incredible Luna and someone Nora cared for. Logan stood from the hunter's side, crows feet now living in the corner of his eyes. Even more so when he smiled. Zeke, now completely silver, moved through the crowd. Grayson was now Alpha of Black Sands. Chadwick never recovered from the damage Kip had caused him. He passed away in his sleep a year after they took down the Alpha council. Polly still full of energy and a ball of light glided towards Nora, Shea following close behind. Nora watched their friends move to the front of the room to meet Jace and her.

"Douglas?" Nora whispered to Jace.

"Running late." Jace shrugged his hand going to her lower back.

She nodded but her stomach turned in on itself. She frowned a little but let Jace guided her into the back office. Jace pulled a chair out for Nora. She felt reluctant to sit. Jace raised an eyebrow at her.

"Something's wrong." Nora sent him through a mind link.

"You are just worried about Mallory, Adam has her, he was going to let her blow off some steam and bring her back for the discussions. They will be here any minute. Do not worry." Jace sent back squeezing her hand.

Nora nodded. She watched everyone take their seats. They had designed this back office just for these meetings. A long dark table was in the center of the room, lined with several chairs, all carved out of wood matching each pack of the council. Red Woods's chair was designed as a fall tree with painted bright red, yellow, and orange leaves. Moonlight's chair was the biggest full moon, City Lights's was a building that sparkled, Black Sands's a dark sandy desert, Dark Water's chair was waves deep blue in color, Silver Mountain's chair was a mountain with a snow cap, the hunters had bow and arrows on their chair, and Cross River had a river carved into it. Nora's eyes focused on Silver Mountain's chair, her mind wanting to know why he was late.

"You know I am not one for long winded things. So let's cut to the chase. Any problems?" Jace said leaning on the chair Nora was sitting in.

"All is good on the hunter's end." Logan said who was about as short winded as Jace.

"Red Woods is all good." Asher nodded.

"City Lights had an issue with some rogues a few weeks back." Polly said, her eyes looking at Shea.

"Rogues?" Zeke spoke up.

"We have not heard of any rogue movement in years." Grayson said his tone mimicked Zeke's.

"They started at Dark Water. A few guards were attacked. Some supplies were stolen." Shea said, nodding to Polly.

"Same thing happened at City Lights, although they were a bit more destructive. They went after our hospital." Polly said.

"Why did you not reach out sooner?" Nora asked her attention on Polly.

"It was a small incident and we handled it. We knew the meeting was coming up." Polly explained, Shea nodded in agreement.

"You should have said something." Asher spoke up, his brow in a frown.

"We did not want to cause an alarm if there was not a need for it." Polly continued talking for herself and Shea.

Nora was watching Zeke, she didn't need to look behind her at Jace. She knew his face was mimicking Zeke's. Rogues have not existed for a while.

"Well it is a damn problem." Douglas said, walking into the room.

He looked worn out and tired. Stress written all over his face.

"Douglas?" Jace asked him, concerned.

"We had an attack as well. They waited for myself and a few members to be gone. Like they knew when the council meeting was. They raided our crops, medical supplies and even tried taking some of the women." Douglas said angry, his eyes fixated on Polly and Shea.

"You should have alerted us the minute an attack happened." Douglas spat.

"Douglas ours were minor." Polly said, trying to defend her stance.

"They are clearly growing!" Douglas growled.

"Woah, everyone breathe." Zeke said, trying to calm the situation down.

"Did anyone leave any of your packs?" Logan asked, his eyes studying them.

Nora felt sick, she felt shaky. The world was going silent around her. She could feel energy coming from somewhere. Her body on high alert. It had not reacted like this in years. Twenty years to be exact.

"Jace." Nora whispered.

The talking around her was blending together into one constant noise. She reached up and grabbed Jace frantically.

"Jace." Nora said louder.

Everyone in the room stopped and stared at Nora. Jace came around to look at her. She was pale, sweat beaded across her forehead. Her eyes flickered from ice blue to amber and then faded out like a flame.

"Something's wrong." She announced.

"Alpha, there's been an attack, a guard is dead. There was movement on the far east side of the pack lands. I couldn't go after them. I have Mallory and we are making it back towards the pack house. Mallory is hurt when she fell. Wyatt needs to be on standby, she may have broken ribs. Alpha I am so sorry." Adam's mind link Jace, hitting him like a ton of bricks.

"Mallory." Nora whispered.

Jace's fist hit the table as the door behind him came flying open. Dante and Matt were both standing in the conference room.

"Lock down." Jace ordered looking at Dante whose face matched his own.

Dante's eyes glossed over as he began to send out the commander to all pack members.

"Matt. Get to patrol now." Jace ordered him, he was out the door before anyone could question.

Nora got to her feet. She locked eyes with Logan who stood at the same time she did. He felt it too.

"Council members, we have had an attack. I ask you all to order your pack members to stay inside the great hall until we can confirm everything is safe." Jace said to the table.

Nora began moving towards the door. She needed her daughter. She needed to know she was ok. She ignored the council members as she could tell a round of questions were about to begin.

"Nora." Jace said his tone was soft because he could feel everything her body was going through.

"I need to get to her now." Nora said firmly to him.

"I got her back." Logan said, making his way to the front.

"Don't go off far, Adam is bringing her through. He will be coming into the community shortly. Meet him in the front. Logan-" Jace said firmly"

"I know if anything happens to her, I die. I got it." Logan said, winking at him as he joined Nora.

"Jace, is there anything you need?" Asher and Zeke both said at the same time.

"A guard was found dead just east of our border. Asher, Red Woods is not far and if they change directions they are coming for Moonlight. Alert your people." Jace said quietly.

"Adam, you don't need to carry me." Mallory argued, they had made it out of the woods and crossed the long grass. She was now able to see houses.

"Hush. We need to move fast and you're injured, princess." Adam said trying to joke but inside his guts were twisting together.

"Put me down now!" Mallory yelled at him and moved in his arms so much that Adam almost dropped her.

"All right!" Adam said anger in his voice as he set her down.

"What the hell Mal." Adam said as he watched her struggle to stand up right.

"I can walk." Mallory said to him, ignoring the look and continuing on ahead.

"Barely." Adam countered catching up to her.

"I am fine." Mallory said through her teeth, she could see movement up ahead.

"You are not. You..are…hurt." Adam said drawing out the words to make a point.

"I do not need any pity." Mallory said, turning on her heels staring at him in his eyes, her hands in fists at her side.

"What the fuck Mallory. No one is pitying you but yourself." Adam snapped back as she got closer to his face.

"You have no right to tell me-"

"I have been watching you do it forever now. Mallory you are the only one doubting, pitying and holding yourself back." Adam yelled, cutting her off.

"Fuck you." Mallory said her body was shaking from anger.

"Mallory!" Nora's voice echoed behind them.

"You mind linked my mother." Mallory said, gritting her teeth.

"I had to let Alpha know. Your what had happened." Adam said defensively.

Nora rushed to her side. Mallory could tell by the way her clothing was barely hanging on to her, her mother had shifted and ran here in wolf form.

"Where are you hurt?" Nora said as she began looking at her head wound.

"Mom, I fell and rolled down a hill. Hit my head and hurt my sides. I am ok. There's something bigger than me being hurt. One of the guards was killed." Mallory said, catching her mother's hand.

"I know. Your father's working on it. We are going into lock down till we find out exactly what happened." Nora said, holding her hand still.

A black jeep that had the doors and roof off pulled up behind them. Mallory recognized his blonde tousled hair, as he stepped out of the car.

"Uncle Logan?" Mallory asked, confused.

"Hey Rebel. Nora I swear you really want to see Jace and I battle it out one day." Logan said to her, shaking his head.

"Sorry I had to get to her." Nora smiled weakly at him.

" Rebel, you're pretty banged up. Come let's get you over to Wyatt." Logan said, winking at her.

Nora began helping Mallory over to the car. Logan gets to the driver seat. Mallory paused as her mother went to help her into the car. Her eyes locked with Adam. Nora followed her gaze.

"Adam?" Nora asked him.

"I am going to catch up with the patrol. I have first hand knowledge of where it happened." He said quietly.

"Ok. Wait for them. Do not go off on your own." Nora ordered.

"Yes Luna." Adam said, bowing his head.

He wasn't coming with her? Mallory thought as Nora pushed her into the car. As the jeep pulled off Mallory locked eyes with Adam. He looked at her once more before starting to make his way towards the woods.

Chapter Four
Lock Down

"Some one saw?" Knox asked as Ronan caught up to him.

"No." Ronan said with a shrug.

He wasn't sure why he was lying. He knew she had seen him. She locked eyes with him from across the field. There was something, something about her. He wouldn't have even stopped what he was doing but he felt this pull. When he looked over he saw her ice blue eyes. She was miles away from him but he knew the color of her eyes. He chalked it up to his wolf zoning in on her.

"You sure?" Knox asked again, looking at him confused.

"There was some commotion. Someone may have found the body but I didn't care to stop." Ronan said nonchalantly.

"Do you care about anything?" Knox smirked as he nodded to the small group of men they had brought with them.

"No, not really." Ronan grinned, the men began moving out.

"Good. It's one of things I enjoy about you." Knox laughed.

"Glad to be of service." Ronan said sarcastically as he began following behind the men.

Knox took his place up front, someone brought him a horse. They moved on foot or horseback for the most part. They needed to be quiet, move like the shadows. Cars and atv's caused noise. They needed to be unheard and unseen. Ronan would let the pack get ahead of him and he would follow behind. He didn't like people and preferred to be alone.

"Where to, Alpha?" Someone from the front asked.

"We need to split up." Knox announced after thinking for several minutes.

"Come again?" Ronan spoke, the crowd moving so he could come up to where Knox was.

"We need to split up." Knox repeated, Ronan was the only one who could get away with questioning him.

"Where are we headed?" Ronan asked intrigued.

"Well all of the council is meeting as we speak. Ronan you said the dead body has been found. So they are now on high alert. They are probably discussing the raids at City Lights and Dark Water. Jace is smart, he's connecting the dots. He is now going to assume that we will go to Red Woods or Moonlight. If he has figured out the pattern." Knox grinned, his wheels turning in his head.

Knox paused for effect. Not only did he like being in power, having control and being in charge. He liked the dramatics of it all.

"So we split up. We need them to think we are larger than we are. We need to draw Cross River out. Have the other packs return to protect their lands. Then we can crush Jace." Knox announced.

"Mick you are to take a handful and go to Moonlight. Burn something. We need to up each attack." Knox ordered him.

"Yes Alpha." Mick said, moving out of the crowd.

Mick was tall and built like an oak tree. His mossy color hair even matched the tree bark. He was Knox's Delta.

"Angela." Knox said a small smile on his face, as a thin but fit woman moved forward.

"Yes Alpha." She smiled back.

"Take the rest of the men except four and move to Red Wood. I want dead bodies." Knox smirked to her.

"As you wish." Angela said bowing and then her eyes set on the crowd.

Angela was Knox's Gamma. She was small and fragile looking but deadly. Her golden blond hair and green eyes drew you in, making her look innocent before the kill. The pack slowly began separating into groups.

"Ronan. I am heading back to gather the rest of the pack. I will bring them back here. You are to stay here with three or four men. Watch, report issues. When the time comes we will bring Cross River to its knees." Knox said, clapping Ronan on his shoulder.

"Stop, I am fine." Mallory said, catching her mom's hand as she went to touch her forehead.

"Don't tell me to stop. What were you thinking?" Nora asked, frowning.

"Just that-

"Good morning." Wyatt said walking into the room, seeing Nora's face and Mallory's, he was almost thankful he walked in when he did. There was clearly about to be an argument.

"Hey Wyatt." Mallory smiled at him.

"Let me take a look at your kiddo." He smirked coming over to her, Nora moved to a side still frowning.

"Ah I'm ok." Mallory grinned, she liked Wyatt he never treated her any different.

"I'll be the judge of that." Wyatt chuckled, walking over to her.

"Judge away. How's Abby and Abigail?" Mallory asked, tilting her head so Wyatt could look at the wound.

"Great. Abby is due any day now and Abigail is trying to follow in Dad's footsteps. She will be the next pack doctor I am sure of it." Wyatt said proudly.

"That's so exciting Wyatt. You be sure to let us know if you need anything for Abby or little William when he arrives." Nora smiled at him.

"Of course Luna." Wyatt said, stepping back.

"All right, let me see the bad stuff." Wyatt said, raising a brow at Mallory.

"Ugh fine." Mallory sighed and winced trying to roll up her shirt.

Nora frowned seeing the purple and came to help her. Nora gently lifted the shirt and fought back a gasp. She tried to choke down the anger. If she had just listened she wouldn't have gotten hurt. She wished she still had her powers if she did she would be able to fix this. She hated that Mallory didn't heal like everyone else. If she had her wolf-

"Mom." Mallory's voice drew her from her rapid thoughts.

"Hmm?" Nora asked, hoping her thoughts didn't show up on her face.

"Can you see if Adam is ok?" Mallory asked quietly.

"Adam?" Nora asked confused, her brows coming together.

"Is Adam hurt too?" Nora asked quickly.

"No, he's just...he's mad at me that's all." Mallory sighed.

"Ok, I will link him in just a minute. How's it look doc?" Nora asked, turning her attention to Wyatt.

"Well." Wyatt said, reaching out and palpating the side of Mallory's rib.

Mallory choked back a yell and tried to remain stone faced but the way her body was fighting it Wyatt knew she was in pain.

"We need an x-ray to say for sure but I am almost positive we have some broken ribs." Wyatt said, rolling Mallory's shirt back down.

"What?" Nora asked, looking at Wyatt as if she didn't hear him.

"BROKEN! RIBS! MA!" Mallory yelled slowly.

"Mallory!" Nora snapped at her for shouting.

"What I know, you're getting old. Just trying to make sure you understood." Mallory laughed and then instantly regretted it, her hand going to her right side trying to hold it in place.

"Broken?" Jace's voice came from behind them in the doorway.

"Hey Dad." Mallory grinned sheepishly

"Broken." Jace said again his tone firm.

"Maybe." Mallory answered looking nervous.

"Damn it Mallory." Jace grumbled crossing the room to look at her.

"We need x-rays to be sure but I think she has some broken ribs." Wyatt said, bowing his head to Jace as he walked in.

"The wound?" Jace asked quickly, his hand going to Mallory's forehead.

"Will heal, it needs to be cleaned." Wyatt answered just as quickly.

"See only slightly broken if at all." Mallory said, winking at her Dad.

"You and your mother." Jace said, shaking his head.

"Her mother." Nora is repeatedly offended.

"Listen I know you're upset that I am hurt but if I didn't fall we would have never found the body. We wouldn't have known there was a threat. Speaking of, did you find out anything? There was someone across the way to the east. I only saw just one." Mallory said, taking her father's hand down from her forehead.

"We are running patrol. Adam is leading Matt to the east to show him where. We have the borders protected and we are increasing numbers." Jace said, still frowning.

"The other packs here?" Mallory asked quietly.

"X-rays and then we'll talk about pack business." Jace said softly to her.

"Fine but did you tell Zeke and Asher? East is towards their packs." Mallory said as Wyatt wheeled in a wheelchair for her.

"Yes. If you were at the meeting you would know." Jace said firmly, being a little hard on her.

"If I was there we wouldn't know about the intruder. Wyatt take me away." Mallory announced as she slowly got into the chair.

Jace shook his head watching her be wheeled out. Nora came up behind him and wrapped her hands around his waist leaning into his back.

"She's so much like you." Nora said quietly.

"As graceful as you." Jace smirked back, Nora pinched his side.

Jace was still focused on the doorway that Mallory just left out of. He was secretly proud that even hurt his daughter's mind went to the safety of the pack.

Chapter Five
Patrol

"We're waiting on orders." Matt said tugging on Adam's arm who was peering too deeply into the forest.

"Yeah I know." Adam said, his voice full of anger.

"Chill out." Matt said, shoving him lightly.

Adam whipped around his eyes glowing, his body shaking; he wanted to fight something. Needed to get this anger out somehow.

"Watch yourself." Matt smirked, his eyes daring him as Ryker pushed forward.

"Sorry." Adam said quickly, he didn't mean to take it out on Matt but he was so angry.

Angry with himself for letting her get hurt. Angry that he snapped at her, angry at her for thinking so lowly of herself. He clenched his jaw, his teeth grinding against each other.

"It's not your fault." Matt said quietly as he watched the rest of the patrol coming out of the forest.

Adam just gruntted his response, his eyes fixed on the large gray wolf that was moving quicker than the rest of them. Adam felt his stomach sink slightly. A chocolate brown wolf flanked its side and Adam let out a breath.

"It's gonna be ok." Matt winked seeing his reaction as he waited for them.

The chocolate brown wolf shifted before Adam could even respond. It was across the distance to them in no time, out running the gray wolf. Sarah cupped Adam's face with her hand. Her other hand went to his shoulder.

"Are you hurt?" She asked quickly, her eyes scanning him.

"Mom." Adam said, rolling his eyes at her.

"That wasn't an answer." Sarah said frowning deeply, she could see he was physically fine but something was wrong.

"Adam." Dante's voice came from behind them.

Adam bowed his head to his father feeling a rush of shame and guilt.

"Beta, I ..-"

"Broken ribs, head wound. What were you thinking." Dante said, listing off Mallory's injury.

Adam didn't respond. The remainder of the wolves caught up. Dante heard them behind him. He shifted his gaze to them.

"Dante, it's not like he pushed her." Matt said, coming to his defense.

"Silence." Dante ordered Matt.

"Silence." Matt mimicked back but due to status he had to follow Dante's order.

"He's going to wish he never silenced me." Matt snickered through a mind link to Adam.

Adam didn't pay attention to Matt's mind link. His guilt eating him away.

"Adam, you will lead the way to where you saw the intruder." Dante ordered him sharply.

Sarah frowned deeply and nudged Dante. He clenched his jaw but as Sarah rubbed his upper arm, the tension from Dante melted away. He let out a sigh not saying anything else. The look on Sarah's face was telling him he was being too hard on Adam. He pulled his lower lip into his mouth making a tight frown. Adam didn't notice and began walking across the clearing. Matt followed next to him. Sarah sighed and shifted back into wolf form.

"Well Kiddo, I can't really splint broken ribs. You're really lucky none of the broken ones pierced your lungs." Wyatt said coming back into the room.

"Do we have to tell them?" Mallory smirked a little.

"He already did." Nora said, coming into the room.

"Hi.." Mallory said in a small voice.

"Wyatt, what's the plan for her?" Nora said, sighing.

"Full body cast. Complete confinement for at least eight weeks." Wyatt said his face was firm and solid as he spoke.

"What?" Mallory asked, going to sit up and flinching.

"Afraid so, If only you had listened to your mother." Nora shrugged a smirk lingering on her lip.

"Mom, there is no reason for me to be there." Mallory sighed.

"There is every reason for you to be there. You are my daughter." Nora said, frowning seeing the small flicker of pain in Mallory's eyes.

"Yeah I know. Everyday I am reminded I am your daughter." Mallory said quietly.

"You. You are not lacking." Nora said firmly.

Mallory felt her lip quiver at the words. She took a breath in. Trying to hold back the emotions that were eating her alive.

"Does the cast cover my ears?" Mallory jested trying to draw the attention off how vulnerable she felt.

"I mean I don't see why not." Wyatt winked at her.

"Perfect." Mallory chuckled and then winced from the pain.

"I'm going to go get supplies." Wyatt said, excusing himself.

"Are you in a lot of pain?" Nora asked her concern all over her face.

"No, not really. Just when I move or laugh." Mallory grinned.

"Have you…Have you checked in with Adam?" Mallory asked before Nora could respond to her pain response.

"They are just finishing up searching the area where he saw the intruder. He should be heading back shortly…You two ok?" Nora asked her, tilting her head as she asked the question.

"We just got into an argument. That's all." Mallory said, biting her lip.

"Couples argue." Nora grinned.

"Ma. We are not a couple or a thing. He's my friend. My best friend. Besides, I don't even have a wolf." Mallory said her voice cracking as she said the word wolf.

"Mal, is this what this whole thing is about?" Nora asked quietly.

"I don't fit in anywhere. I don't belong with the hunters, I am not coordinated, and I do not belong with the wolves." Mallory laughed, pointing at her ribs and then flinching.

"I don't belong with the humans." Mallory said, starting to ramble.

"I don't have super awesome powers that you once had. That everyone hoped for-"

"Mallory." Nora said, trying to stop her rant.

"Even if I did love Adam like that. I have no wolf. No wolf means no mate. At any point another female with a wolf could walk in and bam. Mate bond. Mallory on the curb…trash." Mallory said in one big breath, tears stinging her eyes as she let it all out.

"Mallory Adam wouldn't-

"And how am I supposed to live up to you and Dad. Dad is amazing and strong and fierce people respect him.

He has a power to him. He is freaking superman. And you..you saved all worlds. Now even without powers you're still helping run everything…and you have a bad ass wolf…I have nothing. I am just me." Mallory said tears slipped down her cheek.

It felt like her chest had cracked open as the words came rushing out like water from a flood gate. Nora wrapped her arms carefully around her, leaning her head into Mallory.

"My girl. You are amazing. -" Nora started to say

"Mom." Mallory attempted to stop her.

"Hush let me finish. Your wolf may still be hiding or even if you don't have one. You still are faster than warriors who have been in training since they could walk. Your aim is Incredible. Even when up against people who have the benefit of sharper senses. You may be clumsy but it is because you are not cautious. You jumped into everything feet first, heart first. You are stronger than humans but just need fine tuning. You hold responsibility and loyalty above everything else. Leading with both your mind and heart. You are what the moon Goddess envisioned for our worlds. Do not sell yourself short." Nora whispered to her.

"You do not need powers or a wolf. All you need is this." Nora said, pressing her lips to Mallory's forehead.

"And this." She said, putting her hand over Mallory's heart.

"I love you mom." Mallory whispered to her.

"I love you too. You are all my stars." Nora smiled at her.

"Alpha said he will need Luna to go address the council. Everyone can start heading home, they will postpone the meeting until everyone can make sure their borders are secured." Wyatt said his eyes still partly glossy from the mind link as he walked in the room.

"Let's get Mallory fixed up and she can help me address them." Nora said, shifting from Mallory.

"In a full body cast?" Mallory said alarm.

"Did I forget to say gullible?" Nora laughed.

"Uh?" Mallory said her eyes shooting over to Wyatt who was holding up bandage materials.

"No full body cast kiddo, just a wrap." Wyatt laughed.

Chapter Six
Waiting

Ronan watched them move through the tree line. He smirked, his hand twitching at his side. He recognized the young man leading them. He was the one in the clearing with the girl with long flowing jet black hair. His mind kept wandering back to her. The moment their eyes locked he felt something.

"We should tell Alpha, they are getting awfully close. " Clay sent through a mind link, his eyes studying the group of men.

"No, it's fine." Ronan answered shortly, he suppressed his wolf's instinct to come forward

"If we are caught it won't be fine." Clay said sharply back.

Ronan turned quickly grabbing Clay by the throat. Within seconds Clay was pinned to the ground. It happened so quickly and was almost soundless. Clay's eyes widened as he realized he was on the ground.

"Beta I am sorry…please." Clay whispered his hand covering Ronan's hand asking him to stop.

"If I say it's fine, it's fine." Ronan growled.

"Yes Beta." Clay whispered, nodding.

"If you're worried, take the cowards with you and fall back." Ronan said, letting go of his throat and spitting on the ground next to Clay.

Clay scampered to his feet, looking around. The three other's shrunk away worried. They were not sure what was worse, being caught or facing Ronan. Ronan was deadly and unpredictable. He didn't call on his wolf when fighting. He used pure ability. Pax was his backup and secret weapon.

Ronan's eyes shifted back to the search party. Part of him wanted to be found. He wanted the fight. Pax wanted the kill. Ronan took a deep breath and sighed.

"Fall back." He sent the message out through a mind link to the four with him.

The men quietly moved back into the forest more. Ronan was annoyed as he moved soundless. He moved like shadows without effort as the others with him were filled with anxiety, walking on eggshells to be quiet. Ronan clenched his jaw. The next time men were left with him he would pick who stayed. He was fighting the urge to kill the ones with him.

They had searched the borders for hours. Matt had to order Adam to stop. He was determined to find whoever killed the patrolman and he partially was blaming the intruder for Mallory being hurt. Mallory, thinking her name, twisted his stomach. The words he spat at her eating at him. He had not meant to snap but he was so frustrated with how she saw herself.

"Where are you off too?" Matt sent him through the mind link.

"Going to work on my apology." Adam sent back flashing him a small smile.

"Alpha knows this has nothing to do with you. Everyone knows Mallory is…spirited." Matt sent back with a smirk.

"It's not the Alpha." Adam sent back letting out a small breath.

"Oh well good luck with that." Matt smirked, throwing him a wink before walking towards his home.

"Patrol in the morning." Matt sent to him as Adam began walking off.

"Bright and early." Adam sent back his eyes looking up at the stars trying to find his words.

"What have you two been talking about?" Dante's rough voice came up behind Matt.

Matt went to open his mouth but smirk and then closed it dramatically, shrugging his shoulders.

"Are you serious! What the hell's wrong with you?" Dante growled, stepping towards.

Matt smirked again and went to shrug when Dante grabbed him by his shirt and yanked him onto his tippy toes. Matt's eyes flashed as Ryker pushed forward.

"You better answer me Matt, I don't have time for your games." Dante growled, ignoring Ryker.

"Life, patrolling, how you're an ass." Matt snickered *through mind link.*

"Why are you talking through…you're an idiot." Dante said letting Matt go.

"Telling you to shut up wasn't a literal command." Dante sighed annoyed.

Matt threw his hands up in the air pointing to his mouth. He the began to open and shut it as if to say well you see I can't talk.

"I should keep you this way." Dante smirked, his smile growing into a grin at the thought of never hearing Matt again.

"You know, using mind link my voice will never get tired. It's just thinking." Matt smirked as he looked at Dante.

"Uh?" Dante asked, confused, tilting his head as he looked at Matt.

"Twinkle, twinkle, little star. How I." Matt started to sing *through mind link.*

"Oh for fuck sake you can talk. If I had to hear your singing in my mind twenty four seven I might give myself a lobotomy." Dante said, waving his hand at Matt.

"Ahh now see, was that so hard." Matt smirked, clapping Dante on his shoulder.

"He's upset that Mallory is hurt. He's hard enough on himself and blaming himself for everything. Go easy on him." Matt said quietly.

"He-

"He saved her, got her back to safety and now is going to apologize. He also patrolled his ass off today trying to find who did this. Take it easy on him." Matt said quietly before giving Dante a nod and heading out.

Dante grumbled watching Matt walk away. He was angry but he knew it wasn't towards Adam. It was towards the person who did this to their pack. He was upset that Adam and Mallory were so close to danger and on their land. The land that was supposed to be safe.

The words Mallory I am sorry kept repeating over and over as he walked to her house. He knew, Mallory I am sorry, wasn't good enough but he was only partially sorry. He just wished she could see herself as he saw her. He stopped under her window, anxiety creeping up as he stepped into the light that poured out from her bedroom. He took a deep breath and picked up a small pebble from the ground. He rolled it around in his hand before tossing it at her window. The ping echoed through the night.

"Come on Mallory." Adam whispered, picking up another pebble and chucking it a little harder at the window.

As the pebbles soared through the air, just as it was about to hit the window. The window opened. A hand catching the pebble. Adam flinched expecting the pebble to hit them.

"You know, tossing rocks at someone's window is a little fairy-talish for you." Mallory smiled and dropped the pebble.

"Can I come up?" Adam asked quietly.

"What's the password?" Mallory smiled, she was so happy he was there.

"Really." Adam laughed, shaking his head.

"Password." Mallory said fiercely.

"What if I just force entry." Adam smirked, mischief flashing in his eyes.

"Well that would be unfortunate. I would hate to kick your ass wounded. That would be sad for you." Mallory grinned.

"I'm coming up." Adam said, grabbing the side of the bricks and pulling himself up.

"No password, no entry." Mallory laughed and then winced in pain grabbing her side.

"We will see about that." Adam said, scaling the wall and reaching her window within seconds.

"Woah! Extra quick today." Mallory teased and blocked the window.

"Let me in." Adam ordered his voice low as if it was a secret command.

Mallory felt her stomach flip in excitement. She narrowed her eyes at him. She shook her head no at him, refusing to move from blocking the window. Adam pulled himself up into the window sill leaning in. His nose inches from hers.

"Password." Mallory said firmly, placing her arms on the window sill saying she was blocking him.

"Mallory I am so sorry." Adam said, his voice cracking a little.

"I am sorry you have given the wrong response to the password. You will now be ejected from the window." Mallory smirked, putting her hands on his shoulders as if she was going to shove him.

Adam shook his head at her. His hand went to her cheek. She was standing in the window. Her hair was down flowing about her. The moonlight coming in from behind him, gave her a glow. Her white nightgown shimmered in it. Mallory leaned into his hand.

"Mallory is the best." Adam said with a smile dancing on his lips.

Mallory pulled her lower lip in and nodded, the way he said it made her chest feel heavy. Like it meant more than just a silly game they used to play when they were kids. She moved aside, allowing him in. His feet hit the hardwood floor and Mallory felt like this time was different then all the other times he had crawled through her window. She felt nerves racing around inside. Adam was her safe space, why was she nervous.

"Mallory I am so so sorry." Adam said, taking a step towards her, his eyes going to the wound on her head.

"Adam, you didn't hurt me. I fell. It's not like you smashed me over the head with a rock and broke my ribs." Mallory said, shaking her head.

"Ribs?" Adam asked moving close others, his eyes fixated on her ribs, he then noticed the way the night gown hugged around them, he could see the shape of the bandages.

"Shit Mal." Adam whispered in his voice full of regret.

"Adam, you didn't push me either, stop." Mallory said, shoving his arm lightly and then winced.

"How many?" Adam asked his hand subconsciously going to her side, he gently touched them.

"I'm not sure. Several. It's going to take some weeks to heal." Mallory said with a shrug.

"Fuck." Adam whispered.

"It's no worse than when I broke my foot. I may heal slower than wolves but I heal quickly for a human." Mallory said, bopping him on the nose.

"I am sorry you're hurt but that's not why I am sorry." Adam said, his hand moving to her hip.

"Oh?" Mallory asked, now physically aware of how close he was to her, this was never a problem before.

"I am sorry I yelled at you but only half sorry." Adam started trying to figure his apology out.

" Well that's some apology. Anyways I am sorry I yelled at you too." Mallory said, giving him a weird look.

"I am only sorry because I yelled at you. I am not sorry for trying to tell you to stop seeing yourself as worthless. You are amazing and strong. Kind, smart. You're a born leader. And a little bit funny." Adam said the space between him and Mallory was getting smaller.

"Adam I -" She tried to deter the overwhelming emotions, she looked down at the ground.

"I just wish you could see yourself the way I see you." Adam said, grabbing a hold of her chin and lifting it up.

Her eyes met his and her stomach flipped inside like somersaults. She could feel every part of herself inching closer to him. The world around them stopped. His head lowered and his lips pressed into hers. The warmness of his lips spread through her and her hand found its way to his hip pulling him closer. His mouth moved against hers pulling on her lower lip making her mouth open slightly. His tongue slipped into her mouth causing a rush of tingles to spread through her. His hand moved to her lower back pulling her against him as he deepened the kiss. His tongue brushing against hers more fiercely and demanding. Mallory moved into him more and then there was pain. She winced, a shooting pain from her ribs shot through her interrupting everything in that moment. Adam moved back carefully. His eyes searching hers and then going to her ribs to see if she was hurt.

"Shit Mallory I'm sorry." He whispered out of breath.

"No, no um it's ok. Maybe um maybe you should head out, it's late." Mallory rambled on in the moment catching up to her and suddenly she felt fear.

"Um ok." Adam said, dropping his hands from her and stepping back.

"You got patrol in the morning and I still need to help my mother with the bits and pieces left over from the council." Mallory said finding excuses.

"Mallory I'm sorry. I didn't mean to well actually I am not sorry for the kiss but if I made you comfortable-

"It's not the kiss Adam." Mallory said a small amount of pain leaking out into her voice.

"Then what is it?" Adam asked going to her.

"I..I don't want to talk about it." Mallory said quietly.

"Tell me." Adam said demandingly, worry slipping into his voice.

"What if you have a mate? I mean what if we do this and she comes along. Your other half. The one you're meant to be. " Mallory whispered.

"Mallory, you don't know that." Adam said, realizing her fear.

"Adam, I don't have a wolf. I can't be your mate. And you, you are so perfect you have a mate somewhere out there." Mallory said, stepping away from him, her voice cracking as she tried to hold back tears.

"You don't know that. You don't know that it's not you." Adam argued.

"We would know by now…wouldn't we." Mallory said, frowning.

"Your parents, my parents, Matt and Lilly Wyatt, everyone has mates and it's different." Mallory argued.

"Matt and Lilly!" Adam said like he had just won a prize.

"Ok.." Mallory said back, confused.

"Lilly doesn't have a wolf. She is a hunter and they are mated." Adam said, following her across the room.

"Adam." Mallory said quietly.

"Listen princess, you do not know if you don't have a wolf. She will show herself and she will be strong and fierce. And we will be mated. I don't care what you say, you are my other half. I feel it." Adam said firmly.

"Adam." Mallory frowned, her own heart breaking because somewhere in the pit of her stomach the fear had taken over.

"I decide what my fate is." Adam said, closing in on her and grabbing her chin.

"I want you. You and all your problems and mishaps and adventures. I know it." Adam said, kissing her forehead.

"You're signing up for a big … .mishap." Mallory chuckled, chasing a tear out of the corner of her eye.

"I know what I am getting myself into. You will see. You are meant to be my mate." Adam said, pressing his forehead to hers.

"Good night princess. Get some rest. You need to heal." Adam said, going to the window.

Mallory choked back her argument and watched Adam leave. She loved him, she had always loved him but something kept telling her that it would be nothing but heart break.

Chapter Seven
Negotiation

"*I* hope all your packs are well. I understand the need to leave. Your homes come first. To those who have stayed to resume the Alpha Council meeting we will only be discussing matters that obtain only to your packs and not all of wolf kind." Nora said, looking out over the room.

Zeke, Asher, Douglas, and Grayson had stayed behind. Polly, Shea and Logan left. Polly and Shea because they were the furthest and Logan needed to get back to the hunters. He felt what Nora had felt. Something was coming and he needed to prepare. His eyes were remorseful as he left.

"Mallory…Before we get started did you see anyone or anything?" Zeke asked quietly, his mind caught up in thought.

"Zeke, we have asked her." Jace said almost defensively.

"Alpha, It's fine." Mallory said being proper to her father in the formal setting.

"Alpha Zeke, I did think I saw one man. He was across the clearing. For some reason my mind thought him to be a rogue but there was something more to him. He was east and that's why I wanted my father to alert you and Alpha Asher. Your packs are the closest to our lands." Mallory said with a small nod.

"Could you see what he looked like?" Douglas asked.

Jace went to speak, he was angry and on defense because he knew that the council knew Mallory's wolf had not appeared yet so her senses were not heightened.

"He had blond hair, reddish brown eyes at least six feet tall." Mallory said recalling the image of him.

"Mallory?" Jace asked quietly, wondering how she could have seen such detail from the other side of the clearing.

Mallory shrugged to him; she was not sure as well. Nora watched her daughter closely. Could it be happening? Jace wondered, looking at her.

"Thank you. We will send the description out to our packs. " Asher smiled at her.

"Ok now on to other things. I will turn the floor over to Zeke. Who had some issues he wanted to bring up." Jace said nodding to Zeke.

"Alphas-" Zeke began to speak but his words got caught in his throat.

Simultaneously his eyes glossed over and his body stiffened. Asher went to say something and in that same second his eyes glossed over.

---

*S*moke flooded the pack lands. The smoke glowing red as heat spread through everything. Ashes began to float down. Lyla was running from house to house banging on doors trying to get people out.

"East side of pack land fire!" Lyla mind link Chance as she throws her shoulder into a door.

The door cracked and she came bursting through. She pulled her shirt up over her mouth trying to breath through the heaviness.

"Hello!" She yelled into the darkness.

She could hear coughing from the back bedroom. She began to move through the black fog carefully, Getting to the door way she leaned in trying to see where the noise was coming from.

"Beta, where are you?" Jaime linked her at the same time as Chance.

"Hang tight We got water trucks coming!" Chance said back, hiding his panic in his voice.

"Joanne's. I can't find her." Lyla sent back quickly as she accidentally leaned on the door frame.

The door frame began to buckle, crumbling against her weight. She tumbled into the room, hitting the floor. The ceiling of the room is now engulfed in flames. Lyla crawled, towards the bed, seeing a foot hanging out on the other side.

"Joanne!" Lyla called out to her.

She didn't respond. Lyla crawled over to her. A loud crack was heard as she reached her. Her lungs are burning at this point. Lola pushed forward, giving her strength and trying to combat her burning lungs. Another crack echoed through the room. Lyla looked but noticed the fire was causing the ceiling to split and any second it was going to give out. She crawled to Joanne's side reaching her and she shook her. She didn't respond. She looked at her chest and it was rising ever so slightly. She needed to get her out of there. Lyla got to her knees and pulled Joanne into her arms. Her skin was on fire, it felt like she was cooking. She began walking back to the door. Another loud crack rang out and a beam from the ceiling crashed in front of her. Lyla stumbled backwards trying to maintain her balance. Her eyes scanned the room. She needed a way out.

"Beta we're here." Jaime's mind link came through.

"Outer room, no window." Lyla said, making her way to the exterior wall.

"Ax!" Jaime yelled, as she rounded the corner of the burning house.

Jaime sprinted to the wall and banged on the wall.

Chance got to the house just in time to see Jaime carrying an ax. He chased after her.

"Lyla!" Jaime shouted as her fist hit the wall again, the wall cracking slightly.

"Here!" Lyla yelled back as best as she could, her voice going weak as the air was getting heavier and heavier to breath, she sunk to the ground trying to get beneath the smoke.

"Move!" Jaime yelled, pulling the ax back and swinging it forward.

Jaime swung the ax with everything she had in her. It cracked the wall. She took a deep breath, her eyes glowing as she pulled on her wolf for strength as she hit the same spot in the wall. The crack became large and a piece of the outer wall fell inwards.

Lyla could see sunlight peeking in through the small crack in the wall as the weight of the air took its toll on her. She couldn't move anymore and her chest felt tired. Her eyes grew heavy. She couldn't breathe.

"Hurry." *She mind linked Jaime as her voice showed how weak she was slowly becoming.*

Jaime was panicking inside as she swung the ax again hitting the outer wall. Another small piece chipping away at.

"Move!" A voice yelled as a loud honking noise came from behind her.

Jaime glanced back to see a truck coming straight for her. She jumped out of the way as the truck went full force into the house. The wall crumbling inward, a large hole breaking open. Black smoke came pouring out of it, clouding Jaime's vision.

"Lyla!" A voice screamed jumping out of the truck.

Before Jaime could even see who the person was they were gone into the blazing building.

*S*omething was wrong. He was going to head back and check in with the rest of the hunters but something told him to head to Red Woods. He didn't even realize he had pressed the pedal completely to the floor. Getting to Red Woods the sky glowed orange. Black smoke started filling the air. His first thoughts were Lyla. His stomach knotted in fear as he raced towards the fire.

He could see the house completely engulfed with fire. His neck where Lyla had marked him began burning. He tried to ignore it but the rush of pain felt like his skin was on fire. In an instant he knew she was in there.

He saw Jaime trying to break through the wall with an ax. He braced himself and sent the truck flying into the wall. His head bounced off the driver side window, cracking instantly. The same crack from the window mirrored the large gash now on the side of his head. Blood splattered from it as he threw his shoulder into the door to open it. He glanced around quickly making sure Jaime was out of the way and he ran straight for the house. He pulled himself up onto the hood of his truck and slid in.

*S*he could see the sunshine now pouring in from the large hole. She couldn't move. She was so weak and it was just enough trouble trying to make sure she was getting air. Her body pressed all the way down to the floor. She had pulled her shirt up over her mouth trying to block the smoke. Her wolf was working overtime trying to repair damage. She was alone in the darkness, her hand still holding Joanna but she was pretty sure she was gone. She was once again in the darkness. Her mind brought up old suppressed memories of being locked away in Kip's dungeon.

"Lyla!" His voice screamed into the blazing darkness.

I'm dead. She thought hearing Logan's voice. At least her mind was giving her one last good memory even if it was fake. She wanted to reach out and touch him to feel him one last time. Tell him how he was the one to save her from her own deep darkness. That she had never thought love would find her but she couldn't have imagined finding anything like how deeply he loved her.

"Logan." She said out loud her hand barely moving to reach out to him.

It was the faintest whisper. The sound of wood cracking and things falling echoed around him. His name was the smallest sound in the world but he heard it. And then he saw her. She was holding on to someone. Her shirt covering her face, her gold blonde hair covered in ash. He saw her reaching out for him. He moved to her the fastest he had ever moved. Kneeling down beside her he pulled her into his arms. Feeling his skin against her she relaxed instantly, her vision starting to fade.

"I got you." He coughed as he went to lift her.

"Joanna." Lyla whispered her eyes closed.

Logan saw the body next to her on the ground and the word shit! Crossed his mind. Lyla passed out. He gritted his teeth and moved towards the hole in the wall.

"Hey!" Jaime yelled climbing up on the truck hood.

"Here!" Logan said, thrusting Lyla into Jaime's arms.

"Logan!" Jaime yelled, the realization that it was Logan made her sick, what was he doing, how long could he last in there.

Logan blindly searched for the body, trying to remember exactly where he had stepped. It felt like any moment the house would collapse around him. His foot bumped something and he knew it was Joanna. He reached down, pulling her towards him. Getting a hold of her he began rushing to the exit. He heard a loud crash coming from behind him and his gut told him the house was about to buckle. He placed Joanna on the hood of the truck. As he tried climbing up it as well. Someone came around and pulled Joanna off the truck, clearing the way for Logan.

It felt like thunder, the ground was rattling as he climbed up onto the hood of the truck. He began crawling across the hood trying to get out as fast as he could. His lungs were burning and not wanting to be pushed. Pieces of debris began falling on his feet as he scrambled to escape. A hand grabbed his shoulder and pulled him out as the hole the truck had made was covered.

Logan hit the ground coughing, air felt like a blessing but his chest burned every time he inhaled and he felt like a boulder was sitting on it.

"Lyla." Logan said in a very heavy breath.

"Jordan's got her." Chance nodded his head that way.

"The other girl." Logan said, lifting his hands up trying to give his lungs more space to breathe in air.

"Logan, why don't you come sit down." Jordan said from the ground glancing up at him.

Logan shook his head. He couldn't sit; he felt like his lungs had no room. He walked a few steps towards Jordan and paused.

"Lyla?" He asked, closing his eyes.

"She will be ok. Her wolf is healing her pretty quickly." Jordan said, standing up and studying Logan.

The gash from the car accident was pretty deep and his head was bleeding like crazy but it wasn't the wound that was bothering Jordan it was how Logan was acting.

"Get me oxygen." Jordan yelled to the ambulance truck.

"Logan, come here." Jordan said motioning for Logan to come to him.

"She's ok." Logan said his lips were starting to turn pale.

"Yes Lyla is ok. I am worried about you right now." Jordan said going to Logan.

"Ok. good." Logan said and his legs buckled.

"Oxygen!" Jordan screamed as he dropped to his knees and began working on Logan.

---

*A*sher's mind link went on longer than a normal mind link. His body was tense and rigid. The emotions he was pouring into the room flooded into Nora. Fear and panic.

"Something is wrong! Asher." Nora said going to walk around the table to him.

"Jace look at Zeke. Something is happ-

The world went dark. Nora fell over and collapsed into the table.

"Nora!" Jace yelled, rushing to her side.

"Get Wyatt." Mallory ordered as she held on to her mom.

---

*T*he world was dark. She had been here before. It was no longer frightening like before. She wanders in the darkness looking for her. She had not heard or seen from her in so long.

"Nora?" A male voice called to her, Nora stopped a feeling of unease washing over her.

She spun in a circle and like a spotlight had turned on she found him. He was on his knees hunched over.

"Logan." Nora said, rushing to him.

"Nora?" Logan said slowly sitting up.

"Where are we?" He asked, his hand going to his head.

"Well normally…this is where I've met the Goddess…it's like limbo or something…wait, Are you ok?" Nora asked, panic setting as she said the words out loud.

"The fire." Logan quietly said Nora's thoughts registering in his head.

"Fire?" Nora asked quickly.

"There was a fire at Red Woods. I was heading back to the base when I got this strange feeling that something was wrong and I went to Red Woods. My neck started burning and I knew it was Lyla. I got to the house and it was covered in flames. Someone named Joanna. Lyla had gone inside to get her out but then got trapped. I got her out but the smoke…I couldn't breathe." Logan said, not sure what it all meant.

"No…You're ok…this is just something…something else. This is not what, I'm not even going to say it out loud. It's not that." Nora said firmly.

"Nora…you don't let Lyla blame herself. This wasn't her fault. You tell her to be strong for the twins. They need their mom." Logan said running his hand through his hair, he felt sick.

"No. You're not going anywhere. I'm not letting you. You hear me." Nora said, her voice cracking a little bit as her voice shook.

"Nora-"

"You're a hunter damn it. You're not going out because of a little smoke. Now shut up." Nora said, getting angry, a warm tear slipped out of her eye and ran down her cheek.

"Nora, can you make sure she's ok? You don't let her slip into darkness. They are still so young." Logan said quietly.

"No. I won't need to because you're going to be fine. Now get the hell out of here and go back." Nora said firmly.

"Nora, I saved her…that's enough for me." Logan whispered smiling,going to give her a hug.

"I said No." Nora said and shoved him in his chest.

A zap of energy flowed out of Nora and landed in Logan's chest. Logan landed a small distance away from Nora and flat on his back. Nora looked down at her hand; she had not done that in so long.

"Zara what was that?" Nora asked, walking slowly over to Logan.

"I don't know. There was no build up like before. We just panicked and bam." Zara answered.

Nora kneeled down next to Logan and his body began to flicker like a light bulb going out.

"Logan!" Nora said going to touch him again.

"Nora it's-

Logan started to say but he faded out. Nora touched the ground where he used to lay and fear washed over her. Did he die? The room began to fade further into darkness. This was not supposed to happen! Nora slammed her first in the ground, angry washing over her.

"You said there would be peace!" Nora screamed as the world went dark.

It was soundless and empty. The world around her was nothing. She held her hand on the floor where Logan's body had been. It was still warm. Her chest felt like it was caving in. Memories of him flashing through her mind, like a memorial. The time she broke his nose, chasing him into that alley. The way he was never afraid of Jace, the smirks, the winks, the condescending laugh. This was not supposed to happen! She hit the ground again with her fist.

"Why!" She screamed.

"Nora." Like her anger had summoned her, the small light floated across the darkness.

"You said it was supposed to be happy ever after. Logan…he's..he's-

"He's not dead, Nora." The light slowly transformed into the Goddess.

"He was going to be. This was supposed to be your goodbye to him. However, like usual you surprise fate. You still have a small fragment of your powers hidden deep within you." The Goddess reached out touching her cheek softly.

Small little zaps of electric shock trickled Nora's cheek. She looked at the Goddess waiting for her to explain.

"The fact that your power is still there tells me we are not done yet. Something is coming Nora. Something like before. Your daughter will be the answer. She will save you all this time." The Goddess smiled.

"No." Nora said, grabbing her hand.

"No?" The Goddess said, shocked.

"No, it almost killed me each time. You are not doing that to her! She will not be that. She is not your sacrificial lamb." Nora said, Zara pushing forward so her eyes glowed, ice blue with an amber ring.

"Do you know who you're speaking to!" The Goddess said, grabbing her hand, bending her wrist backwards.

Nora dropped feeling the power the Goddess sent into her. Her wrist wanted to break. Nora shut her eyes tightly.

We got this. Zara growled, pushing her strength into her.

Nora opened her eyes. Amber beaming brightly, the ice blue color gone. She locked eyes with the Goddess letting out a yell as she stood.

"You will not use my daughter as your pawn." Nora screamed.

The struggle of power went back and forth. The Goddess trying to hold on. She could feel Nora's powers trying to come back.

"Enough!" The Goddess said, taking her other hand and pressing Nora's head.

Nora 's eyes rolled back into her head and she fell backwards onto the ground.

"I am not using your daughter as a pawn. This is just how it is." The Goddess said, stepping over Nora.

"See for yourself." She whispered and the world went black.

Pain radiatedthrough Nora's head as the world came alive with images. Women with jet black hair with amber colored eyes flashed into her mind. They locked hands with one another, old to young. The heads flying backwards as energy passed from the old to the young.

"They will be cursed to hunt their own forgotten kind. Powers passed down mother to daughter. They will lie dormant until they are needed. Locked away deep inside the hunter until a threat arises. They will remain strong and powerful. Fast with heightened senses but the powers will come and go. That way we are not more of a target." Whispered words floated around her.

"Some may never have them. May we get to a point in life where they won't need them."

Nora jolted upright looking at the Goddess as her vision cleared. She was shaking from the rapid fire memories.

"So you see this is not my doing." The Goddess grumbled.

"Fortunately for you, your daughter, she has you!" The Goddess said.

"Don't disrespect me again or we will no longer be an alliance. I am rooting for you Nora and your daughter has a special place in my heart. Get her ready." The Goddess said walking away.

"Wait. Can't it just be me." Nora shouted, getting to her feet.

The Goddess shook her head and snapped her fingers. Nora was thrown back hitting the ground.

Chapter Eight
Chaos

*N*ora's face hit the table as she sank to the floor. Landing on her back her eyes shot open. She was staring in the brightest pair of ice blue eyes. His hand on her face, his dark eyebrows in a frown as he tried to hide his concern. She smiled at him, putting her hand on top of his. Then as if she remembered it all. She jolted up right.

"Fire." She said looking to Asher who was still in a mind link.

"Fire?" Jace asked, confused.

"Red Woods is under attack, send help. Asher, he needs to get out of his panic, fear trance." Nora said, walking over to him.

"Dante." Jace said his eyes looking across the room to him.

"On it." Dante nodded, rushing out of the room.

"Matt. Logan's hurt." Nora locked eyes with him, fear flashing across them.

"Fuck, I'm going." Matt said, looking quickly at Jace who nodded for him to go.

"Asher!" Nora yelled, shaking him.

He didn't budge. Jace growled, coming to help her when he paused by Zeke. He was doing the same thing. His stomach sank.

"Nora…Zeke." Jace said, connecting the dots.

"Get in touch with Levi. Matt's going to Red Woods, send Dante to Moonlight." Nora said, reaching back with her hand.

Jace looked at her confused and watched her hand fly into Asher's face. The loud smack echoed across the room. His face instantly turned red and swelling up. His eyes shot open a loud growl emerged out of his mouth as he went to go after who attacked him, claws out. His claws going straight for Nora's throat. Jace saw it coming and jumped over the chairs trying to block his way.

"No! Mom!" Mallory yelled as a wave of energy came out of her.

Everyone in the room was thrown into a wall. Zeke hit the wall and his eyes shot open.

"Fire." Zeke said out loud.

"Mom." Mallory said looking down at her hands, her body shaking slightly.

"No.." Nora whispered looking at Jace.

"No? What was that?" Mallory whispered as Zeke started to get up.

"It's ok baby, we're gonna figure this out." Nora said, moving around Zeke.

"Is..Does she?" Jace asked, looking from Nora to Mallory.

"Maybe…I don't know, when I was out the Moon Goddess spoke to me. But before that I found Logan in the darkness where I usually go when I see the Goddess. Logan was dying and I zapped him. I thought my powers were coming back but..she said it's passed down mother to daughter. It only appears when needed." Nora whispered her voice holding pain.

"I have questions." Mallory announced.

"I think we all do." Zeke said, trying to regain his thoughts.

"We can't do this now. Someone is attacking Red Woods and Moonlight as we speak. Logan said there was a fire. Lyla almost didn't get out. I do not know what's going on at Moonlight. We need to send help. Matt is going, have him take reinforcements. Have Dante do the same. Zeke and Asher you need to go to your packs." Nora said locking eyes with Asher who was still in a daze.

"Asher go." Nora said firmly.

"Right." Asher said looking down at his hand, his claws still out as everything slowly came back to him.

Zeke nodded and rushed out the door. Asher followed quickly behind him. Nora locked eyes with Jace dread pitting in her stomach.

"I need to go contact the other packs and up security." Jace said, looking from Nora to Mallory.

"It will be ok." Jace said quietly, he walked over to her and placed a quick kiss on the top of her head like he would do when she was a child before walking out the door.

"We are heading to you. Keep your distance and send back any information that you see. I need to know what Jace is thinking and doing. We are going to take them down shortly but we need to be ahead of them." Knox sent through a mind link to Ronan.

"He has sent out troops too, I am assuming Red Woods and Moonlight. It's happening now. Angela and Mick need to be made aware so they can stay out of sight." Ronan said, looking down from the tree tops.

He had heard them coming from a good distance; they were in wolf form and moving fast. Two sets of groups both running each and branching off in different directions. He recognized the dark gray wolf in the lead of the first pack and then the red wolf of the second. Jace had sent his Beta and Delta out to help. It was a rookie move.

"Then do it. They are heading east towards Red Woods and Moonlight?" Knox asked once more, confirming.

"Yes." Ronan groaned, having to repeat himself.

"We will be there by nightfall." Knox sent back his tone sharp.

"Mick, Angela, Cross River heading towards Moonlight and Red Woods, be discreet and stay out of sight." Ronan sent them.

Part of him could care less if they got caught. Angela's pretentious attitude drove him insane and Mick, he tolerated. He leaned back against the tree, the wind ruffling through his hair. His thoughts wandered back to her ice blue eyes. He wondered who she was there? Was she just a pack member? Was she a higher up's daughter? Who was the boy with her? His wolf growled at the thought of the boy.

What's your problem? Ronan grumbled at Pax.

Girl. Pax grumbled back at him.

Girl…Ronan said back but Pax dismissed him.

Mallory took a deep breath in. She squeezed her eyes shut trying to find the feeling she felt when she got frightened. When she thought Asher was going to hurt her mother. She clenched her jaw and her fist into a tight ball. She let out a long breath becoming frustrated.

"I don't know what it was but I can't do it again." Mallory groaned, slapping the side of her leg with her hand.

"It's ok. You will feel it build in the core of your stomach. It will build and then usually with a touch you can release it. If your powers are like mine, you can also draw energy from people with the same touch." Nora said calmly.

"But I didn't touch anyone. I just was so afraid Asher was going to hurt you. Maybe it's just a fluke…Maybe you did it " Mallory said, throwing her hand up.

"It wasn't me. It will take time. It will come. I will help you ok." Nora reassured her.

"It wasn't some random attack. They attacked two packs at the same time. Whoever it is, is trying to send a message." Jace said firmly, walking into the office.

Nora watched his face scrunch up with frustration as he tried to explain that this was all something bigger to whoever was on the phone.

"Polly, your pack was attacked. How can you not think it is something bigger. They literally moved from your pack and downwards. Douglas is concerned. I am waiting to hear back about the damages done to both Red Woods and Moonlight. They are increasing the damage since they hit Dark Water and City Lights." Jace said, sitting down in the chair behind the desk.

"Dead body here at Cross River and now fires in Moonlight and Red Woods, not empty buildings either. The fires were meant to weaken and kill. We have at least one casualty from Red Woods." Jace said his hand clenched in a fist.

Nora heard him say causality from Red Woods and her heart tensed in her chest, fear pitting her stomach making her feel nauseous. Jace's eyes shot to Nora and he realized what was wrong.

"Her name was Joanna. Logan, Lyla, Jaime, and Chance are all okay. Jordan has Logan stable in the hospital. Lyla too." Jace sent a mind link quickly to her.

She felt a little relieved but she wanted to be there for her friends. She was debating asking if they could go.

"Polly, the best move right now for everyone is to stay in their pack lands and make sure they are safe. We are going to get down to the bottom of this and then we will meet and make moves. It might be quick so make sure you're on standby. I have spoken to Dark Water as well as

Grayson and Douglas who are on their way back to their packs. I have told them the same message and they agree as well." Jace said resting his forehead in his hand.

He was drained, exhausted. It had been so long since anything major had happened and he had hoped it wouldn't happen again. He was worried that this was going to be something big. Cole shifted inside to let Jace know he also sensed it.

"So what's the plan?" Mallory spoke up as her father hit the end call button.

"Lock down, extra patrol, upping security. Matt and Dante are trying to help at each pack. Matt was pretty shaken up with Logan being hurt but he will be ok. Lyla is doing ok, I think the stress of Logan getting hurt put a delay in her healing but her wolf is working hard on fixing them. Moonlight is in rough condition. They are sorting through the ashes. They had buildings and homes on fire. They have people missing and no confirmed death yet. Lyla saved Red Woods. It was meant to be so much worse." Jace said quietly, trying his best to think of anything.

"We will help wherever we can." Nora said, moving closer to Jace.

"Have you guys figured out what all that was?" Jace asked, bringing up Mallory's powers from earlier.

"It was most likely a one time thing." Mallory blurted out.

"The answer is no, it's tricky. You remember how I was when I first started using them. Fear triggered it. That's how I started as well. It will happen slowly…hopefully." Nora said quietly, touching her daughter's shoulder.

"Yeah maybe. Did Adam go with Dante?" Mallory asked, she needed to talk to him.

"No he's out patrolling, he is taking command of it, with the help of Wyatt and Sarah." Jace smiled a little proud.

"Oh..can I-

"No." Jace said, cutting her off.

"Dad-

"Mallory not now, we do not know what's happening. Yes you have been trained to fight and can defend yourself but you do not have the powers of a hunter or wolf on your side…yet. You are also still recovering. We need to be careful right now." Jace said quickly.

"Figures. I do not need to be a wolf to protect myself or have dumb hunter powers. I knew you thought like everyone else." Mallory said, trying to control the emotion coming over her.

"Mallory, I just want you safe." Jace said, trying to make her see that right now no one might be.

"Mallory-

"I'm going to go to my room." Mallory said, cutting off Nora as she walked out of the office.

"I didn't say she wasn't capable." Jace groaned.

"But you didn't say she was." Nora frowned at him.

"Ugh I don't have time for all of this em-

"Alpha, they have her." Matt's mind link came blasting through Jace's brian.

"What? Who?" Jace sent back quickly, his body on edge.

"Hannah. Red Wood's Luna. They've taken her captive. Who ever attack Red Woods took their Luna." Matt sent back quickly.

"Asher? Where's Asher?" Jace said standing, his eyes still glossed over as he was still in mind link.

"He left, his wolf took over and he's gone." Matt sent back a little out of breath as if he had been chasing someone.

"Send someone to make sure Asher isn't running into his death. Stay and help Jaime take control and set up safety." Jace linked.

"Yes Alpha." Matt responded quickly.

"They have Hannah." Jace said his eyes coming back to normal as he looked at Nora.

"Who?" Nora asked her body tensing, she needed to do something but had no clue how to act.

"Who ever attacked. Asher took off-

Before Jace could continue he was hit with another mind link. Nora tensed up seeing it. She watched the same wave of emotions pass over his face as the first mind link. His phone began ringing and Zeke's name flashed across it. Nora grabbed it from the table, hitting the answer button.

"Zeke?" Nora asked quickly.

"Nora? Where's Jace? I need help." Zeke said his voice was calm trying to mask his panic.

"He's in a mind link right now, what can we do?" Nora asked quickly.

"They took her." Zeke said, the panic slipping through.

"Who did they take Zeke?" Nora asked quickly but her stomach already knew.

"Jessica. They have my mate Nora…She's pregnant." Zeke said, trying to control himself.

"We will find her." Nora said as Jace's eyes returned to normal and locked with Nora's.

He held his hand out for the phone and Nora handed it over. Her hands went to the top of her head as she let out an exhale trying to calm herself.

"Zeke, we will do everything in our power to help you get her back. This was planned, they want something. They took Hannah from Asher as well. They won't hurt them. They need them for whatever it is they want." Jace said, trying to keep Zeke level headed.

"Zeke, you're her mate. You can sense her. You can feel if she is safe. Take a deep breath and try to feel her." Jace said in a calm but firm tone.

"Dante's coming to you he's gonna help track them. I will send more people if needed. We will find her Zeke." Jace said quietly as he hung up.

"You're not going anywhere alone." Jace said, looking at Nora.

"Asher?" Nora said worried, she felt better that Jace was able to talk to Zeke.

"He shifted and Xander took over. Matt is trying to track Xander; he's shifted and taken off after him." Jace let out a breath, everything was spiraling.

"Can we send any more people?" Nora asked quietly, trying to think of anything that could help.

"We sent as many as we could to make sure we won't be vulnerable." Jace said a silver lock of hair falling down into his eyes as he was trying to put something together.

"Zeke sent almost all of Moonlight when Lance had me, Asher has stood by us through everything as well." Nora said, trying not to add more stress.

"Ok. Let's think. We can figure this out. Let's figure out where they would be heading." Nora said, going to the maps.

"Ok, Ok. They started off at Silver Mountain, then Dark Water, City Lights-

Loud sirens began to blast. Echoing through the pack lands.

"Mallory, go find her. I will find out what that's about." Jace said moving to the door.

"Alpha, Luna perimeter breach." A mind link was sent and shook Nora and Jace.

Chapter Nine
Sirens

Roan watched movement coming from behind them through the trees. He could hear slow steady walking. They were trying to move soundlessly as they approached them. Ronan motioned for everyone to stay in their hiding spots till he gave the command. The select few he had with them pressed into the shadows blending in. Night had fallen and they had been waiting there long enough.

Ronan saw her blond hair ponytail swing behind her as she walked into their hiding place. She was pushing a woman in front of her. The woman had ropes tied around her wrists and her mouth was gagged. He knew looking at the ropes that they were drenched in wolf bane. He could see the red raw marks from it against her deep brown skin. She was in pain but she kept it hidden. Her chocolate brown eyes searched the area. Her clothing was covered in soot and there were pieces of ashes in her tightly curled dark hair. She had a power to her and Ronan knew right away this was someone's Luna and mate. He sighed before hopping down out of the tree.

"What the fuck is this bull shit?" Ronan asked, getting to his feet.

"What's it look like?" Angela grinned.

"It looks like fucking mess." Ronan groaned, his eyes looking to the trees as more movement was coming.

The men with Angela fanned out around the clearing making way for the more that was coming. Mick walked up the center holding another woman with strawberry blond hair and gray eyes.

"Why do we have women hostage?" Ronan grumbled, getting a headache.

"For leverage, Ronan. Leverage." Knox's voice came from behind him.

"What leverage are we needing?" Ronan asked, turning on his heels to look at Knox.

"The very beautiful woman Angela is holding Zeke's mate and Luna to Moonlight. Mick is holding Asher's mate and Luna to Red Woods." Knox began explaining.

"Kind of figured that." Ronan said not hiding his annoyance.

"Moonlight and Red Woods are Cross River's biggest allies and hold the biggest packs next to Cross River. So now we have their Lunas and if they do not bow before me…they will not have Lunas anymore." Knox grinned looking at each woman.

"So we are hiding in the woods outside of Cross River with Moonlight and Red Woods Lunas. Don't you think Moonlight and Red Woods are on their way here right now." Ronan said not hiding his aggravation.

He knew Knox was impulsive and not the planning type but now he was about to get them all slaughtered.

"I hope they're on their way." Knox laughed.

"All right, I kind of wanted to plan my own death but sure this works." Ronan said sarcastically.

"Here let me put your mind at ease. We are going to walk into Cross River-

"Why walk, we stay here any longer and they'll just find us or Moonlight or Red Woods." Ronan laughed.

"You're lucky you're my Beta. We are going to walk into Cross River parading the two Lunas infront of us and make them surrender or else we kill them. Jace may not give but his Luna will make him. She wouldn't be able to let two innocents be lost. It's simple. When Moonlight and Red Woods get here we will have captured Cross River too and they will have to buckle as well." Knox said is tone very serious.

Ronan let out a breath, becoming more frustrated with the plan. The plan was stupid but he decided to stay quiet. Mick and Angela loved destruction and chaos. They didn't think for themselves.

"Problems?" Knox asked, looking at him curious.

"Nope none at all…I guess fuck it." Ronan said, clenching his jaw.

"Ronan, you're staying here." Knox said, his eyes narrowing at him.

"Yes Alpha." Ronan said, throwing his hand up.

"You will keep a select few with you in case any stragglers attempt to escape. Capture them or kill them. I don't care." Knox nodded to Angela and Mick who began moving towards Cross River.

"Jason and Kai stay behind. You two are the fastest and the ones I can tolerate the most." Ronan ordered.

Jason and Kai nodded, stepping out of formation and going to stand by Ronan. Ronan watched them leave, shaking his head. If they all get killed he could go back to rogue life.

"Find something to do." Ronan ordered Kai and Jason, as he leaned back against an oak tree.

Nora rushed out of the office door heading for the stairs. She needed to make sure her daughter was okay. Her stomach squeezed inward with fear. Her hand grasped the railing as she used it to steady herself, her feet moving faster than her body. Her mind screamed Mallory as she got to the third floor landing. She rushed to the door, slamming into it as not being able to stop. The door busted open. Mallory jumped back away from the window.

"Mom." Mallory said quietly, as she motioned for her mother to come to the window.

"Look." Mallory said pointing.

Nora hurried to the window and looked out. She saw them. They were moving half in wolf form and half in human form. The ones in wolf form had gray glowing eyes. They were marching from the east spreading out. Attempting to surround Cross River. Their leader's destination seemed to be locked on the pack house. Two females out in front of them as if they were being paraded down the road. Nora recognized them instantly.

"They have Hannah and Jessica." She whispered out loud.

"The Luna to Red Woods and Moonlight…How?" Mallory whispered.

"I don't know. You need to hide, we need to get you out of here." Nora said quickly.

"Adam." Nora sent out in a mind link.

"Luna we are being surrounded. The main group is at the front gate but there's movement in the back of the pack lands." Adam sent back.

"Where are you?" Nora sent it back to him.

"Trying to take a group of soldiers around the back of the leader's group. Trying to entrap them before they do it, to us." Adam sent back.

"Jace, we are being surrounded. There's a group coming towards the pack house with Hannah and Jessica. They have gray glowing eyes. I can see from Mallory's room." Nora sent it to Jace.

"I know I am heading out there. You and Mallory stay back. Be safe." Jace mind linked back.

"What is going on?" Mallory demanded watching the scene from her window.

Nora moved to the window to see Jace heading out there. A man moved forward pushing past Jessica and Hannah. He had red brown hair that was cut short and hung loose around his ears. He had a familiar smirk on his face as he pulled a knife from his belt. He said something to Jace and then moved towards Hannah. He pressed the knife to Hannah's throat and then motioned for the person holding Jessica to do the same. Nora studied Jace, her heart pounding in her chest.

We need to do something! Zara screamed inside of her.

"Nora…I..I have to surrender. I cannot let them kill Zeke's and Asher's mate. I need you and Mallory to escape. Run." Jace sent it to Nora as Nora watched him drop to his knees.

"Oh God." Nora whispered.

"Mom?" Mallory said quietly.

"We need to go, come on." Nora said, grabbing Mallory by the hand.

"I love you." Nora sent to Jace as she pulled Mallory out of the bedroom and began racing down the hall.

Cole growled inside of him so fiercely that he could feel his own chest rumble as he walked outside.

"Alpha, wait for me." Wyatt sent to Jace, his tone panic.

"They're knocking on the pack house door. Have the men try their best to spread out around the territory. Secure our borders. We will try closing them in." Jace sent back to Wyatt.

Jace locked eyes with their leader. His mud brown eyes filled with excitement and his red brown hair reminded him of someone. Jace narrowed his eyes as he walked to the end of their driveway to meet him.

"Let them go." Jace ordered.

"Funny that you think you can order us around." He laughed as he reached towards his belt.

"Funny how you think you can come on my land without an invitation." Jace growled his eyes glowing ice blue as Cole pushed forward, begging to be let out.

"We have an invitation." He laughed again, twirling his knife around his finger and pointing at the two Luna's.

"If you do not release them-" Jace started to say.

"What? You'll do what. You are one person. Yes I am pretty sure you could kill several of my men. Go ahead I need to weed the weak ones out but you will not get to me and you will not stop the blood I will be spilling from these two beautiful Luna's throats. Their blood will be on your hands and your friendships shattered. Who should I kill first?" He snickered walking towards Jessica and Hannah.

He looked at Jace and took his blade and pressed it into Hannah's throat. Images of Hannah's dead body laying on the ground blood seeping out of her. Asher's face and how crushed he would be rushed into his head. Asher had waited so long to find his mate and now he had found her it would wreck him. Jace clenched his jaw and watched the man nod to the person holding Jessica and soon a blade was pressed against her throat.

"Surrender." He grinned.

Jace's hands went to fists. How can he surrender and jeopardize his pack? How could he not surrender and save these two women? The man pressed his knife into Hannah's throat just deep enough that a small red bead of blood rolled out across the blade and down her neck.

"Surrender or I will kill them. I will then find your Luna and gut her in front of you. I will cut her from navel to neck and let you see her insides fall out in front of you. I will kill everyone you hold dearly." The man said his eyes turned sinister as he spoke.

Thoughts of Nora and Mallory flashed through his mind as he felt his jaw stiffen. He had no choice. He couldn't let them.

"Nora…I..I have to surrender. I cannot let them kill Zeke's and Asher's mate. I need you and Mallory to escape. Run." Jace sent it to Nora as Nora watched him drop to his knees.

"Fine. I will surrender." Jace said quietly, he knew that Red Wood and Moonlight would be on their way here, he just needed to hold out.

"Kneel." He said eagerly.

"Who are you? What pack is this?" Jace asked, looking at all of them.

"Knox Alpha of the Shadow pack, now kneel." Knox grinned triumphantly.

Jace let out a long breath as he kneeled. He was not one for dramatics but he needed to keep everyone safe and this was the way so be it.

"Let them go." Jace said from his knees.

"I love you." Nora's mind link came through and he prayed that she had listened and was getting herself and Mallory to safety.

Knox nodded and three of his men came up to Jace. One kicked him forward and he fell over to the ground. The others grabbed his hands and bound them with ropes. Jace winced as the ropes began to burn. He instantly knew it was wolfsbane.

"Now I said I wouldn't kill them. I never said I would let them go. Help him up, boys. We will have a tour of his pack lands. Maybe find his Luna." Knox winked.

"If you touch her I will kill you." Jace said as he was yanked up to his feet.

"Funny from the position you're in I would be careful as to what I would say to me, threats are not acceptable." Knox said, threatening him.

"They're not threats. They're promises." Jace said his voice was ice cold.

"Let's go show your pack their strong Alpha." Knox said as he began walking towards the pack house.

Chapter Ten
Run

*N*ora's hand hit the back door, her other hand gripping Mallory's tightly. She peeked out before rushing out. If she could get to the woods she could get Mallory and herself out. Her plan was to escape and come back with troops.

"Luna." Matt's voice chimed in her head as she crept towards the woods trying to keep her position lower, hoping the darkness will cover them.

"Matt. Jace he's surrendered. They have Jessica and Hannah." Nora said his eyes locked on the heavily treed area in front of her.

"Dante and I are rushing back. Asher is headed that way; he is in wolf form and feral. I'm on his tail. Get out and get to the hunters. Lilly will be waiting." Matt said even his mind link sounded out of breath.

"Mom." Mallory's voice came from behind her panic and it pulled her out of the mind link.

Nora stopped moving and pulled Mallory behind her as three large brown wolves came out of the forest, eyes glowing gray, teeth snarling. Nora watched them slowly trying to surround them Nora took a deep breath and spun Mallory to her.

"Mallory. Look at me. Look at me." Nora said, trying to get Mallory's attention as she undid the necklace around her neck.

"Mom, there's three of them. Mom?" Mallory stammered out as Nora slipped the black onyx over her head.

"I know, I'm going to shift. Zara is strong and fierce. I need you to run. Run through the woods, Run hard and fast. Your quick baby. I've seen you run from Adam. You need to run with everything in you. If I don't catch up, keep going. You need to get to Lilly at the hunters. You need to do that." Nora said, grabbing her face with her hands.

"Mom, I can't leave you." Mallory said, grabbing Nora's hand.

"You need to, you need to go get help." Nora said, kissing Mallory's forehead quickly and stepping back from her.

"I love you. When I shift you run." Nora said her eyes glowing bright ice blue with a ring of amber.

"Mallory." Nora said not seeing her daughter respond, Nora's bones beginning to pop and snap out of place.

"Ok…I'll get help." Mallory said shifting a part of her so afraid to leave her mother behind.

Nora shifted quickly and in her place stood Zara. Her bright white coat shimmering in the starlight, her eyes glowing just as bright as the moon. She let out a low deadly growl and nodded for Mallory to run. Mallory hesitated and Zara growled at her. The wolves focused in on Zara and Mallory reluctantly took off running.

Mallory ducked into the woods running with everything she had. She didn't look back. If she did she knew that she wouldn't be able to leave her mother to fight the three wolves alone. She knew her mother was strong, fast, and capable. She needed to be that too. She needed to get help. She dodged a tree branch and blocked her face from a branch that tried to reach out and scratch. Her eyes locked on everything in front of her as she ran as hard and fast as she could. Her eyes became blurry as she pushed herself to run faster than she had ever. She could hear something coming behind her. Their footprints hit the ground hard behind her. Her lungs burned in her chest as she tried to ignore it and push herself to keep going.

A blurred image was moving towards her, she blinked trying to clear her vision when her foot caught a tree root sending her flying into the ground. She landed on her stomach, her forearms scraping the ground and the skin on her knees cracked open on impact, blood seeping out. She could feel something approaching behind her as she tried to get up. A loud growl made the hair on the back of her neck stand up as she almost froze from the power of it. Mallory got to her knees quickly turning and coming face to face with a dark brown wolf. Its mouth slightly opened as drool dripped down from its curled lip. The gray eyes glowed into hers as she scooted back away from it. It seemed to smile at her as if taunting her.

The large wolf stepped towards her, a low growl rumbling through its chest feeling like it was rattling the ground around her. It ducked its head at her and snapped its large jaws at her. She just needed to get more space between her and the wolf. Her heart pounded in her chest as she slowly tried to creep away. The wolf leaned back ducking its head further down as if it was going to pounce on her. She got to her feet and went to run when another wolf appeared in front of her blocking her in. The wolf was a dark red and looked extremely out of breath. It was frantic and searching for something. It locked eyes with the dark brown wolf.

Mallory tried moving out of the way but the dark brown wolf snapped at her, keeping her in the area between the two wolves. The dark red wolf backed up and went to lunge. Mallory found herself ducking and the wolf went over her head. It landed in front of Mallory letting out a loud growl and lunged for the dark brown wolf. At the last second Mallory noticed the dark red wolf's eyes glowing red with an amber ring and knew they were from Red Woods. She was torn between staying with the wolf and continuing her journey for help. If Red Woods were close by she had to let them know what was happening. She took off running.

Her body was feeling weak, her legs burning, her arms felt like jello. She could hear the wolves behind her fighting. She kept going, she had her mother's voice in her head telling her to run. A red wolf came bolting out of the east, it was running like something was chasing it and came to a tumbling stop in front of Mallory. It's ice bright blue and Mallory recognized him.

"Ryker." Mallory said out of breath.

Ryker tilted his head at her as if confused at why she was out in the middle of the woods.

"We've been attacked, Dad had to surrender. They have Asher's and Zeke's mates. Mom told me to run to the hunters. There's a wolf back there fighting one of the wolves that invaded. My mom, she was fighting three. I need to go for help." Mallory said, leaning over a little bit trying to catch her breath.

Ryker studied her as if trying to process what to do next. He could hear the fight going on. He ducked his head as if hating making the choice. He walked over to Mallory and nudged her with his head as if to say keep going. He moved her with his head. Turning her from the direction she was running for and pointing her slightly right. He then pushed her forward as if to say go that way.

A rush of rumbling like an earthquake hitting the ground was heard. Mallory could hear the slamming of feet. More was coming. A large gray wolf ran past Ryker not even hesitating to stop. Ryker let out a huff and nudged Mallory as if to say he wasn't leaving until she started going. She nodded to him before starting to run again, this time in the direction that he pointed her. She glanced over her shoulder just in time to see Ryker take off.

Mallory ran as hard as she could despite her body feeling weak. She just needed to find the road. If she could get to the road, she knew how to get to the hunters. The trees started becoming further apart from each other and the sky was clouded with darkness. She felt like she had been running for hours. A loud thunder-like noise was coming from her left. It was constant and growing the closer she got. Stumbling forward she grabbed a hold of a branch. She was trying to catch her breath and trying hard to not let her legs give out. She grasped it tightly, her hands getting splinters from the bark. A loud snap was heard as the branch gave away under her weight. She felt her feet give away against the soil as she went tumbling forward.

She landed into cold freezing water. She tried to grab onto the side of the river but the thunder she was hearing was the river and it was fierce. It pulled her away from the sides of river banks. Pushing her hard and fast down stream. She tried grabbing a hold of rocks passing by but they were too slick and sharp only cutting her hands. She tried hard to push against the river's currents but her body was so weak from running she barely was keeping her head above water. She saw a large rock coming up ahead. It poked up out of the water like a large iceberg. She tried to steer herself towards it but the river began to swirl her around in a circle. She tried to reach out to it as she came to it but the current spun her. Her back hit against the rock. The force of it, throwing her head back into it and the world went black.

Chapter Eleven
Lost

*H*e wrapped his hand around her jet black hair. A loud hair raising growl erupted from Jace as he struggled against the chains he was now in. Knox stood in the middle of the hall, his hand dangerously close to Nora's neck as the other yanked her head back. He could hear the wolves surrounding the pack hall. The rest of Cross River inside and kneeling, mostly women and children. What Knox had not expected was that Moonlight and Red Woods would bring their armies. He snapped his fingers and Angela scooped up Hannah and Mick did the same to Jessica, forcing them to their feet and placing a blade to their throats. Knox dragged Nora by her hair to the center of the hall, a blade on his hip.

"Let them in." Knox announced.

Soldiers at the door pulled the doors open and in charge the dark red wolf, a bright red wolf, and a dark gray wolf. Jace recognized all three of them. He tensed up. If Asher did anything a bit rash he could lose Nora, they could lose them all.

"Asher!" Jace yelled at the dark red wolf hoping to make him see anything other than red.

"Shift! Shift or we will kill all of the Luna's" Knox announced.

Matt shifted instantly, afraid to do anything to get Nora hurt. His eyes locked with her, his stomach twisting.

"Luna are you ok?" Matt asked, his body twitching as he resisted the urge to lunge forward at Knox.

"It's ok, I'm ok." Nora smiled weakly at him.

Knox tugged on her hair trying to make Nora make a sound but she clenched her jaw, her hand automatically going to his as she held it in place so who couldn't tug anymore.

"Hang tight we will figure this out." Matt sent her through the mind link.

"Dante where the fuck are you? We are in the great hall. Some psycho has has Nora, Hannah, and Jessica. They also somehow have managed to round up all the women in children. Mallory is running to the hunters." Matt gave Dante a fast mind link, trying to keep it hidden that he was.

"We are just getting to the pack lands. Sarah and the rest of the men are heading around back to the great hall. I have some of Moonlight with us. How many are there?" Dante sent back.

"I don't know. Right now there's only a handful but they have blades to Nora's, Hannah's, and Jessica's throat. They have Jace covered in wolfsbane and chains." Matt said keeping his head low so know one would notice his eyes.

Knox snapped his fingers and pointed to Matt. Matt held up his hands as two men came to him and knocked him down to his knees.

"Hey!" Nora yelled as she pulled against Knox.

"It's ok Luna, I was working on surrendering anyways." Matt said to her with a wink.

"Care for that one a lot huh?" Knox whispered in Nora's ear.

"If you keep struggling I will have them gut him." Knox snickered.

Nora went stiff in his arms, her eyes going to Jace fear flashing in them. They had never been in this situation before and she was powerless. Jace tried to stand again but the man standing next to him pushed him back down, rubbing the chains into his skin. Matt was bound with wolf bane ropes and dragged up to Jace.

"Evening Alpha." Matt smiled.

"Shut up." The man slammed Matt into the floor.

"Oh I like it rough. The ropes could be just a little more tighter." Matt smirked.

"Get him to shut up or he dies." Knox said to Nora but looking at Jace.

"Matt shut up." Jace ordered him.

Jace's eyes locked with Xander. He was watching him debate. Seeing if it was possible to get to Hannah in time.

"Xander let Asher come back. You might get to Hannah but it wont save her. You will kill Jessica and Nora!" He yelled trying to stand up against the chains weighing him down.

Zeke shifted instantly hearing Jace. He hit the ground in human form, his body shaking as he stood.

"Asher he is right!" Zeke growled looking at the dark red wolf.

He watched the dark red wolf begin to twitch and finally Asher appeared. His body shaking, sweat covered his body like he had been fighting for control.

"Hannah." Asher said breathless locking eyes with her.

"I'm ok. It's ok." Hannah whispered to him, giving him a small smile.

"What do you want?" Asher yelled, turning to look at Knox.

"Bad guy..what do bad guys want…money, power, control. Same deal. I want Red Woods…I want to destroy Cross River." Knox said grinning.

The hall door busted open, wood shattering out into the room. A large dark gray wolf came bursting through, flanking his sides were several other wolves, all eyes glowing white except the one glowing ice blue. The back door to the hall busted open, another swarm of wolves came rushing in. The deep chocolate wolf leading the way, her eyes glowing ice blue, and she looked fierce. Her eyes locked with the dark gray wolf as a silent order was given to surround the room.

"Well this is lovely, is everyone here now?" Knox laughed looking at Jace as he pulled Nora closer to him.

"I suggest everyone in wolf form turn human so we can all talk otherwise this is going to get bad really quickly." Knox continued as he pushed his knife into Nora's throat.

He nodded to Angela and Mick, they pressed their blades to Jessica and Hannah's throat.

"If by the count of three there is anyone in wolf form, one of your lovely Luna's are going to be gurgling on their own blood." Knox nodded to a man hanging behind both Jace and Matt.

The man moved towards Matt, a blade in his hand. Nora saw it and began to try to move away from Knox fearing the worst. The blade pressing against her throat.

"Shift!, Cross River Shift!" Nora shouted fearing that Matt was going to be an example.

Dante was the first to shift and then Sarah, the rest of Cross River followed suit but Moonlight was still in wolf form. Zeke almost froze, his eyes locked on Jessica. The man watched Knox, he did not call him off. He took the blade and pressed it into Matt's arm and ran it down it. A thin red line appeared on Matt's arm and began to seep blood.

"The next cut won't be so forgiving." Knox said, his voice low and deadly.

"Zeke. Asher, this is you now!" Jace yelled trying to bring them back to the world.

"Moonlight shift!" Zeke orders snapping back into reality.

"Red Woods shift." Asher followed suit.

---

*H*e was waiting for orders, when the sound of running wolves caught his ears. He motioned for them to hide and just in time as a swarm of wolves came rushing by.

"Alpha, incoming." Ronan sent through a mind link, trying to hide his I told you so tone.

"Well come on down, back up." Knox snickered back.

"Damn it." Ronan muttered out loud.

"Let's move out, we are to follow and be back up, let them get to the hall and get in place, then we are going to surprise them." He said to the men that were left with him.

The men shifted into wolf form and began tracking. Ronan hung back just a second because something caught his ear. He nodded to the one wolf staying behind with him to go on. The blonde wolf looked reluctant but followed orders. Ronan found himself drawn to something. He began moving quickly through the trees the sound of rushing water coming to his ears. Pax became restless as he got closer to the sound. Ronan was confused by the anxicty he was feeling and needed to know the cause of it. Getting to the river bank he felt the urge to dive into the water. He watched the rapids, they were strong and fierce. The water clashed up against the bank splashing his feet. He shook his head, what was wrong with his wolf, why did he want the river?

A flash of black ebony hair came up out of the water. It was just a glimpse of her hair but he locked in on it. She was floating being tossed around as she fought against the current. His body twitched watching her, his wolf telling him to dive into the water. His head telling him to walk away this was not his problem. Then he saw it, the large rock peeking out of the water. She tried to swerve away from it but got spun round backwards. She slammed into the rock, her head going back and smashing against. The loud crack coursed a vibration through his bones, as he watched her go limp. Before he could even process what he was doing, he dove into the water.

The water was freezing and it was dark. He fought against the current trying to get to her. A wave making him duck under water. His wolf fueling him the strength to be strong enough to reach her. He came up out of the water just in time to see her be pushed downward. He ducked under the water below the current getting away from the pulling of the waves. He could see her as he squinted in the water. He pushed himself, his hands outstretched towards her. She was unconscious floating through the water. He knew he had limited time to reach her. His fingertips brushed her arms as the water pulled her away from him again. Pax pushed a surge of strength to him as his eyes glowed brightly and he moved forward. His arms captured her as he pulled her into him and pushed up out of the water.

Coming to the surface he took a deep breath in and then began trying to move to the river banks. The water fought him relentlessly. Getting to shallow water he found his footing and began moving through the water. He scooped her up in his arms cradling her to his chest as he made it to dry land. He placed her down on the rocky soil looking her over. He held his breath trying to see if she was breathing.

"Shit." He whispered at the lack of her chest rising and falling.

He began compressions on her chest. Her body rocking back and forth as he pressed on it. His mind counted each compressions he did.

She hurt, everything hurt. Her body felt like it was being stabbed with a thousand pins and needles all at once. The air touching her skin hurt. She sat up slowly, looking around and she found nothing but pitch black darkness. She pulled her knees up to her chest letting out a long breath. Where was she? She couldn't see her hand in front of her face. She shut her eyes as her whole body throbbed in pain.

"Hello?" She called out in the darkness.

She didn't know why she thought there would be an answer but it felt like the thing to do. She felt silly for doing it but maybe something would come of it. She got to her feet slowly.

"Child." A soft voice called to her.

"Me?..Who's there?" Mallory said, spinning in the darkness, trying to turn to where the sound was coming from but it seemed like it echoed all around her.

"Yes you. Come into the light." The voice said and as she said the word light, a light appeared.

"Ok…" Mallory said walking to it, her body slightly hunched from the pain.

As she stepped into the light all the pain in her body was gone. She was surrounded by a comforting warmth.

"You are the perfect combination of your mother and father. I see both their strength in you. Alot more trusting though." She said stepping into the light as well.

She was something dreams were made out of. She looked like starlight and shimmered like the sun. Mallory shielded her eyes to the glow that surrounds her

"You know my parents?" Mallory asked, looking down.

"Your mother is one of my favorite children and I admire your father's control and strength." She smiled.

"Where am I?" Mallory asked, looking around.

"The in between." She answered quietly.

"In between what?" Mallory asked, confused.

"Life and death." She answered flatly.

"What!" Mallory said, her hand going to her chest as if she was searching for her own heartbeat.

"It's one of the few ways I can speak to you without interference. Mallory you're going to go through some very tough things. You're needing to find yourself. You need to find the hunter in you and the wolf." She spoke quietly.

"I am not either. I have no powers, I have no wolf." Mallory answered bitterly.

"You are your own worst enemy. You believe it so much you cannot let yourself see what is hidden by the curse on your family. You have so much hate towards your own self that the curse doesn't even have to put up much of a fight." She said disappointed.

"What?" Mallory asked, confused trying to process everything that she was saying.

Suddenly she felt pressure on her chest. Like someone was pushing on it. She winced at the pain, what was going on. She grabbed her shirt in her hands as the pressure increased.

"What's going on?" She winced asking the woman, as her chest began to hurt more and more.

"Oh..hmm well it's about time he showed up." The woman said, shaking her head softly.

"What? Who?" Mallory asked, her breath becoming erratic as she tried to stop the feeling in her chest.

"It doesn't matter. You won't remember. I'm sorry Mallory but it's the only way. You need to forget who you think you are to remember who you are meant to be." The woman said, walking over to her.

"What?" Mallory asked, looking at her as she came towards her, the woman had her hand stretched outwards.

"Fate's calling Mallory." She said and tapped Mallory's forehead.

As her finger tip touched Mallory's forehead the world went black and Mallory tumbled back into the darkness.

Chapter Twelve
Fate

"*D*amn it. Come on!" Ronan said in frustration as he pressed down hard on her chest.

She hadn't been under water that long. Pax was whimpering inside of him like he was losing a part of himself. It was driving Ronan insane he couldn't think. He pressed down hard, he felt a crack knowing it was one of her ribs. He paused, going to give her a breath. He pinched her nose and went to place his mouth over hers. Water hit him in the face as she began coughing. He reacted quickly, rolling her onto her side. More water poured out of her as she coughed. She began to struggle, trying to sit up.

"Hey, hey easy." Ronan said, helping her sit up.

"Breathe." He said quietly to her as she winced, taking a breath in.

He knew she had to hurt from how hard he had been pressing on her chest. He knew there had to be some ribs broken. He watched her slowly breathe. She didn't realize it but she had leaned back into him. Her body was shivering from the cold. Although he was wet, the amount of heat coming from his body was incredible. She nuzzled back into him, wincing.

"Help." She whispered not knowing she was saying it, she was cold and everything hurt.

"I'm going to help you, hold on." He said trying to figure out what his next move was.

She leaned back into him looking up at him. Confusion flashing across her face as her ice blue eyes stared into him. Her brows came together and her eyes narrowed.

"Who are you?" She said trying to get her wits about her.

"I'm Ronan…You were in the river, not conscious. I got you out and got you back." He said calmly.

"River?" She said as flashes of falling in the river and then darkness came across her mind.

"Yeah." Ronan said, his voice now confused as he nodded to the river.

She looked to the river and then she remembered hitting her head. She sat up straighter pain shooting through her as her hand went to the back of her head. Her cold wet black hair stuck to her hand and then she felt it. The warmness of blood. Ronan's eyes went through the large wound and he felt a rush of panic. He moved her hand out of the way as he tried to see how deep and bad it was.

"It's ok, let me see." He ordered his voice firm but held a touch of softness to it.

She leaned forward slightly, her body starting to shake from the cold air rushing around her. Ronan parted her hair and saw a good wound on the back of her head. It was bleeding but it was slow. He gritted his jaw. He needed to get her help.

"Is the pack ground secure?" Ronan sent a mind link to Knox.

"Yes, we're putting the rest of them in the dungeon. Jace impressively has a hold building that's like a jail. It was unused and most likely from his father's time. I set the Alpha's in wolfsbane secure cells and kept their Luna's in another." Knox announced proudly of himself.

"I'm coming." Ronan sent back, he wanted to ask Knox what happened now but he really didn't care. Right now all he wanted was to save this girl.

"Nice of you to come join us." Knox snickered back.

Ronan didn't say anything to her as he pulled her against him and began carrying her. She struggled in his arms.

"Put me down. Where are we going?" She said trying to fight him but she felt so weak and couldn't control the shaking her body was doing trying to get warm.

"To get you warm and help your head. There's a wound there. You'll be ok but it needs to be tended to." Ronan said his voice every matter of fact.

"Ok." She shivered, she was too cold and hurt to much to fight him

Her eyes felt heavy as she tried to focus on where he was carrying her to. He pulled her closer to him, his own wet clothing he knew wasn't helping much. He gritted his teeth, how far could he possibly be from a house?

"Hey, stay awake." He ordered as he shook her lightly.

"It's so cold." She said quietly, her teeth chatted together.

"What's your name?" He asked her as he crossed from the forest and now could see houses and civilization.

"Mmmm." She groaned her bones aching and she was too fuzzy to think of her name.

"Mmm?" Ronan half chuckled as he began to move a little quicker, he glanced down her lips were blue and she was losing consciousness.

"Mmm..I don't ..know." She whispered, all she could think of was the noise M made.

"Don't know. How do you forget your name?" He laughed now nervous, his eyes narrowing in on the first house.

His voice got distant,she could hear him asking her questions but couldn't make out what he was saying. She just wanted to give into the darkness. She didn't want to hurt anymore.

Ronan looked down and became angry. She was passing out on him. He growled as he got to the first house. She felt the growl as it vibrated through his chest causing her to lightly shake. Ronan rushed to the first house he could see. The lights were off and it looked empty. He didn't even bother trying to open the door, he kicked it open. The wood buckling and the door jam splinting from the force of his kick. He stumbled through the door looking for a light switch. He threw his shoulder into the light switch turning them on as he entered the living room. He set the girl down on the couch. Her black hair sprawling over the side of it.

"Send me a medic." Ronan mind linked Knox.

"Excuse you?" Knox responded back.

"I need a damn medic sent to the first house on the east end, now." Ronan growled through mind link.

"Christ what's got you all worked up." Knox said, ignoring Ronan's tone.

"Medic." Ronan growled.

"Sending. Remember whose Alpha." Knox threatened.

Ronan ignored the threat, he looked around the room spotting the fireplace. He grabbed a few pieces of wood from the stack and tossed them into it. Grabbing the long matchstick he struck it on the side of the fireplace causing it to set fire. He then tossed the match into and the wood slowly caught fire. He looked back at the couch being so far from the flames. He clenched his jaw walking over to it and then began dragging the couch across the living placing it closer to the fireplace. His eyes fell on her, he had never felt this type of panic or concern for anyone.

Clothes. She needs her clothes off. Pax growled in their mind.

Ronan was about to argue with Pax when it hit him he was right. She couldn't get warm with the wet clothing clinging to her. Ronan grabbed the bottom of her wet shirt and slowly tried pulling it up over her head. He watched the back of her head worried about the wound. He eased her head back down, he stood up looking over her. She was perfect. Her skin was sunkissed and freckles dotted over her body. He shook his head as he quickly undid her jeans and slipped them off. The soaking wet pants hit the floor with a thump. Ronan grabbed the blankets on top of the couch and put them down around her. Her body began shaking more even while she was out.

"Beta?" Justin's voice ran through the house, as he looked around.

"In here. Hurry." Ronan called from the living room.

"She's got a head wound and I can't get her warm." Ronan said as he entered the room.

"Ok. Let's have a look." Justin said calmly as he walked over to the couch.

A concern looked passed over his face as he took in her blue colored skin. Ronan clenched his jaw as the sound of a growl rumbled through his chest.

"We gotta get her warmer." Justin said, ignoring the growl.

"How?" Ronan said, becoming annoyed.

"Um well the fire's good the blankets. Still not warm enough." He was muttering to himself.

"How are you our medic?" Ronan growled.

Justin suddenly hit him in the forehead. His hand pressing into Ronan's forehead. Ronan clenched his fists together, as he glared at Justin.

"Justin-" Ronan started but was cut off by Justin touching his face.

"You. Take off your clothes." Justin said tugging on his shirt.

"What the hell?" Ronan yelled, shoving him lightly.

"You're hot, she's cold. If you want to save her, take your clothing off and get under the blankets with her." Justin said to him as if he was stupid.

"I uh?" Ronan asked his hand to going to his pants.

"Or shit I'll do it, she's cute." Justin said, grabbing the bottom of his shirt.

"You won't be doing nothing." Ronan said as he grabbed him by his shirt and twisted in his hand.

"Woah easy Beta." Justin said, throwing his hands up.

"Just shut up and fix her head." Ronan growled as he pulled his shirt up over his head.

"Yes Beta." Justin said, going over to her to look at her head.

Ronan was down to his boxers, debating on whether to keep them on or take them off. He wanted to take them off because they were wet and she didn't need anything else cold against her but at the same time he wanted some type of boundary between them. She was already confusing him and stirring up feelings he had not felt before.

"What is she?" Justin asked, looking at the wound in the back of her head.

"What?" Ronan said, walking over to see what he was looking at.

"Well she's not a wolf or else this would be healed. She heals faster than a human though. The size of this and the way it looked like it was originally seems like it would have needed sutures but her body is already working on pulling itself back together." Justin said, ignoring a naked Ronan.

"Move so I can hold her." Ronan ordered.

"Where did she come from?" Justin asked curiously as he stepped away.

"I pulled her out of the river." Roan said, sitting behind her and pulling her into him.

She felt like ice as he wrapped his body around hers. He felt her shiver against him. He placed his arms around her holding her closely. Justin had disappeared and came back with more blankets. The girl's color was slowly coming back to normal.

"So?" Ronan asked his tone demandingly.

"I brought some antibiotics in case she develops pneumonia. I have some pain meds because she looks like she's gonna hurt. She is bruised pretty badly, nothing looks broken. " Justin said, holding up pill bottles.

"Set them down somewhere. Tell whoever's house that it is mine until further notice." Ronan announced.

"Yes Beta, most of the subjects are locked away." Justin said, peeking over Ronan's shoulder, take a look at her head again.

"It looks good, it's going to need to be cleaned out once more but with her temperature being so low. I think maybe we should start an IV with some fluids warmed up." Justin said quietly.

Ronan was watching her. The way her dark eyes lashes fanned across her freckled cheeks. He found himself smiling looking down at the small little brown dots that ran across her cheek bone. The brown speckles traveled up over the bridge of her nose and down the other side. He found himself wanting to stay holding her like this. Justin scanned her forehead with a thermometer getting her temperature. He nodded at the thermometer as if saying it did a good job.

"Knock, Knock." Knox's voice came from the doorway as he walked into the house.

"Alpha." Justin said, bowing his head, showing respect to Knox.

"I came to see what has the Beta so worked up." Knox grinned coming into the living room.

Ronan stiffened; he hadn't expected Knox to come out here. He honestly wasn't thinking about anything other than keeping the girl safe.

"Oh…a girl. Hmm. Where did she come from?" Knox asked, his face confused as he tried to read the girl.

"I pulled her out of the river. She was hurt." Ronan said flatly, Pax was just under his skin for some reason thinking Knox was a threat.

"What is she?" Knox demanded.

"She's human." Ronan answered, his voice held a tinge of anger in it.

"Really a human. You are all worked up over some human girl." Knox half laughed when he said it.

"She's mine." Ronan's eyes narrowed looking at Knox, his eyes glowed slightly.

"Watch yourself Ronan." Knox said, his voice turning deadly.

"She's mine." Ronan growled, sitting up slightly, if he needed to he was prepared to fight Knox.

"Ronan." Knox said, shaking his head.

"Relax, no one wants your human. I think humans are disgusting and should be dealt with." Knox grinned seeing Ronan get upset.

"Knox-" Ronan growled trying to figure out what exactly he meant but Knox put his hand up stopping Ronan from finishing his sentence.

"You can have the girl. She is yours. When we do eventually take over, humans will be slaves, so here's your first one. Since you're so fond of her." Knox said, waving him off.

"I'm taking this house for now." Ronan said as Knox glanced at the girl some more.

"Don't care. Take what you want. We're running this place now. We have Cross River, Red Wood, and Moonlight all done. Dark Water and City Lights are run by women and will be easy to subdue. Black Sands are weak, the only one I might be worried about is Silver Mountain but that's not something for now." Knox said quietly.

"I'll meet you in the morning to go over game plans on getting Silver Mountain under control. I believe Douglas might have a son." Ronan said quietly.

"And there he is." Knox smiled at Ronan's comment.

"See you in the morning. Hope your pet makes it. I actually haven't ever seen you worked up like that before. Worried me for a second." Knox said, turning on his heels and moving to the exit.

"Justin fix the Beta's door before you leave." Knox ordered.

"Yes Alpha." Justin said quietly.

Chapter Thirteen
Cold

"*Jace.*" Nora whispered from her cell, she just wanted to hear his voice.

"Nora?" His voice carried down the long hall of cells.

She instantly felt relieved. He was in here with her. She let out the breath that she had been holding in.

"Are you ok?" Nora called back to him.

"I'm just fine. You?" Jace smiled, hearing her voice made him feel instantly better.

"I'm fine, we will figure this out. I am here, Jessica, and Hannah are here. The wolfsbane affects them more than me. They're ok but weak. Asher and Zeke?" Nora asked moving closer to the bars but not close enough to touch them.

"They're here. Asher made himself pass out from trying to get the chains off of him and Zeke tried as well but it had the same outcome." Jace said, his voice frustrated.

"Are you ok?" Nora almost whispered, she was afraid something was wrong.

"I'm fine." Jace grumbled.

"She's got out." Nora said, wanting to tell Jace that Mallory had gone to get help, that she got out of there in time.

"Good. She's strong…Adam is still missing. Dante and Sarah are in cells somewhere else in this mess. I don't even know what the next move is." Jace said his frustration finally slipped out.

He was locked away in a cell he couldn't get out of. His daughter had gotten out but he was unsure if she was safe. His pack was endangered, Cole was slipping away from him the more and more the wolfsbane got into his system. He squeezed the bar with his hands, the silver burning into him. His father had made this prison impossible to escape and it was big enough to hold packs, never mind a few prisoners. He was so bent on destroying his enemies he was prepared for everything possible, well besides his own son turning against him.

"Maybe Adam will find her." Nora whispered her thoughts on her daughter.

"He always does." Jace whispered back, taking his singed hand off the bar.

The last little bit of light crept out of the cells, the darkness slowly taking over. Nora let out a sigh feeling the weight of it creep in on her and the helplessness.

---

*H*e watched her sleep. He was so afraid that if he took his eyes off of her that something would happen. Pax was overly worried and whimpered every so often. It was becoming annoying. Pax was normally quiet and indifferent on most things. The only time he was really vocal was right before a kill and it was more excitement. Her black eyes lashes fanned across her freckled cheek. He found himself tracing the small line of tiny brown speckles over the bridge of her nose and down to her other cheek. He was memorizing every inch of her face, her pouty rose colored lips begging for his. He quickly shut his eyes and leaned his head back trying to breath for a moment.

She flinched, she was weak and tired. She could feel her body hurting. She couldn't remember what happened. She remembered darkness but nothing before the darkness. She was cold, so cold. She moved slightly and something was warm. Like the warmth from the sun or hot bath. She needed it and moved into it more. She let out a soft sigh as she did.

He heard her sigh and he lifted his head back, his eyes opening as he looked down at her. He felt himself stop breathing as he was worried about what would happen next. He watched her dark eyelashes flutter as they opened and he froze looking into the purest blue eyes he had ever seen. He felt his heart speed up in his chest and his wolf began to howl like crazy.

"Mate." The words fell out of his mouth before he could even stop himself.

He was taken back, his stomach knotted inside of itself. Mate. How could it be? They were not supposed to have a mate. Pax became active in him trying to take control. Ronan usually had a handle on Pax and Pax was just there. Now Pax wanted out, wanted to be in control. Pax pushed forwards making his eyes glow gray. She let out a shape inhale and pushed away from him. As the blanket fell away as she scurried over to the corner of the couch she let out a small shriek realizing she was naked. She snatched the blanket from him and covered herself. She went to glare at him but then her mouth dropped open. He was completely naked, her eyes wandered over him, her eyes tracing the scars that riddled his body until they fell on his face.

"Oh god." She yelled and covered her eyes.

"Explain!" She yelled holding the blanket close to her.

"You were cold." He blurted out confused by the way she was acting.

"And! You're naked! I'm basically naked! Where are we? Who are you?" She demanded pulling the blanket tighter to her.

Ronan let out a loud sighed and stood up. He shook his head grunting to himself as he walked out of the room.

"Hey! Where are you going?" She yelled as she stood up pulling the blanket around her before following him.

The adrenaline coursing through her made her push the horrible pain she had aside. She marched after him following him into a bedroom.

He was standing next to a dresser still naked looking through the draws. He had tossed clothing on the floor as he searched for something.

"Hey! Did you not hear me." She yelled again walking over to him.

"I heard you." Ronan said, pulling out a t-shirt and holding it up to him.

"So…" She said, frowning at him.

"Look, do you want me to answer or do you want me to get dressed? I am perfectly fine being naked if you want answers first." He smirked, turning to look at her.

"I..um..I" Mallory stuttered out not sure what to say because no matter how hard she tried to, she couldn't tear her eyes from him.

She wanted to trace the scars and ask why they were there? What had happened? Did it hurt? She wanted to touch them with her mouth. She felt her ears and cheeks turning red.

"What's your name?" Ronan smirked seeing her flush.

"My name…I uh." She became really confused when she couldn't think of her name.

She panicked not knowing her name, her hand going to her head as she turned quickly. The intense rush of pain from turning made her feel light headed and the world started to go dark. She stumbled backwards and began to fall.

"Woah, woah." Ronan said, moving quickly, his heart panicking in his chest.

She fell backwards into Ronan's arms. He pulled her close to his chest cradling her.

"Hey I got you, I got you." Ronan said to her as she blinked looking up at him.

The word echoed in her mind as she looked up into his cognac colored eyes. Water, the sound of waves bounced around in her mind. She remembered a rock and then nothing. Her hand went to the back of her head as she looked up at him.

"You got me out of the river. I hit my head…Who are you?" She said not moving out of his arms.

"Ronan." He said quietly, not making any movement to let her go.

His name settled in her like something familiar. Something that was hers. She looked at him trying to figure out why it felt so good to be close to him, why he felt safe and like she was meant to be held by him.

"What's your name?" Ronan asked his eyes, studying hers as he watched different emotions pass through them.

"I…I…I can't remember. I can't remember anything. I don't know who I am or where I am?" Mallory said starting to panic, she went to move away from but he tightened his grip seeing her getting upset.

"Hey, it's ok. Look, we can figure this out." Ronan said, trying to make her feel better.

"Do I know you?" She asked hoping for some type of answer.

"No…But I promise to help you." Ronan said quietly.

"Ok." Mallory whispered.

"Ok." Ronan said back with a nod of his head.

"Um you should get dressed…I think I could use a shower." Mallory whispered.

"Right. Ronan said with a small smile as he helped her up right.

"There's a shower through the doors there. I'm going to see if I can find some clothing for you and me. I'm not really sure what's in here." Ronan said as Mallory stepped away from him.

She nodded slowly and began walking to the bathroom door. She paused in the doorway, something about what he had said confused her.

"Is this not your home?" She asked quietly.

"No, I'm borrowing it for now. Hey be careful washing up, your ribs are hurt and you have a gash on the top of your head. I'm going to get dressed but I will be right out here if you need anything." Ronan told her firmly.

She looked at him before stepping into the bathroom. She closed the door behind her. Something was not right. There was something going on. Her gut was telling her she was supposed to be doing something important. A nagging voice in the back of her mind told her not to trust him but there was this underlying want and need to be near him. This undeniable pull to him. Shower and then she would figure the rest out. Shower carefully.

Chapter Fourteen
Hope

He groaned the smell of earth and dirt invaded his nostrils. He began coughing. His lungs forced pieces of mud and grass. He rolled onto his side, pain rushed through him. He opened his eyes staring up at the forest trees. The moonlight was the only light in the darkness. He tried sitting up. The world spun as throbbing pain pulsated at the back of his head. He reached up his fingers touching the top of his head and something warm and sticky like syrup was there. He brought his hand to the front of his face. His hand was stained red. His vision was blurry as he waited for the world to stop spinning.

"Alpha." Adam sent through the mind link.

There was nothing. Silence. It was like when a phone line was dead. You picked up but there was no dial tone.

"Dad." Adam tried to mind linking his father, sometimes Alpha would disconnect but his Dad would never.

No answer.

"Mom!" Adam tried to mind linking Sarah.

"Anybody?" Adam linked the higher ranking wolves.

"Adam?" Wyatt's voice chimed back in his head.

"Wyatt!" Adam nearly screamed through mind link his heart was excited to hear someone.

"Thank god your ok Adam! Where are you?" Wyatt sent back.

"The woods just outside of our territory. I was chasing someone, then it all went black. I can't reach my mom, dad or Alpha. What is going on?" Adam sent back.

"We've been taken over. He goes by Knox's. His pack of rogue's got a hold of Jessica and Hannah, then

Luna; forced all three packs to surrender. They have all higher ranking wolves chained in wolfsbane." Wyatt sent quickly back.

"That's why I can't get a hold of anyone. Where are you? Did you not get caught?" Adam asked his mind trying to process everything.

"No, I am. They found out I am the medical doctor here. The one they have for their own pack doesn't know much. They have me tending to the wounded but are watching me closely. Are you hurt?" Wyatt sent back.

"I'm bleeding from my head. I am dizzy and my vision is finally going back to normal." Adam answered back.

"Where's Mallory?" Adam asked quickly before Wyatt could respond to his previous mind link.

"I don't know. She's not with the wounded. She's not locked up in the dungeons. I haven't been down to see Alpha or Luna but my hope is she escaped. You sound like you have a concussion. How bad is the gash?" Wyatt answered him.

"I need to find her." Adam mind link as he got to his feet.

"Adam, you need to be careful. How bad is your wound? You're not going to be of any help if you're hurt and make yourself worse." Wyatt sent back, his tone more fatherly.

"It's healing now that I'm up. Landon is going to take care of it. Do we know anything about where Mallory was last?" Adam said his body itching to move.

"I'm not sure. I will see if they will let me go check on our people and try to find out. If she did get out she would be going to the safest place possible and to get help." Wyatt sent back as he thought to himself.

"I'm going to see if I can find her. I'll bring back help. Tell my Mom and Dad I'm good." Adam sent to Wyatt.

"Be safe." Wyatt sent back ending the mind link.

Adam let his vision come back to focus. His body no longer hurting as Landon pushed all his energy on to healing quicker. Once they realized Mallory could be in trouble Landon stepped it up.

Find her! Landon muttered inside of Adam's mind.

Need your help with that. Adam said back sarcastically.

Adam shut his eyes and inhaled deeply. Landon instantly picked up on her.

Shift! Landon commanded

You're lucky I want to find her just as bad else we be fighting. Adam snapped back.

Adam felt Landon push for control and he reluctantly gave him. The shift happened in seconds, it was the quickest he had ever shifted before. Once Landon was completely free, he locked in on Mallory and took off.

The warm water rushed down over her. Her body craves it. She trembled under the water, the water hurt but felt good at the same time. She looked down over her body. She had bruises everywhere. Her ribs were covered and it almost hurt to breathe. She noticed a slight yellow tinge to come of the bruises on her ribs. They were old. She had been hurt before. She looked at them confused. She didn't remember anything or anyone.

What is my name? She asked herself, why didn't she know? She leaned her forehead against the wall in the shower. She felt like she couldn't breathe. The more she thought about not knowing what was going on or who she was, the nagging feeling that something was wrong ate away at her. She couldn't shake the feeling that she was supposed to be doing something important. Her mind raced as her chest tightened. She began breathing faster and harder. Her chest felt like it was going to collapse. The rapid breathing caused pain to shoot through her and she began to get light headed. She couldn't breath, she grabbed onto the shower curtain trying to keep herself up right. The shower curtain ripped away from the bar as she went stumbling forward.

A loud bang echoed through the bathroom and as she winced preparing herself to meet the tile floor. Her body never hit the floor, instead warm arms embraced her pulling her into him.

"I got you." His voice was calm and steady as he tried to hide the concern in his eyes.

She looked up at him still in so much pain and tried to inhale.

"Breath look at me. You are fine. You are safe." Ronan said, trying to calm her down.

He knew that she had sent herself into a panic and the pain she was feeling was from moving her chest way too much. She shook her head no as tears filled her eyes.

"Breath in, slowly. I'll do it with you." Ronan said, trying to calm her.

She needed to slow her breathing, she kept trying to inhale but didn't realize she was causing herself to hyperventilate. She shook her head, refusing to listen to Ronan. He needed to do something to get her to stop thinking. Her hand came down grabbing his forearm and she dug her fingernails into his arms, tears leaking down her cheeks. He grabbed her face with his hands and pressed his lips to hers.

Her mind went blank, the amount of sparks and shivers from him simply touching his lips to hers exploded

in her brain. He pulled back slowly a small smirk on his lips
as he watched the expression on her face.

"There, can you chill out now." Ronan half laughed.

"I…I-" Mallory went to say quietly.

"You're ok." Ronan said quietly, his thumb rubbing
her cheek softly.

"I am?" Her voice softly whispered the question.

"You will be. I need to get a real doctor up here.
Your ribs look terrible." He said his eyes still focused on her
face.

"I don't remember anything." She said her voice
was still shaky.

"It's ok. We will figure it out. I got you." Ronan said
the confidence in his voice made her feel better, she
trusted that he would help her.

"Ok…So you don't know me?" Mallory asked, she
knew he had said that he had found her in the river but the
way his touch felt against her skin, the way he instantly
calmed her and made her feel safe; something deep within
her knew him.

"No…but I want to." Ronan said quietly his voice
was deep and held unspoken promises.

She felt her breath get caught in her throat as the
words came out of his mouth. Her stomach twisted with
excitement and her heart fluttered. She leaned closer to
him wanting to brush her lips against his once more. She
wanted him to kiss her again. He watched her eyes and
knew the look. Her lip quivered reflecting the want in her
eyes. His thumb traveled down from her cheek and under
her chin, tilting her head slightly up. He brought his mouth
down to hers, his lips brushing hers softly as if he was
testing the water. She moved into it and it was all he
needed. He pulled her onto his lap, his mouth capturing
hers completely. Her hands moved from his arm to the

back of his neck as if she didn't want to let go. He pulled on her bottom lip slightly and as she opened her mouth his tongue found his way into her mouth. Their tongues moved against each other as his hand traveled down her naked wet back. Goosebumps covered her skin as she began to kiss back with just as much desire and want as him. She inched closer to him, the feeling of his hands and body against hers felt like nothing she had ever felt before.

Ronan broke the kiss, his mouth moving from her lips to her neck. She let out a small exasperated exhale. Pax came forward, the urge to bite down and mark her was overwhelming. She moved against him, pressing her neck into his mouth as if asking for it. He nipped at her flesh and she shivered against him with a soft moan, tilting her head so he had more access to her neck. He felt his fangs come down and everything in him was telling him to mark her.

Mark her! She's ours! Pax growled inside of him.

He pulled back away from her neck slowly trying to calm himself down. He felt her hand on his face and she pulled him to her. Her mouth kissed him hungrily. He kissed her back trying to slow the pace. He needed to get control of himself. He was so close to the edge of saying fuck it and letting Pax have what they both so desperately wanted. He pulled back from the kiss, his hand going to her cheek. She pulled back her eyes dazed as she looked at him, questions filled her eyes.

"We really need you to get looked at." Ronan said quietly, his finger brushing her cheek.

"Looked at?" She whispered back confused.

"Your ribs, they look really bad. Were you hurt before?" His eyes looked now at the yellow tinge on some of the bruising.

"I...I don't-"

Mallory! The word screamed in her mind and she almost fell forward into Ronan. The voice was familiar but yet she didn't recognize it. The name though it felt like it belonged to her.

"Mallory." She whispered the name, she knew it was hers as soon as it came out of her mouth.

"Mallory." Ronan said in the same tone she had whispered.

"Mallory, I think that's my name. It's s my name." Mallory said quietly to Ronan.

"Mallory." He smiled saying it, her name was as beautiful as she was.

"Do you remember anything else?" Ronan asked her, eager to know more about her.

"No…other than I am just now realizing I am completely naked." Mallory said her eyes went wide as she went to scoot away from him.

"Shut your eyes." She blurted out as she wiggled.

"It's a little late for all of that." Ronan laughed but let her get up, holding her arm steady so she wouldn't fall back over.

"Shut them!" Mallory said, trying to frantically reach a towel.

"You need to be careful, you're injured!" Ronan said sternly, his hand still holding on to her as he snatched a towel and held it out to her.

Mallory was taken back by his tone. Her eyes narrowed in on him as if she was going to argue with him but then was confused as a towel wrapped around her and he tucked it in.

"I'm going to have someone come up and look at you. Maybe Cross River will have a better medic." Ronan muttered going to the bathroom door.

He frowned looking at the door; the door jam was splintered and broken. He shrugged, not his house, not his problem.

"Where are you going?" Mallory called after him.

"Getting you clothes and changing mine. Turn the water off." He yelled back.

Mallory looked confused and then turned to see the shower was still one and water was slowly starting to seep out of the tub. She felt her cheeks redden as she quickly turned the water. A small spark of hope came to her though. She knew her name. She needed to know more and quickly.

Chapter Fifteen
Cell

    *H*annah groaned starting to come too, pulling Nora away from the bars. Her mind going to caring for her. She was taking the wolfsbane hard. She must have never been exposed to it before. Nora touched her forehead. She was getting warm. She frowned, she needed to talk to someone.

    "Hello!" She shouted into the darkness,trying to get a guard or someone's attention.

    "Nora?" Jace's weak but voice came down the hall to her.

    "I'm ok. I need someone for Hannah." Nora said to him quickly.

    "Hello! Hey!" Nora shouted louder and then began knocking her chains against the bar.

    "Nora, you can't let them know how you're holding up." Jace whispered back quickly.

    He was worried that if they knew she was resistant to wolfsbane that they would do something worse. It affected her but not as badly as others.

    "Well I can't just sit here." Nora said back, still taping her cuffs and chains against the bars.

    "Act weak!" Jace said in an angry voice.

    "What's going on in here!" A new voice shouted down the halls.

    Nora sank to the ground leaning up against the wall but still tapped her wrist against the silver bars. She made herself look bad.

    "Hey you what's with all the noise?" The guard said coming up to the cell.

"You've dose her with too much. She's starting to run a fever. She is not conscious." Nora said, making her voice soft and sounding like it was a struggle.

"So?" The guard said huffing at her.

"I want to speak to your Alpha." Nora said softly, trying to hold back her anger.

"Yeah all right. I'll tell him." The guard jokes, laughing at her.

She needed to do something. Hannah wasn't going to make it much longer if she didn't. She shut her eyes and stood up.

"I want to speak to your Alpha now." Nora growled, stepping to the bars and grabbing a hold of the silver.

The guard's eyes grew wide and he stepped towards her. He narrowed his eyes at her for the first time really looking at her.

"How?" He whispered, trying to lean in enough to see her.

"Your Alpha, now." Nora said as the bar hissed as she squeezed her fists around.

The guard didn't say another word and backed away from the cell, his eyes still holding their stare with Nora until he bumped into the wall. He then took off down the hall. Jace watched the guard run by and his stomach twisted.

"Nora." He said her name demanding answers.

"I needed attention, I've got it." Nora said into the darkness.

"What did you do?" Jace demanded, trying to find the strength in himself to get up.

"I just showed them how strong I am." Nora whispered.

"You're going to get yourself hurt." Jace growled, getting angry with Nora.

"I'll be fine if I don't do something Hannah will get hurt." Nora said back.

A pair of rushed and clumsy footsteps followed by a pair of angry footsteps were heard. The sounds of footsteps echoed down the hall.

"You better not be wasting my time." Knox muttered as he reached the cell.

"Alpha I am not. There's something different with this one." The guard fumbled in front of the cell.

"You there..Luna of-"

"Nora, Luna of Cross River." Nora said, stepping forward her voice strong and her stance determined.

"Ahh. I've heard stories about you. I mostly took them as exaggerated made up nonsense. The Luna who became an Alpha and took down the Alpha Council and before that Kip of Red Woods." Knox said, leaning closer to the silver bars.

"The Luna from Red Woods is getting sick with the amount of wolfsbane your guard have drenched her in. She needs to be released from the chains and rinsed off." Nora said, trying not to take the bait Knox was putting out there.

"Oh …we need too?" Knox grinned.

"I'm assuming you're keeping all of us alive because you want the cooperation of our packs. Right now they are submitting to you because you have their Lunas, Alphas, and Betas under lock down. What is going to happen if one of the Lunas dies?" Nora asked quietly, stepping up to the silver bars and wrapping her hands slowly around the bar.

Knox watched how Nora had no reaction to the silver bars. He stepped up and brushed them not believing and winced. He narrowed his eyes at her.

"What are you?" He whispered to her.

"Take the chains off Hannah." Nora said her voice was calm and steady.

"You have someone come down and take a look at the Luna from RedWoods. Give her medical attention if needed. Nora here is right about needing the packs to comply. Nora and I are going to go for a walk." Knox smirked.

The cell down opened slowly and Nora inhaled as the guard came in and undid her chains. They were then replaced by a simple set of cuffs. These ones were pure silver. The guard wore gloves handling them. Another guard came in and began removing the chains from Hannah.

"Wyatt or Abby." Nora said to Knox.

"Who?" Knox asked, confused.

"Send down Wyatt or Abby. They are skilled with medicine." Nora ordered.

"You know sweetheart, I am playing nice but very few get to tell me what to do. You should be careful with what and how you say things to me." Knox said glaring at her.

Nora was silent as she was trying to read him. He reminded her so much of Kip. She almost cringed saying his name. It was almost eerie.

"Come on, let's walk and talk." Knox motioned for her to follow.

"Alpha are you..um do you need someone to come with you just in case?" The guard asked nervously.

"No, I have everything she loves locked away. If the Luna from Cross River decides to act out, I will start slaughtering her pack. Also have an IV set up with wolfsbane brought in. We will hook her mate up to one if she does anything." Nora felt her stomach twist inside her.

Knox began walking down the cell and the guard moved aside for Nora to pass by. Nora walked by him, the guard watching her carefully. Knox walked past the cell holding the Alphas. Asher was still unconscious, Zeke was barely holding on, and the wolfsbane was finally starting to affect Jace; he was sitting on the ground propped up against the cool wall. Knox grinned, stopping just in front of the cell. Nora caught up to him and glanced at the side.

"Jace." She said going to the bars.

"Nora, What's going on." Jace demanded forcing himself up right and getting up slowly.

"Oh, Nora and I are just going on a stroll. She is quite strong. I wouldn't expect any less from your mate though." Knox said with an overly happy smile on his lips.

"It's ok. How's Asher? He looks rough." Nora whispered.

"He's fine, stupid but fine." Jace grumbled as he glared at Knox.

"Hannah's gonna be ok. Jessica is still out but holding on just fine." Nora told Jace with a reassuring smile.

"Where are you taking her?" Jace demanded looking at Knox.

"The thing is you are not in the position to be demanding anything from me. Keep with that tone and I will gut her right here, right now, and in front of you. I will leave her to bleed out slowly with her entrails hanging out of her. You will have a front row seat to her slow painful death." Knox said, his voice dropping as he whispered his threat.

He took a step towards Nora taking a piece of her dark hair in his hands and twirling it around his finger. He watched Jace grit his teeth trying to hold back whatever threat he had behind his lips.

"You know she's very beautiful. The Moon Goddess certainly blessed you. Beautiful, strong, and desirable. Killing her isn't the worst thing I could do to her." Knox said his finger was now running down the side of Nora's neck.

Jace let out a growl and lunged forward, his arm snaking through the silver bars, burning his arm as he tried to get to Knox.

"Make sure the IV is set up." Knox laughed, grabbed Nora by the arm and led her away from the cell.

It's fine. She mouths to Jace. It's ok. She tried to tell him to calm down. To stop hurting himself. That she would be just fine. Jace began pulling on the bars. The sound of his skin burning echoed down the hall. Knox began to laugh hearing the hissing noise. The sound reminded her of throwing water on a campfire.

"You might not be so blessed. He's kind of dumb." Knox laughed.

He yanked Nora out into the sunlight. The brightness burned her eyes. She went to shield her eyes but remembered the cuffs. Although they didn't cause her to fall out, the silver was taking its toll on her. It did burn and hurt. She could no longer pull on Zara for strength and she couldn't communicate with her or the pack. She was cut off and weakened by a simple piece of metal.

Knox pulled her along a few feet and then stopped spinning her towards him.

"So it's true." He said quietly, his mouth frowning but his eyes showing uncertainty.

"What is?" Nora asked, her own frown appearing on her face.

"You're a hunter..or at least part." Knox grumbled.

"It wasn't hidden knowledge." Nora said sarcastically.

"Hunters are about as good as humans." Knox muttered.

"Where do you come from?" Nora asked, turning to look at him.

"I will be asking the questions." Knox said firmly.

"So is this an interview?" Nora smirked.

"Do you like your tongue where it is? You don't need to talk to answer questions." Knox said, stepping towards her, his eyes glowing gray.

"Rogue's eyes don't glow." Nora said studying him just as hard as he was her.

"We were rogues…in the beginning. Then we found each other. All the unwanted bits and pieces, packs casted out. I brought them together. Became their Alpha. Now look at us. The unwanted and forgotten, controlling it all." Knox smirked.

"What pack didn't want you?" Nora asked quietly.

"It doesn't matter." Knox said shortly, as he turned away from her.

Nora watched him shift his stance and began walking away. She stood there not sure what she was supposed to do. She glanced at the forest. It wasn't far. She could probably make it. If she could get to Logan, warn the other packs.

"You run, they die." Knox said quietly.

"I won't even chase you. I will just give an order and they will all die. I don't need more pack members." Knox said, continuing walking away.

She could hear what Zara would say inside of her telling her to run, to fight, to just go ahead and end him now. She gritted her teeth wanting to do it. She was weak, she was putting on a good show but she could feel the silver taking its toll. Yes she was half hunter but she was also half wolf. The wolf side was becoming sick. She let out a small breath and began to follow after Knox.

Chapter Sixteen
Wolf

"I need a medic. A real medic not ours. Get me who's in charge of Cross River's medical." Ronan sent out a mind link to Kai.

"Yes Beta." Kai sent back.

He pulled the shirt down over his head just as he heard the bathroom door click open. She walked out of the bathroom, her eyes catching a glimpse of his bare chest and stomach. She felt a tingle run through her. The thought of running her hand down over them made her feel flush as she tried to look elsewhere. Her mind went to them sitting on the bathroom floor herself naked in his lap. The way his mouth felt on her skin. She could feel her cheeks getting hot.

"You ok?" Ronan asked her, seeing her walk slowly out.

"Yeah, it just hurts now." Mallory said walking out into the room more, trying to chase the thoughts of him away.

"I have someone coming to look at you." Ronan said his face studying the way she moved.

"I'm fine really." Mallory said moving out of the bathroom doorway.

"You'ro getting looked at." Ronan said, making his way to the bedroom door entrance and pausing.

Mallory gavo him a weird look but he nodded for her to follow him. She didn't like being told what to do but the way he said it, she didn't feel up to arguing. She did hurt a lot. She followed him out into the kitchen and found him looking into the fridge.

"Hungry?" He asked from the fridge.

"Yeah actually. What time is it?" Mallory said, looking to the window.

"I think it's morning or afternoon. I don't know." Ronan said, pulling stuff out of the fridge.

"What day is it?" Mallory asked, her voice cracking a little.

The panic of not knowing anything settled in again. She was starting to freak out. Every time she felt better she remembered she didn't remember anything. She was alone in a house with a stranger, in a place she didn't know.

"Hey, hey, hey. It is friday. It is ahh see ten am. The day is the eighteenth. The month is June, it's hot outside. The sun still shines and the stars and moon come out at night. Your name is Mallory. I am Ronan." Ronan smirked a little as he watched her calm down.

"Ok." Mallory said breathing.

"Ok." Ronan winked at her pulling out lunch meat, bread and cheese.

"Sandwich?" Ronan said, holding up the stuff.

"Yeah sandwiches sound good." Mallory smiled.

"See your name is Mallory and you like sandwiches. We are getting somewhere." Ronan chuckled.

"Why do you feel familiar? Why do I trust you?" Mallory asked sitting at the island, the question was more supposed to be to herself but it came out loud.

Ronan took a deep breath and made two sandwiches, passing one to her.

"That's a complicated question." Ronan said quietly.

"More complicated than not remembering anything about myself?" Mallory laughed.

"Maybe." Ronan said back.

"Well I'm not getting anymore shocked then not knowing who I am so lets start explaining." Mallory chuckled.

"You're my mate." Ronan said out loud for the first time since his wolf forced it from his lips.

"Mate? So like we're dating?" Mallory asked quietly, the word meant something, she knew it for some reason.

Everything was telling her it held special meaning and that she wanted a mate.

"Um no…we've just met, remember." Ronan laughed at the irony in telling her to remember.

"Shut up. Ok so how are you my mate, if I don't know you." Mallory laughed back but was still trying to hold on to her serious tone.

"I think I know the word. Something in me tells me I wanted a mate. That's different from a boyfriend." Mallory said, trying to make her brain focus on finding an answer.

"If you know that then you have to know about wolves." Ronan said hopefully, it would make this all so much easier if she knew already.

"But you're human so that seems a bit strange." Ronan said looking at her like something on her was going to tell him the answer.

"Human…right because you're an alien." Mallory said with a chuckle.

"No   I'm a wolf." Ronan said slowly hoping it would trigger something.

"Oh..Ok. You're a wolf." Mallory repeated back slowly, bells were going off in her head, some sign of warning. The danger light was flashing and she began scanning the room for a way out.

"Yes. Well I can turn into one. His name is Pax." Ronan said quickly trying to explain, he could feel her guard go up and was trying to delay the freak out.

"Mhmm. Well you sure are talented." Mallory smiled brightly

"Talented?" Ronan asked, looking at her as she began to back away.

"Yeah I bet you could start a business for parties or something." Mallory said, still backing away her eyes glancing to the door.

"You don't believe me." Ronan said looking at her dumbfounded.

"No…No…of course I believe you. I just need to go. Um to the river. Maybe if I revisit the river, something might make me remember more." Mallory said, also really thinking that might be a good idea.

"We can do that but you need to stay here until you get looked at." Ronan said, coming out from behind the island.

"No, I think it might be better if I do it alone. I got to the river alone, having you there might be a distraction. You should stay and practice turning into a wolf." Mallory said, closing in on the door.

"Practice turning into a wolf? You don't believe me!" Ronan said, now moving towards her.

"I said I did. Now sit and stay." Mallory said, ordering him like a dog.

Ronan growled and let Pax push forward, his eyes glowing bright gray as the growl echoed around the room.

"Shit." Mallory whispered as he eyes grew wide and bolted for the door.

"Damn it." Ronan muttered, taking off after her.

Mallory grabbed a hold of the cold metal door knob and yanked hard. The door flung open and she went to run out of it. She slammed into something hard and was thrown back. She landed on her butt going to fall further back into the ground but Ronan caught her mid fall. She blinked looking up at a blond-haired man with bright blue eyes. He was tall as he towered over her.

"Mallory?" Her name fell out of his mouth.

"Are you ok-" Ronan started to say but then his eyes narrowed at the blond-hair man.

The man returned the glare and went to reach out and touch Mallory. The blond-haired man's eyes glowing ice blue as he locked eyes with Ronan. Ronan growled and stepped in front of Mallory blocking the way to her.

"Move!" The man yelled at Ronan.

Mallory looked at both of them, their eyes both glowing as they bowed up at each other. She then saw fangs begin to descend. Her eyes widen as she watches them slowly turn into monsters. She quietly backed away. She needed to find another way out.

"What did you do to her!" He yelled into Ronan's face.

"Nothing! How do you know her!" Ronan yelled back just as fiercely.

"You don't know who she is? Aren't you a part of this take over?" He asked, confused.

"Yes…who is she?" Ronan asked, looking back to see if Mallory remembered anything.

"Fuck." Ronan whispered as he realized she had disappeared.

Ronan didn't turn around to say anything else to the man and began trying to find Mallory. The blond-haired man followed after him.

Mallory rushed into the bedroom, shutting the door and locking it. She needed a way out. She didn't know what those things were. All she knew was she had stumbled into some type of nightmare. Maybe she was dead and this was hell. She scanned the room to find the window and ran to it. She threw open the window and went to dangle her leg out, when the door busted open. The wood from the door frame shattering on to the ground. Mallory jumped at the noise, almost hitting her head on the window sill.

"Mallory!" Ronan called, rushing into the room, pausing when he saw her half way out the window.

The look on his face stopped her in her tracks. Everything was telling her to duck out the window and take off but the way his eyes held hers, froze her in place.

"What are you?" Mallory asked her voice just above a whisper.

"I wasn't joking. I told you I can turn into a wolf." Ronan said putting his hands up like he meant no harm.

"Hey kiddo." The blonde-haired man said, stepping to the room.

Ronan shot him a glare but he didn't want to react with anger, Mallory was on the verge of taking off. He looked to Mallory and saw something flash across her eyes.

"What did you do to her?" Ronan asked, trying to keep the anger out of his tone but was having trouble doing it with Pax growling inside of him.

"Come on kiddo, get back in here and let me take a look at your ribs." He said again to her, cracking a smile.

Kiddo…the word rang through her head. She was sitting on a hospital bed, her ribs hurting but she felt embarrassed someone was with her but she was worried about someone who wasn't there. He walked into the room and said hey kiddo to her.

"I know you." Mallory said quietly, bringing her leg back in the window.

"You've helped me before." She said, tilting her head at him.

"It's me Wyatt." Wyatt smiled at her nodding his head.

"What did you do to her?" Ronan growled, going to step in the way of Mallory and Wyatt.

"I could ask you the same damn thing. Why doesn't she know me." Wyatt snapped at Ronan.

"Wyatt." Mallory said, repeating his name trying to pull up some memory.

Another memory flashed in front of her eyes. She was little and crying. She was holding her wrist. There was a boy, he was hugging her as he called for help. Wyatt came. She remembered him talking to her, making her laugh and then without her even knowing he had popped her wrist back in place.

"I know you. My wrist. I was little, you fixed it." Mallory said, squinting at him as she began walking over to him.

"You fell out of a tree. I had to put it back in place. You were always a fearless, brave little girl." Wyatt smiled at her.

"You know me." Mallory said excitedly.

"Your part of Cross River." Ronan whispered, looking from Mallory to Wyatt.

Wyatt nodded looking from Mallory to Ronan, his glare returning as he laid eyes on him.

"What did you do to her?" Ronan said bowing up in front of Wyatt.

"Me. What did you do?" Wyatt growled back.

"Stop. He saved me." Mallory said, coming away from the window and stepping between them.

"I fell in the river and hit my head. I do not remember anything. Things are starting to come back but Ronan saved me. Now I need answers." Mallory said to Wyatt.

She didn't know why but she felt the need to protect Ronan. Everything was overwhelming and the more she tried to remember anything about herself the more she found nothing. Ronan growled again and she reached back and placed her hand in his. Ronan was shocked by the action and looked down at her hand in his. Pax immediately began to calm down.

"Are you hurt?" Wyatt asked his eyes, glancing back to Ronan not sure what to make of all this.

"The wound on the top of my head is healing. My ribs and chest hurt but I'm ok." Mallory said quickly.

"You have broken ribs from a fall two days ago. You remember nothing?" Wyatt said motioning for her to sit down.

"I had to perform CPR. Her ribs might be worse." Ronan said firmly, trying to mask his concern.

"A fall?" Mallory said trying to remember, she sat down on the bed.

"Yeah you were out with Adam and-" Wyatt started to explain.

"Adam." Mallory whispered the name pulled at her heart.

"Mallory!" Her name was screamed inside of her head as she watched herself roll down the hill.

"The head injury is old that's why it's not as bad either." Mallory said out loud.

"I remember falling. I remember you." She said looking past Wyatt to Ronan.

"Me?" Ronan asked, coming to her side. He had not met her before.

"You were standing across the field. I remember your eyes." Mallory said quietly as Wyatt stiffened up hearing it, he didn't say anything but looked closely at her head wound.

"It's healing. I'm going to need to see your ribs." Wyatt said, motioning for her to lift her shirt.

Mallory nodded and went to raise her shirt but a loud growl erupted from Ronan. He stepped towards Wyatt. Wyatt locked eyes with him and was about to go off, he was sick of him acting like he knew Mallory but then it hit him.

"Great." Wyatt said, clenching his jaw.

"Ronan, I don't understand this whole growling, wolf thing but you called for him to look at my ribs. He's ok. I trust him and I know him. I might not remember but he is safe." Mallory said to Ronan trying to calm him down.

"Great what?" She asked Wyatt worried that her ribs might be worse.

Wyatt just clenched his jaw more and motioned for Mallory to raise her shirt. Ronan bowed up behind Wyatt. Wyatt felt it and was done. He spun around to look him in the face.

"She is like my niece. The only thing stopping me from ripping out your throat here is that your her…your her..-" Wyatt said, stopping as if the word he was trying to say tasted bad.

"Niece? What is he to me?" Mallory asked, now becoming annoyed and standing up.

Wyatt and Ronan were now in a staring contest and on the verge of fighting. Mallory stood anger and frustration finally taking over her.

"That is enough! I don't understand any of this bullshit and frankly I kind of remember you and for some reason I trust you but that doesn't mean there is some stupid war over me. As far as I know you both are psycho and I need to leave." Mallory yelled at them with her hands in fists at her side.

"Hey kiddo relax." Wyatt said, turning from Ronan and looking to Mallory.

"You're going to hurt yourself, sit down." Ronan said his tone was a little more assertive than Wyatt.

"I want answers now." Mallory said her eyes locked on them, she felt a power building in her core.

Ronan felt it too he looked to Wyatt who, if he had felt it was hiding it well.

"You are the daughter of the Alpha of Cross River. I am the Gamma. I have known you since before you were born. I have mended every boo boo you have ever gotten." Wyatt laughed a little.

"She's Jace's daughter." Ronan said as his stomach knotted.

Ronan's mind started racing, his mate was his enemy. Knox was the first thing he thought of. He thought she was a human. He would kill her. He looked over at Mallory trying to hide his expression. Knox would torture her and kill her infront of him and her parents just to show off his power.

Keep her safe. Pax whimpered inside of him the whimper was of sadness but under it was anger.

"So I am a wolf?" Mallory asked, trying to process what Wyatt had just said.

"Your wolf hasn't surfaced yet." Wyatt said quietly.

"That's why Knox thought she was human." Ronan said quietly, feeling a little bit relieved.

"So you're not a part of our…pack." Mallory asked quietly, finding the words slowly as they were coming to her.

"No he is not." Wyatt snapped looking at him.

"Mallory I-

"His pack invaded our pack lands, has taken our pack hostage and is holding your mother and father in a cell. We thought you had escaped. " Wyatt said quickly, his gaze burning into Ronan as he spoke.

"What..." Mallory whispered and flashes of her running through the woods flashed through her mind, the urge to go faster and quicker becoming overwhelming. She was trying to get help, trying to get to someone.

"But I guess her being your mate has now put a hiccup in your plans." Wyatt said bitterly to Ronan.

"I-" Ronan started to say but Mallory held up her hand.

"Ok, werewolves are real, there are packs. I am supposed to be getting help. The bad guy is something to me...this is a lot. Ok first things first. Where was I getting help from?" Mallory asked, recapping everything to get her thoughts.

"I'm not sure. Red Woods and Moonlight are also captured. Silver Mountain is too far north and Black Sands too far south. We need help now." Wyatt said thinking out loud.

"You, you're going to help me." Mallory said, looking at Ronan.

Ronan's mind was racing since this whole conversation started and he needed a way to keep her safe. He now needed a way to get her out of here. Knox left him alone for the most part maybe he could maybe leave.

"I'm thinking." Ronan said quietly.

"Mallory, let me look at your ribs." Wyatt said his own voice sounded distant, he too was trying to think of a plan.

"Your wolf isn't present so we can still pass you off as a human. Knox is willing to let that slide because you're mine." Ronan said thinking out loud.

"Yours." Mallory said, narrowing her eyes at him.

"Yeah. He doesn't know your my mate and he thinks wolves should own humans. It's going to work out to our benefit. He won't question you." Ronan said, trying to defuse her anger.

"Ok so can we just leave then?" Mallory said as she lifted her shirt to expose a very black and blue torso.

"Maybe, I need to find a good enough excuse." Ronan said and then frowned deeply seeing Mallory's torso.

"I'll need to wrap your ribs." Wyatt said, reaching for his bag.

"Ok but make it quick." Mallory said, her mind trying to remember who told her where to go.

Ronan took a deep breath, he needed air. This was a lot. Of course, the Moon Goddess would see to it that his mate would be the enemy. After being told he would never have one. He began walking out of the room.

"Where are you going?" Mallory asked nervously as she watched him start to leave.

"Just to get some air." Ronan said quietly, he wasn't sure if she was worried he was leaving or worried that he was going to go tell.

Mallory smiled weakly and watched him go. She caught Wyatt looking at her trying to read her.

"I know, I know you and I don't know him but I trust him more than you for some reason." Mallory whispered.

Wyatt nodded quietly as if he understood and began working on fixing her up.

Chapter Seventeen
Scheming

*T*he summer air hit him in the face with a warm humid slap. He didn't know if it was the air or the rush of not knowing what to do but it made breathing so much worse. He didn't know what to do. He was trying to come up with some plan, anything to get her out of here. His whole body was tense, stomach knotted with the thought of Knox finding out. He had never cared about being doomed to not having a mate. He thought that he was the lucky one. No one to fuss or worry over, but now…now he had one and he wasn't going to let anyone take her from him.

"What's my Beta up to?" Knox's voice chimed in Ronan's head and Ronan winced at the sound of it.

"What do you need?" Ronan sent back, he was always short with Knox so it wasn't out of the normal.

"I need your assistance at the Cross River Pack house." Knox said not even paying attention to Ronan's tone.

"Now?" Ronan sent back.

"Now." Knox sent ending the mind link.

"Fuck." Ronan said out loud running his hand over his face.

He turned to go back inside as Wyatt was coming out. Ronan stopped looking at him confused.

"Where are you going?" Ronan asked him harshly.

"I have to go check on the others. I am actually getting to go down into the dungeon and check on my own people." Wyatt said quietly, waiting for Ronan to move out of his way.

"Wait, you can't go. What about her." Ronan said angrily.

"If you really are her mate, I trust you will take care of her. Get her out of here and quick." Wyatt said quietly.

"You're just going to leave her." Ronan growled.

"She trusts you. If anything happens to her I wont be the only one waiting to hurt you. I can't stay, they will know something is up." Wyatt growled back.

"Knox has just summoned me. It's fine, I will figure it out." Ronan said, stepping out of Wyatt's way.

"Figure out what?" Mallory's voice came from the doorway.

"I need to go meet with Knox." Ronan said with a grumble in his voice.

"Ok so let's go." Mallory said like it was not a big deal.

"No. I need you to stay here. I can't risk you being exposed or in danger. If you're the daughter of Jace then someone is going to recognize you quickly and Knox will end up finding out. If you could just stay here. I will go see what he wants and be back. Then we can leave." Ronan explained his reasoning as he watched Mallory's face change from angry to acceptance as he finished.

"Kai. I need you to come to the house on the outskirts of the territory now." Ronan summoned Kai.

"I'm going to wait till Kai comes, then I will head to see what Knox wants." Ronan said to her quickly.

"Kai?" Mallory asked, looking out around them, she was trying to see if anything made her memories come back.

"He's one of my pack members. He is strong and reliable. He also doesn't ask many questions." Ronan said quietly.

"I have questions. What's your packing doing taking over mine?" Mallory said, folding her arms across his chest, wincing from the movement but she tried to hide it.

"Knox hates Jace. He wants to conquer all packs and rule. Bla bla bla. Cliche bad guy power move." Ronan said, rolling his eyes.

"And your reason." Mallory said anger coming forward.

"I didn't have one. Just part of the pack." Ronan shrugged.

"Oh you sound like a great person and strong person." Mallory grumbled at him.

"You have know idea." Ronan groweld back.

"Beta, I got here as soon as possible." Kai said, running up to the house.

Mallory frowned looking at Kai, she was getting angry the more she sat there and thought about things.

"Kai, I need you to watch Mallory here until I get back. " Ronan said, frowning as well, he could feel the anger rolling off Mallory.

"She is...human?" Kai asked, confused looking at her.

"Yes and the only thing you need to know is to keep her safe until I get back. If a hair is so much misplaced on her head, I will gut you." Ronan threatened him as he narrowed his eyes at him.

"Yes Beta, got it." Kai put his hands up defensively as if to say he got it.

"So now I'm a prisoner too?" Mallory asked, she felt this rage starting to burn in the pit of her stomach.

"No but I need you safe. Safe means out of sight. Just stay. I'll explain more when I get back." Ronan said, now getting annoyed with her sudden mood change.

"Let's go inside..Mallory." Kai said motioning to the door.

"Fine." Mallory snapped, turning her back on Ronan.

Kai glanced at Ronan before dodging his glare and heading inside after Mallory. Ronan growled before storming off.

"*H*ave a seat." Knox grinned as he brought Nora into the dinning room.

Nora looked around the room confused. She was shoved down into a chair. She looked up at Knox who was squeezing her shoulder.

"Sit." He muttered as he moved from her.

Knox moved to the head of the table and he snapped his fingers. Plates of food were brought out. Nora looked confused by everything. Someone placed a plate down in front of her. She looked at it as if it was poisoned and then back to Knox who was still staring. He looked at the chair in front of him and then as if deciding he wasn't going to sit there, he moved back to Nora.

"What? Is a sit down dinner not a thing that's done here?" Knox grinned.

"Hannah." Nora said quietly as Knox sat down next to her.

"Your medical person is on the way down there now." Knox said, picking up a fork.

"So explain to me this hunter wolf thing." Knox said, picking up a green bean and placing it in his mouth.

Nora looked down at her plate. It made her stomach growl. Green beans, mash potatoes, and steak. She looked hard at it. Knox reached over and stabbed a green bean with his fork off of Nora's plate. He picked it up and stuck it in his mouth.

"You're wearing the only poison here doll." Knox winked at her.

"Explain." Knox said, picking up a thin piece of meat off his plate and popping it into his mouth.

"Do you not know how it works?" Nora said her eyes were still on her plate.

"Do you not know the meaning of explaining?" Knox said, his grip tightening on the steak knife he was holding.

"Well you see when two people love each other very muc-" As Nora started to explain sarcastically, her hair was yanked back and the steak knife was pressed to her throat.

"I'll watch you choke on your own blood and not think twice about it. If you couldn't tell before I could care less about rules and I don't think my actions out. So the fact that I am even pausing to explain, you should be grateful. So." Knox said letting go of her hair and letting his knife nick her as he pulled away.

"Let's try again. Explain." Knox growled.

"I am half hunter, half wolf. My mother was a hunter and my father was a wolf." Nora said lying, she could tell Knox didn't know much and she was smart enough not to tell the truth.

"Wasn't there more to it than that?" Knox asked quietly.

"Not really." Nora said, looking back down at the food.

"So you, one single half-breed, took down Kip and then the council." Knox said, putting down his silverware.

"It was a group effort." Nora said glancing at him, she could feel the small drop of blood on her neck beading up, her wolf side suppressed but her body was still trying to heal.

"Mick!" Knox screamed, spit flying out of his mouth, hitting in her face.

"Yes Alpha?" Mick came stumbling in.

"Get me someone she cares about now? Does she have children?" Knox screamed.

"Ok..um..who is she?" Mick said, confused, he had been busy sampling the wine cellar.

"The Luna of Cross River you fool." Knox snapped.

"What is going on?" Ronan asked, walking in to the strange dinner.

"The Luna here is refusing to answer my questions so I want someone who she cares about. Child, Children, something that's going to hurt." Knox said, snatching Nora by the hair again.

"She has no children." Ronan said quickly.

"What?" Knox snapped his eyes, going to Ronan.

"No children." Ronan said again.

Nora looked at Ronan. She was trying to figure out if he knew she had a daughter and was trying to help or if this was some game.

"Just how do you know?" Knox growled.

"What…pssh Alpha you know Ronan um Beta here knows everything. That's his job; he spends way too much time studying our enemies and organizing plans to even care about life itself. That's why he has no friends or a mate." Mick laughed.

"Thanks Mick." Ronan said, gritting his teeth.

"Anytime Beta." Mick grinned.

"You can go." Ronan said dismissing him.

"Great! I have a couple friends I want to get back to." Mick said, wiggling his eyebrows.

"Those friends better be willing participants." Ronan growled looking at Mick.

"Maybe…maybe they will be." Mick chuckled as he went to walk past Ronan.

Ronan stepped in front of Mick, his eyes glowing. He shoved Mick back and looked at him demanding a better answer.

"You know Beta I don't know why you threaten anyone with your wolf. You never let him out. Some of us are even wondering if you have one at all." Mick said bowing up to him.

Ronan half chuckled and Mick looked confused as he shook his head. Ronan threw his head back and launched it forward into Mick's nose. A loud snap echoed throughout the room as Mick's nose cracked. Blood splattered across Ronan's face. Mick swung in response, hitting Ronan in the jaw. Ronan's head whipped to the side. Mick went to swing another blow and Ronan caught his fist with his own and then crushed it. A series of loud pops was heard as Mick let out a horrible yell, trying to pry his hand out of Ronan's. Ronan backed him up against the wall. Mick hit the wall and a crack appeared that ran up the wall as his back was pressed further into it. Ronan dropped his hand, the fingers dangled out of place from their sockets. Ronan took a step back and then threw his elbow into Mick's face, his head ricocheting off the wall and back into his fist. Mick saw stars as everything went black and he sank to the floor.

"Ok so what did you need?" Ronan said, turning back to Knox.

"Well thank you for the dinner show but as I was saying. She is not answering my questions." Knox said like a toddler complaining to their parents.

"What do you want to know?" Ronan said annoyed, he kept looking at Mick and was suppressing the urge of kicking him while he was unconscious.

"She is half hunter, half human." Knox announced, like he had found the ultimate secret.

"She's what?" Ronan said, stopping in his tracks and turning to look at Nora, bells going off in his head. If she was half hunter then that means Mallory is as well.

"She is half hunter." Knox said slower like he was explaining it to a child.

"Ok so what do you want to know?" Ronan asked, returning to his annoyed personality.

"Well the rumors. I want to know if they are true. How did this one mere half-breed take down Kip and then the council. Stories of her having some magical powers." Knox said looking back at Nora picking up the steak knife again.

"She has no magical powers, if she did we would no longer be occupying this territory. Kip was a hot head and underestimated her. He thought she was a human and when he took her he did not think she was strong. Hunter blood running through her, she could be as strong as an omega. Kip didn't count for Jace uniting with other packs and his own pack turning on him. She also linked the …hunters." Ronan said the word hunters leaving his mouth made his brain click, he could get Mallory to them to make her safe.

"The council?" Knox grumbled, the explanation was right but annoying.

"Same thing. The biggest factor is Silver mountain turning on them. Also the only magical power she has is a resistance to wolfsbane and silver due to her being half hunter which Kip as we are overlooked." Ronan said, pointing to her cuffs.

"This is why you are my Beta and allowed to have a crappy attitude." Knox laughed.

"Thanks." Ronan said smuggle, he was itching to leave.

"So what do we do now?" Knox grinned.

"If you are bent on being high king you need larger packs. Send men to Redwood and Moonlight to gather the remaining pack members. We have their warriors but not their elderly, women and children. Then have the Alpha's renounce their title but naming you Alpha of each pack, that way you can avoid anything that could go wrong with the transition of power. We then move on Black Sands, they are still the smallest pack. Next Dark Water, City Lights and saving Silver Mountain for last." Ronan rattled off the plan, he was still Beta and if he drifted from the plan then Know would know something was up.

"Excellent. Perfect." Knox laughed, putting his steak knife down.

"Remember about Dark Water." Ronan said bitterly.

"Yes, yes we can burn it to the ground." Knox said, waving him off.

"Burn it?" Nora asked, looking at Ronan.

"Never you mind, we might need to find something to make you weaker." Knox said thinking out loud.

"I want to go to Red Woods." Ronan said firmly.

"Really? You're never usually the participating type. Yes when there's a battle or fight or take down plan you are in but grunt work?" Knox said quietly.

"The quicker we get the little shit out of the way the quicker we can get to City Lights. We all have our agendas." Ronan said firmly.

"I get it. That's fine." Knox said, nodding.

"I need to take someone from Red Woods." Ronan said thinking out loud.

"Oh?" Knox asked, watching Ronan's brain work.

"Yes they will need reassurance that their Alpha is alive. I need to take the Luna. She can be a negotiating ticket and proof. If they don't cooperate I can also slaughter her infront of them." Ronan said, nodding to his own statement.

"Perfect! Perfect! Perfect!" Knox laughed, hitting the table.

"Ok well I am going to be leaving right away. I suggest you do the same with Moonlight. I don't recommend Mick or Angela." Ronan said a smirk on his face as he looked at Mick.

"Well who then?" Knox grumbled.

"Let Kai go. He's strong, listens, knows boundaries and we want this to go smoothly. Angela enjoys chaos too much and if we have one slip up with any of this the whole thing could go to shit." Ronan muttered.

"Fine." Knox said quietly.

"Try not to mess things up while I'm gone." Ronan muttered walking to the exit of the room.

"You know Mick is right. You would be so much more if you let your wolf out every once in a while. Might help with your attitude." Knox said, striking a nerve.

"My wolf, my say." Ronan said walking out of the room.

"Honestly, I've never seen anything like it. I have never seen his wolf. He fights completely in human form, with the occasional claws or fangs but never fully shifted. He is fierce. I can't imagine what his wolf would do." Knox muttered to Nora.

Nora nodded trying to still figure the Beta out. He covered for Nora but then came up with a full proof plan to take down every pack and let Knox succeed. There was something off.

Chapter Eighteen
Separating

"*I* need to go to the bathroom." Mallory announced moving off the couch.

"Ok." Kai said getting up as well.

"Um, what are you doing?" Mallory asked, turning and glaring at him.

"Coming with you." Kai answered, shrugging his shoulders.

"Um like hell you are. You stay here." Mallory said, firming her stance to show how serious she was.

"Beta said stick with you so…we're going to the bathroom." Kai said very matter of fact.

"No. You can wait right here else we're going to have problems. He said keep me safe he didn't say be a peeping tom and stalk me to the bathroom." Mallory said forcely.

"Fine, I'll be in the hall." Kai muttered as Mallory stormed out of the room.

The bathroom door slammed with such force it knocked a picture on the wall. She flipped the little lock on the door, her mind saying there! As she did but in reality she knew if he was a wolf, he could just break down the door. She walked over to the mirror looking into it. Her blue eyes staring back at her. She kept her gaze fixated on her own reflection as if it was going to tell her the answers she needed.

What are you doing?

Mallory whipped her head to the side, looking at the door. It was still locked and shut. She shook her head, everything was starting to get to her. She turned the faucet on, letting cool water pour into her hands. She lowered her face into her palms splashing cool water over her face. She let the water droplets run down her face dripping into the sink. A small sigh escaped her. She needed to do something. She looked back up at her reflection. Something was off. She leaned into the mirror and suddenly the bottom of her iris started turning amber in color, it flooded her iris like the sun rising until the ice blue was gone and her eyes glowed amber.

"What the fuck." She whispered, grabbing a towel and wiping the water off her face.

She looked back at the mirror and her eyes were normal. She needed to get away. She backed up from the mirror and light caught her eye. There was a window in the shower.

"You ok in there!" Kai called knocking on the bathroom door.

"Fine, privacy!" Mallory yelled at the door.

She climbed into the shower and then began moving the random shampoo, conditioner, and body wash bottles out of the ledge of the window. She then took a deep breath and pushed the window open. The window creaked as she opened it. Her mind yelling shit, shit, shit as she glanced at the bathroom door, waiting for Kai to come bursting in. She paused her heart pounding in her chest but when nothing happened, she let out a breath. She hoisted herself up onto the ledge and dangled her leg out. It wasn't far from the ground but her ribs throbbed from just pulling herself up. She swung both legs out and told herself all she needed to do was hop.

She went to jump when she heard the bathroom door bust open. The noise scared her and she fell. She hit her ribs on the way down causing her to let out a yell in pain. She braced herself for the impact of the ground praying she didn't hit her ribs once more. The ground never came.

"Mallory." A familiar voice said panicked as two strong arms pulled her into his chest.

Mallory blinked and found herself looking up into a pair of hazel eyes, a mixture of relief and worry flooded his face.

"Thank god I found you." He said, looking her over.

"You're not hurt are you?" He said again trying to look at her while still holding her.

"A little." Mallory answered, he felt familiar, his voice she knew.

She kept looking at him trying to process who he was She was searching her mind hard for a memory, something to tell her who he was. She saw the relief in his eyes and she knew she meant something to him. He set her feet on the ground but his hands moved to her waist to steady her. She couldn't find anything that gave her a clue who he was to her. His hand moved to the side of her face and he rubbed his thumb across it gently.

"I was so worried." He said quietly, his head leaning down as his breath brushed her lips.

He moved his mouth closer to hers going in for the kiss and Mallory froze, something inside of her wanted to shove him away but something was keeping her still. A loud growl erupted and he was thrown backwards away from her. He landed on the ground and Mallory's view was replaced by a very angry Ronan. Every muscle in him was tense. He was towering over the man inches away from attacking him. Mallory reached forward, she needed to help the man but she didn't know why. Her hand wrapped around Ronan's forearm and she tugged him back. Ronan turned around anger rolling off him, his eyes glowing as he looked at Mallory.

"Don't." Mallory said to him, she knew deep down inside that even though Ronan looked like he was going to kill someone he would not hurt her.

"Who is he!" Ronan yelled.

"Get away from her!" The man yelled, getting to his feet.

Ronan ignored him, looking at Mallory still for an answer.

"I…I don't know. I know I am supposed to but I can't think of who he is." Mallory stumbled out, still holding on to Ronan tightly.

"Mal…It's me..Adam." Adam said confused, was she pretending?

"Adam." She said out loud hoping it would trigger a memory.

"Run Mal!" A small boy laughed as he chased her through the woods.

The leaves were bright colors of orange, red and yellow. She ran fast not looking back hoping she would beat him. He always beat her. A long tree root stuck up out of the ground as a small Mallory pushed herself to run faster. Her foot catches the root and falls forward, her knee scraping. She fell and curled up holding her knee. Adam found her quickly and bent down looking at her knee. He saw the blood and scooped her into his arms carrying her out of the woods.

"Who are you?" Ronan growled again.

"We grew up together." Mallory said almost like she was asking.

"Yes. Your my best friend Mal…your-" Adam stopped talking looking at Ronan.

"Who are you?" Adam said, now becoming defensive.

"None of your damn business." Ronan growled trying to step forward but Mallory's grip tightened on his arm.

"His name is Ronan." Mallory said, stepping in between Adam and Ronan.

"Adam, I hit my head when I fell in the river and things are all messy right now. All I know for sure is Ronan saved me and I was going to get help." Mallory said quietly.

"His pack attacked ours, forcing your father and mother to surrender along with Moonlight and Red Woods. His Alpha held a blade to your mother's throat threatening to cut it along with the other Luna's if no one surrendered." Adam yelled.

Mallory clenched her jaw. She knew that she should be upset, that she should be angry but she didn't feel anything. What he just said were words right now and all she could tell was she trusted Ronan.

"I know-" Mallory went to say.

"Know what,Mallory let's go." Adam yelled at her again.

"Yell at her again you won't have a jaw to move next." Ronan said, his voice low and deadly as he went to move around Mallory.

"So you save her from a river and you think you have some claim to her." Adam said bowing up again.

"She's mine." Ronan growled.

"Shut up! Shut up! Shut up! I am not anyones and no one gets me. You Adam, I know we have a connection but I don't remember you and I trust Ronan. So we are leaving that as it is." Mallory elbowed Ronan in the gut as she held her hand out to Adam, as if it would stop him from moving closer.

Ronan winced at the blow to the gut but didn't move from staring down Adam.

"If you both want to help me, I need help remembering where I was going and how I can help save them. I know I feel no connection to this place yet but I know that's what I was doing." Mallory groaned.

"We can go to one of the remaining packs. Your parents had allies everywhere. We can get help elsewhere." Adam said, holding his hand out to Mallory.

"We need to take you to the hunters." Ronan said countering Adam.

"Hunters?" The word vibrated in Mallory, this was something she knew something she felt.

"Knox is sending someone to Moonlight to gather the rest of the pack, I am supposed to go to Red Woods to do the same. I managed to get the assignment so I can sneak you off. I also arranged for the Lunas to go as well. Knox will then make the Alpha's renounce their title, giving it to Knox. He will then be an Alpha four times. I need and I can get you to the hunters." Ronan said letting them know the plan.

"If he becomes an Alpha four times over he's going to be almost unstoppable. We don't even know what bloodline this rogue comes from." Adam said as things become serious.

"His father's name was Kip, some link to Red Woods." Ronan said, answering Adam blowing the comment off as he was trying to think of a solution.

"Kip from Red Woods." Adam repeated.

"Yes." Ronan said, becoming frustrated with Adam.

"As in the man that kidnapped your mother and was trying to create monsters to take over the world." Adam said sarcastically looking at Mallory.

"The hell if I know. Amnesia remembered." Mallory said, making a face at him.

"Seriously." Adam was annoyed that Mallory couldn't remember anything.

"None of that shit matters right now. Ok you, you need to get yourself down into the dungeon and get to the Alphas. You need them to renounce their titles naming someone else preferably someone not here, as Alpha. That way they cannot be forced into giving the title to Knox." Ronan said, taking apart his own plan.

"Ok…That could work." Adam said, replaying the words Ronan just spoke in his mind.

"You can do that?" Ronan asked, his eyes narrowing at Adam.

"Fuck you. Yes I can do that but can I trust you to take care of Mallory." Adam said, gritting his teeth as he looked at him.

"Fuck you. Yes, I will protect her at all costs." Ronan growled.

"And why, why should I believe you? How do I know that this isn't some twisted trap of Knox's." Adam said, stepping closer to him, Mallory still separating them.

Ronan pulled her back into him causing space between Adam and her. He moved her to the left, stepping forward. Before Mallory knew it she was being held by one hand on her waist by Ronan as he stepped protectively towards Adam.

"She's my mate." Ronan said, daring Adam to challenge him.

The words she's my mate struck Adam. He froze trying to understand them. His mouth dropped a little bit as he stared at Ronan.

"What?" Adam said, his mind refusing to process it.

"She is my M-" Ronan started to say but as the word mate started coming out of his mouth Adam's fis t landed on Ronan's jaw, sending him back a step.

"Fuck." Adam muttered, shaking his hand.

"Woah, Woah, Woah!" Mallory yelled, grabbing Ronan by the back of his shirt as he went to go after Adam.

"That's enough." Mallory said getting in between the two of them.

"We have bigger things going on than who I belong to. Which honestly you both can go fuck yourself." Mallory said, hitting them both in the shoulder.

"You, I can't go tell people I don't remember right now to renounce their titles. We need to work together so we can save our home. Go get to my parents and relay the message. You..For some reason I trust you. You get me out of here and to the hunters. We need back up and need help now." Mallory ordered.

"Mal." Adam started but saw the look on her face and he frowned.

"You take care of her. I swear anything happens to her and I will kill you." Adam said fiercely.

"I will." Ronan said quietly.

"I'll see you soon Mal. Happy early birthday." Adam said, stepping into her and pulling her into a hug.

"Thanks." Mallory said, a part of her felt sorrow why didn't she remember him.

She watched him walk away not sure if she was making the right choice but everything was telling her that she needed to stay with Ronan and this would be the one way she could help and maybe remember.

"Ok lets go." Mallory said, turning to Ronan.

Chapter Nineteen
Want

*A*dam's stomach pitted in a knot as he moved quickly through town. He was heading for the dungeon. He knew that Knox would put them in the old dungeon versus the small holding cells they had below the pack house. He needed to be quick. He was going to get the message to Jace and then try to meet Mallory over at the hunters. Mallory. Her name bounced around his head. The way she looked at him with no recognition, like she had never known him. The small glimpse of hope he felt when she remembered a memory but then it quickly faded. She was supposed to be his forever. Even if her wolf never surfaced. Even if his wolf never called her name. It was supposed to be them versus the world. She was supposed to be his. He felt rage building up inside of him, the knot turning into this burning sensation that felt like it was going to erupt out of him. He needed to do something. Before he could stop himself his fist went flying into a nearby tree. A loud crack was heard as his knuckles were instantly pushed back into his hand. Blood began oozing out of the small scrapes that now riddled the top part of his hand. He could barely move his fingers. He looked down at his hand and didn't connect to the pain.

She had a mate Ronan. The name left a bitter taste in his mouth. How dare someone else be her mate. Was it real? What if he was making it up? What if it was all part of some overall plan? He shook his head trying to get rid of the thoughts running around in his. He needed to focus, he couldn't get caught. Even if Ronan may be some evil mastermind, he did know that if the Alpha's did renounce their titles to someone else then they couldn't be forced to give them to Knox.

"Adam!"

Stupid. Owen muttered.

Adam turned slightly to see who was calling his name. He too agreed with Owen. He was stupid, he should have kept going. Adam turned and relief went through him.

"Wyatt!" Adam said, walking to him.

"What are you doing?" Wyatt asked, the excitement turning into concern.

"Your hand. Let me see." Wyatt said, looking down at Adam's hand.

"Did this happen when you got away?" Wyatt asked, picking up his hand.

"No." Adam answered, frowning.

"So...trees piss you off?" Wyatt smirked.

"No...Mallory, apparently she has a mate." Adam blurted out.

Wyatt took the opportunity of Adam being distracted and pulled on his fingers. The quick snap popped all of his knuckles back in place. Adam pulled away as soon as Wyatt let go holding in several choice words.

"So that Ronan is her mate." Wyatt frowned as well.

"So he says. He also says that I have to get to the Alphas to get them to turn over their titles so that Knox does not force them to give him the title of Alpha of Moonlight, Red Woods, and Cross River." Adam said, resisting the urge of rubbing his hand.

"Come with me. I am needed down there to check on Hannah. No one would suspect you if I say you're there to help me." Wyatt said motioning for Adam to follow him.

"If Knox becomes Alpha of four packs he will be unstoppable." Wyatt whispered, shaking his head as he started walking.

It wasn't long before they were walking past guards outside the entrance of the dungeons. They nodded to Wyatt and looked suspicious at Adam but didn't say anything. Walking in from the bright outside, they were blinded in the darkness. Their eyes struggled to focus as the world took on a weird green hue. Adam noticed the temperature change as soon as he started walking in. It almost felt like he was going underground. It had been so long since he had been down here. Jace would catch Mallory and him playing down here when they were little and would scold them.

"Adam." A weak voice called out from behind iron bars.

"Mom!" Adam said running to the bars, the silver burning his skin as he stuck his arm through it to grab hold of her hand.

"Adam, are you ok?" Sarah said, sounding tired.

"I'm good. Are you ok? Are you hurt?" Adam said as he wrapped his hand around hers.

"I'm fine they've dosed everyone they considered strong with wolfsbane, so just tired. What are you doing? Did you find her?" Sarah asked quietly.

"She's ok. She's going to get help. I'm going to help Wyatt check on everyone. We have a plan, don't worry." He whispered to her getting closer to the bars.

"What do you mean?" Sarah said, searching his face with her eyes.

"It's going to be ok. Where's Dad?" Adam whispered.

"They have him in a cell further down." Sarah whispered.

"Rest. It will be over soon." Adam said to her quietly.

"Adam." Wyatt urged him.

"I love you, I'll see if I can check in on Dad." Adam said to her, she gave him a weak smile and nodded.

"I love you too." She said letting go of his hand.

Adam kept looking back at the cell that was holding his mother feeling useless and pathetic not being able to save her. He swallowed down the feeling and told himself it won't be for much longer. Wyatt nodded to a cell to his right as he kept going. A guard came forward and opened a cell for Wyatt. Adam paused looking into the cell Wyatt had nodded to. He saw Jace, his Alpha weak, collapse into the ground. Asher was barely awake, he looked drained. Zeke looked like he was inches from being unconscious again.

"Alpha." Adam whispered into the cell.

"Adam?" Jace whispered, his eyes trying to adjust to see him.

"Yes Alpha." Adam said a small amount of hope in his voice.

"Adam what, what are you doing down here?" Jace coughed.

"I need to talk to you. All of you." Adam whispered.

"What's wrong?" Jace said, straightening up.

"Knox, he's going to come down here and force you all to renounce your titles of Alpha. He is then going to have you name him Alpha of each pack. Then he will be an Alpha four times." Adam said quickly, but then frowned deeply as he noticed the IV port coming out of his arm.

Adam's eyes traced the IV line up to a small bag hanging from a pole. He knew without reading it they were pushing wolfsbanes through Jace's blood stream. Adam suppressed a growl as he glanced at the guard watching Wyatt closely.

"If he is in control of all of our packs, he can command them to do whatever he asks. Never mind the strength of each pack." Jace said, trying to sit up more.

"We need to stop him." Asher mumbled quietly.

"How." Zeke said breathlessly.

"The only way is to give your titles to someone else. Someone who is not here. Someone safe." Adam said his eyes locked with Jace.

"Did you mean it about the hunters?" Mallory asked as she waited to find out what the next steps were.

"Did you really just climb out a window?" Ronan growled.

"I asked my question first." Mallory said with a small smile.

"Yes. We need to get going. I have to go pick up the Luna of Red Woods and then we can head out." Ronan said, walking over to her.

He stopped in front of her, studying her. His hand slowly went to her side. As his fingertips brushed her waist, she flinched anticipating him touching her ribs. He instantly frowned.

"Are you trying to have one of your ribs puncture your lungs? Should I bother trying to save you at all? Maybe I should take you to a cliff so you can just jump off of it." Ronan growled his eyes glowing as Pax pushed forward. He stepped closer to her, his breath brushing her lips.

"Are there other options?" Mallory smirked.

She knew she should be afraid of him, everything about him screamed danger but she couldn't help but feel excited being this closer to him. Her heart raced in her chest as her eyes were captivated by his lips so close to hers. He smelt amazing like mahogany, something warm, she wanted to bury herself into his chest. Her skin seemed to vibrate, she was much too aware of his hands lingering on her waist. Her body begged to feel his touch on her bare skin. She could feel her cheeks getting warm.

"I could say fuck it. Let Knox do what he's doing. Take off with you. Lock you away." Ronan said his voice just above a whisper, his lip brushed hers as he finished the word away.

Mallory went to lean into his lips but a twig snapping from behind them, Ronan turned quickly a deadly growl erupting from his chest as his hand landed on the throat of the person.

"Beta it's me, it's me." Kai yelled trying to get air, as Ronan's hand quickly began cutting off air.

"You idiot. You let her get hurt. I said, keep her safe." Ronan growled his eyes narrowing at Kai.

"She had to go to the bathroom and insisted on going alone." Kai pleaded.

"You tried to go to the bathroom with her!" Ronan roared.

"Ronan." Mallory said, reaching out and putting her hand on his shoulder.

"He's turning blue." Mallory said softly, her hand now rubbing his shoulder.

"So." Ronan said his eyes still locked Kai as his eyes began to roll back in his head.

"If he's dead, he can't help you." Mallory said in a sing-song voice.

Ronan grumbled hearing Mallory's voice and let go. Kai hit the ground grasping, his hand going to his throat holding it looking up at Ronan. Ronan clenched his jaw looking down at Kai. Ronan extended his hand down towards Kai offering him help. Kai took it and Ronan pulled him up. As he helped him up Ronan grabbed ahold of Kai's thumb. A loud snap was heard as Ronan yanked back on

Kai's thumb. His thumb broke instantly. Kai let out a loud scream as he looked down at his bent thumb.

"Ronan!" Mallory yelled.

"Next time I say keep someone safe and you don't it won't be your thumb that is snapped." Ronan threatened Kai, ignoring Mallory.

"Yes Beta." Kai was trying to choke back the pain.

"Straighten your thumb out and get to the dungeon. Retrieve the Luna from Moonlight and head there to get the rest of the packs. If the pack won't come, kill the Luna. I am going to Red Woods." Ronan said, reaching back and grabbing a hold of Mallory's hand leading her away.

"Kill the Luna." Mallory said, yanking on his hand.

"Ronan!" Mallory yelled at him as he dragged her to the front of the house and to a driveway.

"You said-

"I said what I need to say to make sure, those I need kept safe are. I am Beta of this pack and have an image that needs to be upheld." Ronan said harshly to her as he opened a car door.

"But you can't be serious about killing her." Mallory said her eyes wide as she looked at him.

"Get in." Ronan said motioning to the car.

"You can't be serious." Mallory said, demanding an answer.

He stepped into her causing her to back up against the car. She was now trapped between him and the car. She felt a fire burning in her belly pushing her to be mad and fight back; but the sheer excitement of being trapped between Ronan and the car, his body less than an inch away sent her mind spiraling.

"Dead serious. I mean what I say one hundred percent of the time. The Luna is a pawn and a piece in the game that I am playing. What I hold important will always come first." Ronan said his voice low as he stepped closer.

Ronan's body was now up against hers sending chills running through her that she couldn't stop. Her eyes focused on his chest because she was unsure what to do or say next. She couldn't think. His finger traced her jawline getting to her chin, he tilted her head up.

"Right now what I hold important is you and keeping you safe. Nothing and no one else matters." Ronan said, his thumb reaching up and brushing her lower lip.

Her breath caught in the back of her throat as her eyes locked with his. A soft ring of gray glow outlined his cognac-colored eyes. His hand slipped from her chin to the back of her neck, holding it firmly. He leaned his head down so that his mouth was less than inches from hers, his nose touching her own nose.

"Now you can either get in the car or I will put you in the car. Ethier options gets me what I want, you choose." Ronan said his lips brushing hers as he spoke.

"One hundred percent of the time?" She whispered her lips twitched into a small smirk as she tried to redeem herself.

Ronan pushed her into the car closing the gap between them. His body pressing completely into hers. His hand that held the back of her neck squeezed gently as his mouth captured hers. The kiss was fierce and demanding. His tongue entered her mouth to claim and conquer. His tongue rubbed against hers as he pressed his pelvis into her. His other hand grabbed her hip and squeezed as if he needed to hold on to her. Her mind was gone completely, she was lost in the pure want of it all. Her fingers entwined into his shirt pulling him close as her tongue fought back. Her other hand's fingers hooked his pants loop holding him to her. Her body screamed for more. To be touched and felt. A moan escaped her lips as he pulled her bottom lip into his mouth sucking on it. Her legs went weak as he let her lip go, breaking the kiss. She was breathless, her chest moving rapidly as if she had ran a mile, each exhale made her breast rub against his chest, sending more tingles through her.

"One hundred percent of the time…now get in the car." Ronan said his voice daring her to argue.

She nodded slowly as she tried to catch her breath. She was lost in the haze and confused about what to do next. His hand moved off her hip as he stepped back slowly. His other hand was still on the back of her neck as she let go of him. With small pressure he moved her forward and guided her into the passenger seat. She sat down still stunned looking up at him.

"Good girl." He said his voice deep and eyes locked on hers, his eyes saying all the things he wanted to do to her.

Chapter Twenty
Close

Knox shoves Nora along. She didn't really understand what Knox had planned. It seems like Ronan did all the planning. She watched him walk past her, he looked lost. She wanted to ask where he was going. He left Mick laying on the floor in the dining room.

"I'm trying to decide what to do with you." Knox said over his shoulder.

"Ideas?" Knox smirked looking back at her.

"Let me go?" Nora smiled back brightly.

"Funny." Knox grinned.

He suddenly changed direction and started heading back towards the dungeons. Nora rolled her eyes at him. She was wondering if she could make it if she ran. He didn't look really fast. She looked around her surroundings looking for guards and pack members of his. She slowed down trying to put distance between them. They were so relaxed for some who had taken over another pack. He did not have a patrol going. He was either too confident or stupid. Her eyes settled on the woods. She could make it. She shifted her stance. Once she got away and got the cuffs off Zara would be back and she would be in a better position to help her pack. She was so focused on the woods she didn't notice Knox had slowed down and was now waiting for her to make a move. She took a small step to the side and suddenly his hand was around her throat. His fingers curled into her skin as he squeezed.

"Run and I will start executing members of your pack. Your Beta's family will be slaughtered, then the one who think's hes funny…Matt. Yes I can tell by the way your eyes dilated. There's a soft spot for this Matt. I will kill him and his family slowly in front of you. Everything you love will be gutted. Right now you need to accept defeat." Knox said to her as he continued to restrict air from her.

Nora's hand went to his as she tried to pry his hand from her throat. She dug her fingernails in his hand making him bleed as she tried to get him to stop. The world was closing in as he continued to choke her.

"I should kill you right here. You're worthless. Half breed. " Knox said as he continued to squeeze.

Nora's vision faded to black as her body slumped. Knox groaned as Nora passed out. He let go and let her fall to the ground. As he let go her body automatically inhaled. Knox huffed looking at her. He let his anger get the best of him now he had to carry her to the dungeon.

Mallory kept quiet as they pulled up to an old stone building. She glanced over at Ronan who seemed like he was contemplating his next move. He let out a small sigh and then looked at Mallory.

"Wait here." He said firmly but was looking at her hard.

"What are we doing?" Mallory said not really responding to the wait here.

"I need to go get the Luna of Red Woods." Ronan said to her.

As he was looking at her he focused on something just passed her window. Knox was walking this way carrying someone.

"Look at me." Ronan commanded.

Mallory looked confused glancing out the window as he said look at me. She saw a man carrying a woman. The woman had long raven colored hair and she looked dead. Ronan grabbed her chin and pulled her face towards him.

"You stay in this car and don't get out. I need Knox not to pay attention to you or focus on you." Ronan said firmly.

"He's the guy who is doing all of this?" Mallory asked anger sparking within her.

"Kind of. Yes He's the Alpha." Ronan said quietly, he was the one who came up with the plan for Knox.

"Kind of." Mallory snapped, not liking the answer.

"Look, I'll explain more when I can. Right now you need to stay put. Once I get the Luna we can leave. I need to get you to the hunters." Ronan said quietly, his voice dropping to a whisper as Knox got closer.

"Fine but explaining starts the minute we start driving again. Mallory said, her eyes narrowing in on him.

"Deal." Ronan said in relief.

He went to leave but something in him twisted, he didn't want to leave her for a second. Pax whimpered inside of him like a lost puppy. He wanted to kiss her but his eyes flicker to Knox. He was now close enough to see everything. Ronan reached over and squeezed Mallory's hand. She looked at him confused but he didn't say anything and got out of the car.

"Ronan!" Knox smiled as he walked over to the car.

"Knox, what are you doing? Why-

"She got mouthy. She's alive. I am returning her to her cell, where she can rot." Knox said quickly.

He looked over at the car, his eyebrow raising as he saw the girl inside. He glanced back at Knox, his eyebrow still raised asking a silent question.

"I'm here to get the Luna of Red Wood to start my task." Ronan said quietly, he knew that's not what Knox was asking but he was trying to bring Mallory up at all.

"Duh what are you doing with that…that … Human." Knox said as his lip turned up, like he had a bad taste in his mouth.

"She's mine. I keep my things with me." Ronan said firmly.

"Geeze, ok. I'll have the guards come up with her." Knox said as his eyes glossed over sending the mind link.

Ronan was becoming impatient. Knox kept looking over at the car. The small seconds were turning into hours it felt like.

"She's got the same color hair as this one." Knox said, moving Nora's head as he moved his arms.

"Have you had the Alpha's name you Alpha of their packs yet?" Ronan asked, changing the topic.

"No not yet. I am going to after this." Knox said, his gaze turning to Ronan.

"We need to do it quickly. After that happens you need to order all the members of each pack that are here to swear an oath to you to ensure the bound." Ronan said firmly.

"Ok. Ok." Knox said annoyed.

"You're the one who wanted this." Ronan said to him shrugging his shoulders.

"It was't just me you had the perfect plan for all of this. It's going to be fine and all of it will work out." Knox said reassuring Ronan.

"I need you to be quick with the whole Red Woods thing. You have been lacking in your Beta duties and I have been letting you but I need your presence with me more." Knox said firmly.

"Yeah well you know I am more of a behind the scenes type of guy." Ronan said his eyes going to the door of the building, grateful that he was seeing movement.

"True." Knox replied, his eyes also going to the building.

One guard came out holding Hannah and the other guard was walking towards Knox. He put his arms out to Knox and Knox dropped her into his arms. The other guard looked at Ronan.

"Back seat." Ronan said nodding to the car.

The guard nodded and walked over the car. As he got to the car, Mallory opened the back door from inside and the guard laid Hannah down. He glanced at Mallory before exiting the car. Knox watched them and Ronan nodded his head to Knox as if he was saying bye and began walking to the car. Ronan could feel Knox's gaze on his back, it felt like his stare was burning him. Pax also was having anxiety in Ronan's head the word go, go, go was playing over and over again. He needed to get Mallory away from him.

"Hurry back." Knox called to him, it was a weird response, like he wanted to say something else.

"I will. Go secure your titles. If we don't have that, this can't work." Ronan told him as he opened the driver door.

"Right." Knox smirked and began walking to the building.

Ronan got in the car, his stomach twisting as he put the car in reserve, trying not to act too quickly to alarm Knox. As he pulled away he clenched his jaw glancing over at Mallory, she was fine. She was safe. He didn't notice. Mallory looks so much like Nora, he was so afraid for a second.

"We better hope your friend has gotten the Alpha's to renounce their titles to someone. Otherwise we have bigger problems." Ronan muttered as they began driving out of the pack.

Chapter Twenty One
Red Wood

*R*onan drove in silence heading towards Red Wood. He could feel Mallory's eyes glaring at him.

"I'm taking Hannah to Red Woods and giving her back to them. I am not going to kill her or bring the rest of the pack back. Once we drop her off we are going to the hunters." Ronan said with a big sigh.

"Really?" Mallory asked her tone and body language changing.

"Yes." Ronan said annoyed as he turned down the road to head to Red Woods territory.

"Thank you." Mallory said quietly.

Ronan nodded his head in response, still not saying much. His eyes fixated on the road. As he pulled into the drive of the pack house, he felt a little uneasy. There was no one around. He didn't see anyone the whole way in. He knew that the warriors were all in Cross River captured but still there should be someone setting up.

"Wait here." Ronan ordered her.

"Why? What-"

"I said wait here." Ronan said, locking eyes with her.

"You're not as scary as you think you are." Mallory said not taking her eyes off him.

"Love, you haven't seen me even try to be scary. Wait here." Ronan said his voice started out light but as he got to the end it was deep and deadly sounding.

Mallory didn't say anything but gave up on the staring contest. She turned her head away from him and looked out the window. Ronan got out of the car slowly. He shut the door and began making his way to the back seat door. That's when he heard it. He had been waiting for it. A loud snap of twig breaking brought his attention to his side. Before he knew it he was surrounded. They were half transformed, claws and fangs were out but they were still in human form. They looked to be seconds away from completely changing. Mallory went to open her door to back Ronan.

"Stay in the car." He growled as he kept his eyes on them.

He heard the door shut and knew Mallory was out of the car. Before he knew it she was standing next to him.

"If shit happens you can't take on all of them by yourself so don't even start with me." Mallory whispered to him in a hushed tone.

"You should listen to what I say." He whispered sharply back.

"We're not here to cause any trouble." Ronan announced waiting for the leader to say something or move forward.

"Then why are you…Mallory?" A woman started to say but was distracted by Mallory.

"Yes, I'm Mallory." Mallory said quietly, she had no clue who this woman was.

"It's me Layla." She said again confused why she was acting like she didn't know her.

"Logan's wife. Beta of Red Woods." Layla said, trying to get Mallory to remember.

Mallory shook her head. She didn't remember her. She was trying her hardest, nothing came. She frowned at nothing.

"I'm sorry. I had an accident and now I don't remember anything or anyone." Mallory started to say but was cut off by Layla.

"Accident?" Layla asked, coming over to her, her hand held out like she was going to touch her.

Mallory stepped off to the side keeping her distance. Ronan stepped in the way blocking Mallory protectively. Layla narrowed her eyes at him.

"Your Luna is in the back seat. They had her cuffed with wolfsbane. Her body did not handle it well. I am assuming she has never had exposure to it." Ronan said, ignoring the look.

"We need to get her to the hospital. It actually survived the fire. Logan is there now." Layla said thinking out loud.

"Logan…" Mallory repeated his name.

"Yes Logan." Layla repeated watching Mallory's face as there were some glimpses of remembrance.

"I need to go." Mallory said quietly to Ronan.

"I need to get you to the hunters." Ronan whispered to her.

"Well then I guess you're going to the hospital. Logan is the head of them." Layla said, her eyes glancing over to the car.

"I'll drive, you ride shotgun and you fill me in on what's wrong with Mallory and the status of Cross River." Layla ordered, as she began walking to the car.

A low growl vibrated through Ronan's chest as Layla went to touch the handle of the driver side door. She didn't mean to but the growl made her hand fall away from the handle. She turned around, her eyes glowing slightly not sure of Ronan's intentions. The remaining pack members inched forward, eyes slightly glowing as well. Mallory grabbed Ronan's arm.

"He likes to drive." Mallory smirked a little bit.

"So I will sit in the-

"You will sit in the back, next to your Luna. Mallory is in the passenger seat. The Shadow Pack has taken over Cross River and by now Moonlight completely. Moonlight, Cross River, and Red Woods Alpha's along with the high ranking wolves are being held in cells. Mallory hit her head on a rock. She doesn't remember anything." Ronan said shortly, his arm making Mallory's hand slid into his as he led her to the passenger side door and opened it into it.

"Ok then." Layla said looking at Ronan weird, she nodded to her pack letting them know that everything will be ok.

"Alert the hospital that Luna is on her way and to get everything ready for her." Layla commanded.

Layla got into the back seat of the car. Carefully she took Hannah's head into her lap. Hannah's eyes fluttered lightly but did not open. Layla was relieved, that it was a good sign. Getting the cuffs off was giving her body some relief. Layla looked at the back of Ronan's head.

"Where do you fit into all this?" Layla asked in a suspicious tone.

"I'm the Beta to Shadow Pack." Ronan said very matter of fact like.

"Shadow Pack?" Layla asked her mind searching through the territories, there was no Shadow Pack.

"A pack of rogues and the unwanted that no one knew about. That has now started taking over your packs." Ronan said his voice maintained the same tone.

Layla let out a low growl as she lunged forward. Ronan was waiting for it. He reached over and tightened Mallory's seat belt. With one hand holding her in place he whipped the steering wheel to the side, sending Layla back. She bounced into the back seat and then was flung into the door. Ronan jacked on the brakes, sending her into Mallorys seat.

"That's enough. If I was here to do anymore damage. I wouldn't have stopped for an introduction. You all would be dead. Check your Luna, shut up, sit down." Ronan orders as Layla pulled herself back into her seat.

"So why are you helping?" Layla growled checking on Hannah.

"Mallory…She is my mate. Knox will kill her." Ronan said quietly, his eyes flickering over to Mallory who was studying him.

"Well that's a damn good reason but how do we know you're not lying." Layla said ready to fight again as they pulled up at the hospital.

"If Adam did his part right, The Alpha's will renounce their titles leaving someone who is not captured in charge of their packs. Saving everyone from Knox gaining three new titles. I am taking Mallory to the hunter's to get back up and I am literally giving you back your Luna." Ronan said a threat in his voice as he listed off the reasons.

"You know that's betrayal. You're betraying your own Alpha." Layla said her voice having an edge to it, it was extremely uncommon for a Beta to turn against their Alpha.

The bond between Alpha and Beta was almost nearly as close as Alpha and Luna. She watched Ronan's face and nothing changed. He shrugged.

"I've never really cared about anything until recently." Ronan said his eyes moved to Mallory who was just taking it all in.

"I can't renounce him. I need to still hold some ties so I can still have inside information." Ronan said, seeing the look on Layla's face.

"You know she is Jace's daughter. Cross River's Alpha." Layla said her tone of voice still sounded like she was testing him.

"Why do you think I am helping?" Ronan rolled his eyes and unclicked Mallory's seat belt.

"Let's go to the hunter's leader." Ronan said his tone less than amused, as he got out of the car.

"Mallory are you ok? Do you really not remember? Are you safe?" Layla whispered to her quickly.

"No. Ronan saved me from drowning. I'm part hunter but feel no connection anywhere. When I saw Adam I had a memory come up but felt nothing but I'm sorry. The only person who feels like anything to me is him. He's safe, he's…something more." Mallory said his voice fading to a whisper as Ronan got to her door and pulled it open, his hand automatically going for hers.

Ronan helped her out, his hand lingering in hers as his eyes narrowed at the pack members coming out of the hospital and rushing to the car. He moved Mallory behind him, blocking her protectively as he watched. The stretcher came out and they quickly loaded Hannah onto it. Just as quickly as they came out they were back inside with her.

"Come on, I'll take you to Logan." Layla said quietly as she walked to the sliding glass doors.

Chapter Twenty Two
Hospital

*T*he hospital was cold and made Mallory want to leave. Something was telling her it was not good. Ronan glanced back at her, he could feel her becoming upset. He stopped and turned towards her to ask her what was wrong.

A nurse came charging out of one of the rooms with a needle and syringe in her hand. She was going to stab Ronan with it. Her heart dropped to her stomach as she felt like everything slowed down.

"No!" She yelled as she pulled Ronan into her, in one swift movement she was in front of him.

She hit the nurse in the stomach with an open palm. She sent the nurse flying backwards on the floor. Another nurse came towards them and they were surrounded, quickly. Ronan let out a deadly growl going to step in front of Mallory.

"Enough." Layla said and they began to back away.

Mallory locked eyes with Layla, her body felt like it was vibrating. Everything in her was hell bent on protecting Ronan.

"My fault. I forgot to tell them to stand." Layla smiled at Ronan.

"Let's go." Mallory said to Ronan, her eyes burning holes in Layla.

"Mallory." Layla said her face almost looked hurt.

"No this was bullshit. He told you the truth and you want to ambush him. No. Come on. We will figure this out on our own. You're welcome for your Luna back. By the way, that was his idea, not mine." Mallory said, stepping out from behind Ronan, her eyes daring anyone to move.

Ronan wasn't sure how to feel. He had never had anyone stand up for him before or choose him. He was abandoned as a child, his father killed his mother in a jealous rage and he was left to fend for himself. This was the first time in his life he was being chosen.

"Mallory, you can't be serious. We are like family." Layla said going to touch her.

"We might have been, but I don't remember you, this place or anyone else for that matter. If this is how you treat your family, I don't want it." Mallory said she was shaking, she was so angry.

"Hey Rebel."

It was a warm soft voice coming from the doorway of a hospital room. His chocolate brown eyes with crow feet at the end of them called to hers and the small smirk on his face, made her mind twitch. The rebellious blond hair of his, she could almost remember pulling it. An image of younger her running at him full force ready to fight popped into her head.

"Uncle Logan." the words fell out of her mouth and his smirk grew into a smile.

"Are you causing all the problems out here?" He chuckled.

"Logan you need to be resting you…almost didn't make it." Layla said, coming over to him.

"Thank god she knows one of us." She whispered into Logan's ear.

"I don't remember but I know your name and you are the first person that feels like…home other than Ronan." Mallory said loudly so she knew that she could hear them.

"Ronan...hmmm he doesn't ring a bell." Logan said, looking at Ronan.

"Ronan, the real reason all the problems are going on out here." Ronan introduced himself, a small smirk on his lips.

"Hey Rebel, Want to come into my suit and explain, Let an old man sit?" Logan said to Mallory.

"Only because I feel I can trust you but she, she stays out." Mallory said hatefully to Layla.

"Mallory." Layla said hurt.

"It's ok, I got her. Go tell your pack to stand down. See to Hannah, Asher needs you to be the leader that you are." Logan said, kissing her forehead.

Ronan pulled Mallory back closed to him, she landed neatly against his chest. He leaned his head down to her ear.

"Are you sure about this?" Ronan whispered to her.

Mallory just nodded trying to stop the overwhelming chills he just sent through her. She couldn't help but want to move closer to him, to want to feel his lips against her skin but she shook her head slightly trying to chase those thoughts away she had to keep focus. She needed to talk to Logan.

"Yes it's fine. You're coming." Mallory said, taking his hand from her hip and entwining her fingers with his.

"There was no doubt about that." He smirked, walking past Layla and following Logan into the room.

"What happened?" Mallory asked, noticing Logan's weakened state, sadness and hurt for him filling her.

"Fire. From what I can tell Ronan could probably fill you in on it." Logan said, adding a small jab in there.

"More of your planning?" Mallory asked, a little annoyed.

"Hey, it was my job, I'm good at my job and It was a pretty good plan. Set fires to the other packs, draw them back home, conquer yours, force the Alpha's to submit by using their mates, Luna's. Using the Luna's was surprisingly Knox but It worked out perfectly. Complete take over in a few hours with no war. It was a good plan till you came along and now I'm working to undo it all." Ronan said, his voice a little proud.

"And why her? Logan asked quietly, he could see it without Ronan saying it. The way he stood too close to Mallory, the way his eyes were judging him and everyone else in the room.

"She's my-

"I'm his mate. Although I believe at one point I got what that meant but I don't know now. Long story short hit my head, memories gone. Now before I hit my head I was going to get help. Ronan found me in the river. Seeing you now, something tells me I was running to you." Mallory said quietly.

Ronan eyed Logan carefully when she said running to him. A tinge of jealousy went through him.

"Mallory doesn't have a wolf yet and she's half hunter." Logan said, looking at Ronan.

"Don't care." Ronan shrugged.

"You understand what all that means?" Logan asked quietly, his eyes still judging him.

"It means it's gonna be hard. Life's hard." Ronan shrugged again.

"All right then. Mallory, you were coming to see me because you're part hunter. With the wolf world under attack the safest spot will be with us. We are the strongest allies the wolves have. We do not have to bend to certain rules or obey certain people." Logan said quietly.

"Layla is my mate that's why I am here. You need to take Mallory to our base, it's in the city. It's hidden in plain sight. Mallory, they know you there. Find Drake, tell him what's happening and he will assemble the troops." Logan smirked a little at saying assembly the troops.

"Ok." Mallory said quietly.

"Your mom?" Logan asked worried, his showing concerned.

"I don't know. I don't ..." Mallory started to say but she began feeling panicked not being able to even recall her own mother.

"The Alpha's are in their own holding cell, shackled with wolfsbane. The Luna's were as well. Nora seemed unphased by wolfsbane. She was ok last I saw her. Hannah has been returned; she was in worse shape. Jessica is being brought back to Moonlight only as a bargaining piece. They are going to round up the rest of Moonlight and take them back to Cross River. Knox will then have the Alphas renounce their title and name him Alpha of all Moonlight, Cross River, and Red Woods. Not to mention being Alpha of Shadow pack." Ronan said firmly, his hand caught Mallory's and he pulled her against him as he explained.

Mallory leaned back into him, she immediately felt calm. She liked the way he could instantly make her feel like everything was ok even if it wasn't.

"Shit." Logan said quietly.

"If Adam was able to get my message to Jace and the other Alphas it won't happen." Ronan said quietly, his arm wrapping around Mallory.

"Meaning?" Logan asked, straightening up.

"I told Adam to tell the Alpha's to renounce their titles to someone who was not captured. That way Knox couldn't force them to make him their Alpha." Ronan said quietly.

"We need to move quickly." Logan said with a nod.

"They were going to move on to Black Sands first, then Dark Water, City Lights, and lastly Silver Mountain. Layla is the Beta here and needs to reach out to them. We need to start moving against them before it is all too late." Ronan said calmly.

"Get Mallory to the hunters. I will have Layla start working on it." Logan said but then began to cough.

"You're not ok are you?" Mallory asked.

"Smoke inhalation…honestly should have died, I think your momma had something to do with that." Logan said, giving her a wink.

"Stay the night, head out first thing in the morning. The pack here won't bother you." Logan said quietly and he took a step back like he was going to fall.

Mallory bolted forward catching Logan by the shirt. His hand went to her shoulder steadying himself. Ronan stepped up a frown on his face at Logan touching Mallory. Ronan caught Logan by the arm and helped steady him back onto the bed.

"Get a nurse in here!" Mallory yelled over her shoulder as she walked over to the oxygen.

Ronan got Logan settled on the bed. As a nurse came rushing in. Layla close behind. Ronan scooted his legs up in it as he laid back.

"Logan." Layla said, rushing over to him.

"I'm ok, just stood up for too long." Logan said with a wink as they placed and oxygen mask over

"Layla…" Logan started to say but pointed at Ronan.

"He needs you to get in contact with Black Sands and then the other packs. Knox's next move is to take over

Black Sands. We're staying tonight and going to the hunters to get back up in the morning. I need an address." Ronan said quickly.

Logan pointed to his jacket pocket. Layla looked over at his jacket and walked to it. In the pocket of his jacket were cards. Layla frowned and walked over to Ronan handing him a card. Ronan looked down at it in his hand the address to a building on it.

"Be there tomorrow. You can stay in the pack house. Take the second room on the right. No one is allowed in there" Layla said with a nod her eyes then going back to Logan.

Layla helped him back in bed and began hooking him back up to the monitors. Logan tried to make a face at her but he was so weak from standing.

"Is he going to be ok?" Mallory asked worriedly.

"He needs rest." Layla said quietly.

Mallory watched him struggle and bit her lip. Something was pulling and pooling deep inside of her. In her core she could feel something building. This energy she had never felt before. There was a small spark of it when she shoved the nurse away from Ronan. Something defensive. She stepped away from Ronan and began walking over to Logan. She felt the energy flowing down her arms and into her finger tips.

"Mallory?" Ronan asked, looking at her moving towards Logan, he could feel this power radiating off of her and it was not her Alpha status.

Logan went wide-eyed as he saw Mallory approaching him, the realization of what was happening hit him and he began to shake his head no at her. The monitors on the machine began going off as his stats began to tank.

"Help! Doctor!" Layla cried out in a panic.

Mallory reached out and grabbed a hold of his arm. As she touched him a force went into him making him lean back into the bed. A light flowed from her fingertips and settled into Logan's chest. The bright burst blinded everyone for a second. As the light faded Mallory let go of his arm and the alarms on the machines turned off as Logan's stats turned to normal. Doctors rushed in confused as Mallory backed away.

Mallory stumbled slightly feeling her body go weak. She felt drained and her legs felt like jello.

"Mallory?" Ronan asked as he stepped towards her.

"What just happened?" Ronan asked to go to her side.

"I..I-" The weakness spread through her as she tried to answer.

The world began to turn to speckled pieces of light as she couldn't see. She reached out to grab Ronan.

"Catch her, she's gonna fall." Logan yelled as he sat up in bed taking the oxygen he no longer needed off.

Mallory went limp as the world went black. Rona caught her as she fell back into his arms. He shook her lightly but she was out.

"Somebody explain now." Ronan growled as he pulled her into him more.

"She's like Nora." Logan said, swinging his legs over the side of the bed.

"And.." Ronan said, becoming angry.

"She can use energy around her to defend herself, heal, and fight. It's part of her bloodline and the first hunters had it. She hasn't turned twenty one just yet. It's coming early." Logan said, trying to figure things out as he spoke.

"Why is she unconscious?" Ronan demanded.

"She used her own energy to heal me. It takes a toll on the body." Logan reassured him.

"What do I do? How do I help her?" Ronan asked, looking down at her.

"She just needs rest. She will be ok once she wakes up. I've seen her mother do it several times." Logan explained swatting the doctors away from him.

"Ok." Ronan nodded and began carrying her out in his arms.

"Ronan…you need to make sure she doesn't ever do too much…this power, it can hurt her." Logan said carefully.

Ronan nodded not really sure what he meant but all he knew was he wanted to get Mallory somewhere comfortable.

Chapter Twenty Three
Scars

*H*e carried her over to the bed and placed her down. He ran his hand over her face and brushed her hair from her face. He saw her eyes flutter slightly and his stomach knotted. She opened her eyes and groaned.

"Hey." He said quietly, his hand going to her cheek.

"Hey." Mallory smiled, stretching a little.

"You ok? You kind of scared me for a second." Ronan said quietly, his voice a little vulnerable as he admitted the fear he felt.

"Hmm why? Oh…oh. I did it again." Mallory said quietly

"Again?" Ronan said, scrunching his eyebrows at her.

"Yeah the energy thingy…my mom said it had something to do with hunters..hey, hey my mom! I remember something!" Mallory said excitedly.

"I don't know anymore but her it was something." Mallory smiled.

Ronan smiled, his stomach twisted inside of him. It was something else he needed to protect her from. Logan's words lingering in his mind but he wasn't going to let her see his worry.

"See you're slowly getting there." Ronan nodded as he stepped back away from the bed, his mind going to the stories he had heard about Nora.

"Once we get to the hunters I am sure more will come back." Ronan said as he looked down at the card in his hand.

He watched her expression change and knew she was becoming upset because she didn't have all her memories. Mallory looked exhausted and he didn't blame her. The world was spinning and nothing was making sense. Ronan glanced over at her. He hadn't marked her yet and he could already feel everything she felt. He put the card down on the dresser near the door. He checked the door twice and then slid the dresser in front of the door. Mallory raised an eyebrow at him from the bed.

"Incase someone wants in." Ronan said quietly.

Mallory nodded lightly and looked down at her hands as if they were going to tell her an answer. She didn't know what she was doing.

"There's a bathroom in here if you want to shower." Ronan said quietly, he wasn't sure what she needed.

"Ok." Mallory said quietly.

"When's the last time you ate?" Ronan asked her.

"Before I climbed out the window." Mallory smirked a little.

"Can I see your ribs?" Ronan asked, crossing the room, he had to keep reminding himself that she wasn't a wolf, that she didn't heal like him.

"They're fine." She answered quietly.

"Do they hurt?" Ronan asked, ignoring her tone, he wanted to know if she was ok.

"A little. I'm more drained than in pain." Mallory said, closing her eyes as she said drained.

"Hungry?" Ronan asked her, trying to find somewhere, that she would let him help.

"Tired." Mallory said quietly.

"Ok." Ronan nodded as he got up and walked over to the dresser.

Ronan began looking through the drawers. He grabbed a t-shirt and held it up looking at Mallory. He then walked over to her and handed her the t-shirt.

"Change, get comfy. I'm going to shower." Ronan said softly, handing her the dark t- shirt.

"Ok." Mallory yawned.

Ronan smiled a little at the yawn, as he began walking to the bathroom he pulled his shirt up over his head. He stretched as he dropped the shirt to the floor. Mallory's eyes roamed over his back as he paused in the doorway. She felt her cheeks getting warm as she couldn't take her eyes off of it. She didn't know when she got up off the bed but she found herself standing behind him Her hand reaching out and touching a long scar that ran down the length of his back. Ronan had heard her coming and chose not to move. His skin flinched slightly as he felt her trace the scar.

"What happened?" Mallory whispered, as her finger tip followed another mark.

"That one was from a blade." Ronan said, trying to suppress the urge to turn and catch her wrist.

"Whip." He said as she traced a thin line.

She stepped closer, her fingertips still tracing the scar. A large circle scar sat on top of his shoulder blade. She stood slightly on her tippy toes and brushed her lips against it. Ronan couldn't take it anymore.

"This-" Malllory began to say.

Ronan couldn't stop himself, he quickly turned and caught her by the wrist. He pulled her into him. Her breath caught in her throat as she looked up at him. His eyes glowed slightly and for the first time Mallory noticed a scar over his eyebrow. She carefully reached her finger forward touching the scar.

"You have so many." She whispered.

"More than you know." He said, sounding like there was more to the statement.

"I want to know." She whispered.

Ronan was taken back by her statement, his eyes searching hers. Did she really want to know? She could see him hesitate.

"What-" Mallory going to ask what happened but Ronan couldn't let her.

He let go of her wrist and his hand went to the back of her neck pulling her mouth towards his. His mouth captured hers, she felt her knees go weak the minute his lips touched hers. Her hand goes to the side of his face as her lips respond to his, kissing him intensely back. She broke the kiss and he went to step back thinking that she was stopping the advances. Her hand caught his hip stopping him from stepping back. His expression was confused as he waited for her to respond. She leaned forward, her lips touching the circle scar that looped over the top of his shoulder. She watched his skin respond in small goosebumps. She kissed along his shoulder to the next scar. A long thin red mark ran down over the front of his chest. Her mouth traveled along It. Ronan leaned back against the doorway as her mouth traveled down over his stomach, another diagonal scar ending at his pants linc.

She kneeled in front of him, her mouth brushed along his pants line, looking up at him she watched him lean his head back as he took a deep breath in, Mallory looked up taking in the sight of him enjoying her mouth sent thrills through her. She wanted to make him moan.

Her heart raced as she became excited at the thoughts running through her mind. Her fingers grabbed along his pants button and began to undo it. She went to pull down on his pants to release him but he caught her hand.

"You sure?" He said breathlessly.

She nodded, going to do it again, his hand still stopping her. She noticed the glow coming from his eyes was intense.

"Once we start, I don't know if I can stop." Ronan warned.

"Then don't." Mallory said as she pulled her wrist away and pulled his pants down.

His member was exposed, she grabbed a hold of him at the base wrapping her hands around him. Ronan leaned into her touch, his hand going to the back of her head taking her hair into his hand. She leaned forward her tongue tracing the tip of him. She looked up locking eyes with Ronan as she opened her mouth and let him full it. Ronan let out a small deep groan as he watched her start moving her head up and down. His hand held her hair tight as she began to move quicker. Her tongue twisted around the top of it as she moved back downwards. Her tongue moved down the side of his length as her mouth continued to move over him. He leaned further back into the door. The sight of her having him in her mouth brought him closer to the edge. He let out a growl as he tugged on her hair telling her to stop. She released him from her mouth and looked up at him. He kicked his pants and boxers aside.

His hand dropped her hair and slid to the back of neck as he moved downwards to help her up. He pulled her against him, his mouth, capturing hers fiercely. His tongue invades her mouth, his hands moving over her ass as he cups it with both hands and then in one swift movement picks her up. Mallory wraps her legs around his waist as he carries her to the bed. He laid her back on the bed straddling her. Her mouth begging for more as he broke the kiss. He began kissing her shoulder slowly working up the side of her neck, his mouth teasing her. Her body began to ache, the urge growing more intense with each kiss. He got to her ear and took her ear lobe into his mouth. He sucked on her earlobe sending chills through her as she let out a small gasp. His mouth moved down the side of her neck and moved down to her over her collar bone. Every part of her body began to vibrate. A small moan escaped her mouth. He grabbed her shirt in between his hands and pulled the shirt split down the middle. The rush of cold air made her shiver as her skin turned to goosebumps.

He placed warm wet kisses down the center of her chest and over the tops of her breast. Finding the clasp in the middle of her jade color bra, he squeezed the clasp, and her breasts were freed. He grabbed a hold of one firmly in his hand squeezing. He flicked his tongue over the top of her nipple teasing it before taking it into his mouth and sucking. Mallory let a sharp inhale that turned into a deep moan as Ronan's teeth pulled at her nipple before he let his lips capture it again. His other hand massaging her other breast. His mouth left her breast and began traveling down over her stomach. He stopped seeing how bruised her ribs were. He was afraid to hurt her. Her fingers entwined in his hair pushing his head back down wanting him to continue. He smirked against her skin as he reached her pantline. He ran his tongue under it and watched her shiver. Her fingers tugged on his hair begging him to stop toying with her. He undid the button of her jeans and she lifted her hips so he could pull them off.

He kissed the side of her thigh, placing soft kissing on each one making her heart beat faster with anticipation. His face linger just above her center and she seems to twitch with anticipation. He placed a small kiss on top of her and he watched her melt. He ran his tongue down her slit and she inhaled her thighs fall outward to let him have more of her. He ran his tongue over her bud, the sensation sending chills through her. She lifted her hips trying to meet his mouth. His warm wet tongue began to rub against her and she tilted her head back in pleasure as the feeling overwhelmed her. A loud moan escaped her as he pulled her bud into his mouth sucking on it, sending her into ecstasy. His hand moved towards her entrance and he slipped a finger inside of her. He began to slowly move his finger. His mouth continued to taste her. A louder moan escaped her as he placed another finger inside of her beginning to move faster. Her hips rising to meet him and moving with him.

He couldn't take anymore, the sight of her, the sound, the taste of her. He needed her. He moved away from her, kissing up her stomach to her breast as he positioned himself at her entrance. She felt his swollen member at her entrance and her whole body begged for him. She locked her legs around him and pulled him to enter her. He pushed in gently a moan escaping them both as he filled her. Her hips began to rock against him as he began to move. He moved faster and thrusted deeply in her. Her body begging for him. Her muscles tensed around him as he could feel her coming to her climax. She pulled him deeper into him with her legs as all of her muscles contracted. Fireworks exploded in her mind as she reached her orgasm. The same rush went through him as he climaxed with her.

He straddled her just a little bit longer after he finished breathing hard. She had a small smile on her face as she leaned back with her eyes closed enjoying the moment. He watched her closely for a second to see if there were any signs of pain. She reached up, running her hand down his chest and patting the bed next to her. He smirked a little as he laid down next to her. She went to roll over but he pulled her against him wrapping his arms around her. She let out a sigh of content before drifting off to sleep.

Chapter Twenty Four
Cursed

She was in darkness again. She had been here before. A light shined like a spot light in the center of the room. Mallory walked to it slowly. Her body is on edge. Stepping into the center of the light she felt a force push through her. The weight of it almost threw her back out of the light. She regained her footing and looked around trying to see what had happened. Again the invisible force rushed through her. She stumbled backwards, losing her footing and falling.

She hit the ground but it was no longer the cold room she was in. She felt dirt under her and it puffed up around her as she tried to sit up. She was in the woods. The trees swayed with the passing breeze. She didn't know how she knew but it felt like fall. The breeze had a crispness to it. Looking closely at the trees she noticed each leaf was getting a tinge of red, yellow or orange. Across the way a small group of children sat in a circle gathered around a woman who seemed to glow with light. Mallory's eyes fixated on her as she began walking towards them.

"There are three bloodlines that started it all. Each one cursed differently but all the same." She reached down, touching each child's head as she spoke.

"Someday, someone will come and fix two of the curses." She said touching the dark haired boy and then the wavy jet black haired girl.

"But one will be forgotten." She whispered, touching the blond hair boy.

"There will be peace for many years…until the two previous cursed have a child. Then the world will begin to spiral. That child needs to remember and be the one to break the third. Or all will be lost." The woman said touching the blond hair boy's head and then locking eyes with Mallory.

"If the curse remains, all will be lost." She said her eyes burning into Mallory then a light radiated out of her sending Mallory back into the ground.

She hit the ground hard, the wind getting knocked out of her as she did. She sat up coughing. She was trying to get the air back into her but the air around her was so thick, she could not breathe it in. A smell invaded her nose. It was burning her nose and smelt rotten. She covered her nose as she stood up. Thick black smoke filled the air. Ashes tumbled in the wind as little sparks of ember floated through the sky. Everything around her was burning. She walked down the road and bodies were stacked in the gutters. Blood pouring out into the road from the homes Everything was dying.

"All will be lost!"

A figure rushed at her from out of the smoke. She tried to back up and get away but she stumbled and fell.

Mallory jolted upright in bed, her body shaking from the dream. She covered her face in her hands and calmed herself. She reminded herself where she was. She was safe, she was ok. A shiver went through her, her body feeling cold. She glanced over trying to find Ronan. He was up pacing the floor. She sat up looking at him. He had been doing it for sometime. His hands at the side of his head as if he had a headache, like he was in pain.

"Ronan?" Mallory asked sitting up more.

"It's fine." Ronan said dismissively as he went back to pacing.

A sweet but metallic smell hit her nose. She immediately knew it wasn't a good smell. She narrowed her eyes as she then noticed blood droplets across the wooden floor. Blood droplets that Ronan was pressing into the floor, smearing across it as he walked. She could see the blood running down his hands, down his forearms and dripping off his elbow.

"Ronan!" Mallory said getting up and crossing the room to him.

"No. No. No. Stay there. Stay back." Ronan said, trying to dodge her.

"Hey, talk to me." Mallory said, stepping in front of him.

"Pax." Ronan whimpers like it causes him pain.

"Pax?" Mallory said wanting to reach out and touch him.

Ronan saw her wanting to touch him and he stepped back. Sweat beaded across his forward as he gritted his teeth.

"My wolf. He wants control. He's wanting me to shift." Ronan said blood started to trickle out of his nose, he had never felt Pax push so hard before.

"Ok, why does he? What happens if he does?" Mallory asked fighting with herself to not go near Ronan.

"He wants you. You're not supposed to have happened. I am not supposed to have a mate. I won't let him hurt you." Ronan groaned as the blood coming from his nose turned from a trickle to a steady flow.

"Ronan." Mallory said, stepping towards him.

"No you don't understand. He's not safe." Ronan said, stepping back and bumping into the wall.

His back hit the wall knocking a picture of red poppies off; it crashed to the ground. Ronan sank to the floor with it as a wave of pain washed over him. He would die before he let Pax out.

Mallory could feel his pain. She didn't understand. Why was he acting like that? How could it be causing her pain? She walked slowly over to him. He whimpered as another wave of pain flooded him. Mallory kneeled before him. She reached out slowly, touching his cheek. Ronan winced as if her touch burned him. Ronan's eyes were completely gray now, the glow seemed to light up the room. Ronan's eyes locked with Mallory and she could feel his wolf.

" Pax." Mallory whispered.

"Out." It wasn't Ronan's voice that came out, but a deep lower almost gut wrenching voice.

"You're hurting Ronan." Mallory said to him firmly.

"Ronan hurts me. Want out." Pax said, almost growling.

"Why?" Mallory asked quietly.

"Mallory mate. Want Mallory." Pax said to her, grabbing her wrist.

"Yes, I'm your mate but you're hurting me." Mallory said motioning to her wrist.

"Pax no hurt Mallory." Pax said letting go of her wrist.

"Ronan thinks Pax hurt. Pax is not like Hamiltion." Pax whimpered.

"Ok. I believe you. I don't think you'll hurt me. But you are hurting Ronan. If you hurt Ronan, you hurt yourself." Mallory said, her hand touching his cheek.

Ronan's head leaned into her hand wanting and needing the touch. He seemed to nuzzle into it.

"Pax you need to let Ronan have control." Mallory said calmly.

"No." Pax growled.

"Do you want to hurt me?" Mallory asked again.

"No. Never hurt." Pax whimpered.

"If you hurt Ronan, you will hurt you and in return hurt me." Mallory said her voice was calm.

"No hurt." Pax grumbled.

"Talk to Ronan for Pax." Pax continued.

"If you stop pushing for control and stop hurting him. I promise I will talk to him." Mallory said with her other hand going to his ear and pushing a lock of tousled blonde hair behind it.

"Ok. Pax trusts Mallory." Pax said quietly and then suddenly the glowing in Ronan's eyes stopped.

"Mallory?" Ronan asked, blinking, a look of confusion on his face.

"Hey, it's ok. Are you hurt?" Mallory asked him, searching his face.

"I'll be ok…how?" Ronan whispered.

"I just talked to him." Mallory smiled.

"You talked to him. You talked to Pax." Ronan repeated.

"Yes. He doesn't want to hurt anyone, he just wants to meet me." Mallory said with a small shrug.

"No. He will never meet you." Ronan growled.

"He won't hurt me. I know he won't" Mallory said defensively, she promised Pax she would talk to him.

"You don't know what kind of wolf he is." Ronan said quietly.

"He could have pushed for complete control. You were gone Ronan. He chose to let you come back. That has to say something." Mallory said defending Pax more.

"Mallory you don't understand." Ronan said quietly.

"Ronan, he's a part of you." Mallory said quietly.

"He shouldn't be." Ronan muttered, going to walk away.

"Hey." Mallory said catching his hand, the wounds from his claws digging into his hands were already healing.

"Explain." Mallory said as he looked back at her.

Ronan let out a long breath before rubbing his face with his free hand. He looked at her as if debating on telling her.

"Fuck it." He muttered to himself before turning towards her.

"Pax has never been out…willingly." Ronan said quietly.

"Why, how does he stay in like that? Wolfs are meant to run and be wild and free. They purposely patrol in wolf form to just let them out for a bit.." Mallory paused as the words falling out of her mouth were memories coming back, her face lit up but then she paused, letting Ronan continue.

"My so-called father killed his mate. His wolf was overcome with jealousy because another man touched her His wolf went feral. It's been going on since my great grandfather. Each mother lives long enough to maybe raise a child halfway. I don't know why they kept reproducing. The night my mother died I begged for it to end. The Moon Goddess in a rage of the aftermath placed a curse on my fathers line to remain mateless…you're not supposed to be, I am not supposed to have a mate." Ronan said a tremble went through him at the weight of his statement.

"I was happy with the curse and angry at my wolf side that I never let him out. The few times I accidentally did, I was stuck in wolf form for days or weeks. He wouldn't give back control and I have no memories of what happened." Ronan grumbled.

"Ronan, that's not fair to him. You don't know if he is even like that." Mallory whispered.

"And I won't be taking the chance." Ronan said looking at Mallory like she meant everything in the world to him.

"Ronan." Mallory started to say but Ronan narrowed his eyes at her.

"I'm not talking about this any longer." He said walking to the far side of the room and then out onto the walk out porch.

The air hit him as he closed his eyes. He took a deep breath then tried to calm himself. Pax had never pushed that hard before. She didn't understand. She wouldn't understand. He needed to pull himself together, she wasn't supposed to see him like that. He looked up at the sky, his eyes narrowed.

"You said no mate." He said his eyes looking at the bright white moon.

He felt like he had been betrayed and lied to. This was not a game. He wasn't going to be like the men before him. He would end it no matter what. He made the silent threat to the Moon Goddess as he loosened his grip on the railing.

"Ronan." Mallory's voice came from behind him, it made him instantly calmer but at the same time now made his guard go up.

"I'm ok." He said quietly, the sun started to break through the horizon.

"Are you?" Mallory asked quietly.

"Always." Ronan smirked, turning around to look at her.

"Are-

"It's morning. We should try to leave before the whole pack is awake. We need to get you to the hunters before nightfall. Save your pack and all." Ronan said, cutting her off and walking inside.

Chapter Twenty Five
Power

"*A*lphas, you need to do something now. We are running out of time." Adam said in a hushed tone to him.

It was only a matter of time till Knox came down here and made them submit, giving up their Alpha titles and naming himself Alpha of all packs. Jace grunted, it had to be someone safe. Someone not there. Someone Knox didn't know about. Jace's eyes began to glow as he took a deep breath.

"I Alpha Jace Knight of the Cross River Pack step down as Alpha and name Mallory Renee Knight as Alpha in my place." Jace said firmly and as he finished his statement he collapsed backwards into the wall.

"I Alpha Zeke Warren of the Moonlight Pack step down as Alpha and name Mallory Renee Knight as Alpha in my place." Zeke said and the strength he was holding on to vanished from him.

"Zeke, what did you do?" Jace asked him, confused as to why he named Mallory as well.

Asher was still in and out of consciousness. Zeeke groaned and kicked Asher's foot with his. Asher's eyes fluttered open for a second.

"I, Alpha Asher Cross of Red Woods name Mallory Renee Knight as Alpha in my place." Asher managed to get out, his body seemed to be spent as soon as the words left him.

"You all named Mallory." Adam whispered.

"Asher. Zeke, why?" Jace asked quietly.

"That fucker wants to be a four time Alpha. When your daughter comes through for us. Which she is yours and Nora's daughter there's no doubt in my mind that she will. He will see what messing with a three time Alpha is like." Zeke said in an angry tone.

"Adam, you need to get to Mallory and help her through this. She's going to need someone by her side. You get out of here and go to her. I'm counting on you." Jace said to him firmly.

"I will. I promise." Adam said.

"Adam!" Wyatt called down the dark hall to him.

"I promise." Adam said to him before getting up and heading towards Wyatt.

"Adam, you need to go. Take this medical bag head out of the dungeons. Act like you're going back to get more supplies for me. Once you get to the hospital, shift and take off. No one knows about you ethier. Mallory's going to the hunters, meet her there." Wyatt told him, grabbing his shoulder as he spoke.

"Come with me." Adam said to him not wanting to leave him behind.

"I can't, they have Abby, she's expecting any day now and Abigail they have her too." Wyatt said with a frown.

"Ok. Ok. I will be back." Adam nodded to him as he took the medical bag from him.

"I know you will." Wyatt nodded to him as he squeezed his shoulder tightly before letting him go.

Before she could even argue with Ronan they were in the car and gone. The sun was barely touching the road as they left Red Woods. Ronan was silent the whole way there. Mallory was fighting with herself to not bring it up. She was so upset for some reason that he rejected his wolf. She kept glancing over at him and he acted like he didn't see her. She was tired of the silent game. She went to call him out on it when she was suddenly hit with a force. She sucked in a huge amount of air as she felt a surge going through her. She grabbed the door, gripping it with her fingers.

"What the hell?" Ronan said, looking over at her.

Mallory arched back into her seat as wave after wave of pure strength pours into her. It was overwhelming and her body was beginning to shake. Ronan pulled the car over to the side of the road. He went to touch her but she felt like she was on fire. He opened his car door and ran around the front of it pulling the passenger door open.

"Mallory!" Ronan said, touching her shoulders as he tried to get a response.

Her eyes began to glow as they flickered in color. The glow was first bright ice blue, it glowed bright and then faded. Another wave went through her and her eyes flashed bright white. Her body relaxing and tensing in between each glow. The white faded and was quickly replaced by red, and then amber. The amber glow was faint but fought for its place. As the glow faded he watched her body relax. She inhaled sharply sitting up.

"Holy shit." She muttered as her body felt different, she felt powerful.

"What the hell was that?" Mallory whispered looking at Ronan as if he had an answer.

"You are radiating power." Ronan said quietly looking at her, his hand went to her forehead; the heat she had been giving off was now gone.

"I feel powerful." Mallory said, shaking her hand as if it had fallen asleep.

"What is this?" Mallory asked as she watched him study her.

"You don't have a wolf?" Ronan asked her, his eyes looking for something.

"Nope, it's just me in here." Mallory said with a small shrug.

"Well I think you just became Alpha, your father named you in his place but the power you're giving off. The colors…no…they didn't" Ronan said quietly.

"They didn't?" Mallory asked, annoyed.

"I think not only did you just become Alpha of Cross River but of Moonlight and Red Woods." Ronan said his hand going to the back of his neck like this might cause problems.

"Why? And why is it bad?" Mallory asked quietly.

"I have never heard of someone being Alpha who does not have a wolf for starters. I don't know what that kind of power will do to you, if it would do anything. Secondly if Knox finds out about you, you now have a bigger target on your back. He also only has to make you crown him Alpha of all three. If it were separate people he would have to hunt them all down." Ronan said the worry in his voice escaping a little.

"Ok so let's not let him find out about me. Problem solved." Mallory smiled, putting her hand to the side of his face.

"Let's get to the hunters to make sure we get you safe." Ronan said his gut was twisting inside of him.

He was angry and nervous they would all put her in danger like this. What were they thinking? Ronan let out a frustrated sigh before getting up and closing tho passenger side door. He walked slowly around the front of the car.

"Kai." He paused, mind linking him, he needed updates.

"Yes Beta?" Kai sent back quickly.

"Updates." Ronan sent back annoyed, that he would even ask.

"We are just getting near Moonlight. We had some delays with Moonlight's Luna. She needed to rest." Kai sent back, Ronan could feel the wincing in the mind link that he knew Kai was doing.

"Take your time. Do not endanger her health. We are still at Red Woods. We are going to be spending the day there. Send updates to Alpha." Ronan orders him.

"Yes Beta." Kai said as Ronan cut the mind link off, at least they were taking time too.

Ronan got in the car and Mallory raised an eyebrow at him asking silently why he had paused. Ronan shook his head back in response letting her know it was nothing before continuing on. The country roads soon turned into congested city roads and before she could have said anything to him they were in the heart of the city. How did everything happen so fast? Ronan pulled up to a red light, Mallory looked at him confused.

"Where are we going?" Mallory asked quietly.

"The hunters' building is somewhere just off the center of the square here." Ronan said, looking around.

"What's the address?" Mallory asked as she moved in her seat trying to read street signs.

"It's there on the card." Ronan pointed to the center console as he squinted, turning down a road.

"Its-

"It's right there." Ronan half laughed looking at an old dark building painted all black.

"How do you know?" Mallory asked, squinting trying to find the address.

"Come on, it just screams secret layer." Ronan laughed, pulling up to it.

"Ok so what do we do?" Mallory asked quietly.

"You go knock?" Ronan shrugged.

"Knock?" Mallory asked again, blinking as she looked at him.

"Or ring the doorbell. Whatever they got up there." Ronan smirked.

"You want me to go ring the bell?" Mallory repeated.

"I'll come with you but yeah you're doing the knocking or the ringing. They know you…remember." Ronan smirked with a wink.

"You know I don't…jerk." Mallory laughed, nudging him as she went to reach her door handle.

Ronan caught her other hand pulling her back. Her face inches from his. She felt a chill rush through her as his skin touched hers. Her breathing caught in her throat as she focused on his lips.

"I go first." He said to her,

"Uh?" Mallory asked, still looking at his lips, she fought the urge to just lean an inch closer so hers could brush against his lips.

"You're not knocking or ringing any door bell. I will. Stay behind me, stay close." Ronan said to her, his voice from as he ordered her.

"I-" Mallory went to protest, confused about his statement.

Ronan leaned in, her lips quivering in anticipation for his. He pressed his lips against hers. It was a soft slow kiss. Mallory leaned further into it wanting more. Ronan pulled back and opened his car door. Mallory blinked; it was a kiss that made her wanting more. He had never kissed her so softly. She knew that it was only a few times but each time it was demanding. She reached for her door handle but the door was already opened and Ronan's hand was reaching out for hers. Mallory put her hand in his and he helped her out of the car. Getting out she looked up at the large building. The large sign swung above the wooden black door reading Societatea Vânătorului. She thought, here goes nothing going to knock. A growl came from Ronan as he caught her hand stepping in front of her.

"You don't listen." Ronan muttered as his hand balled into a fist and he knocked three times on the door.

Mallory almost giggled at the frustration Ronan expressed. He looked at her making a face of disapproval and she busted out with a small giggle. His frown deepened as he turned to her. Mischief sparkled in her eyes as she watched him bow up.

"Really?" Ronan whispered to her as he pulled her close, his hand slipping around her waist.

"You're really cute when you think you're in charge." Mallory smirked, her eyes wanting him to play the game back with her.

He stepped into her more, pressing her body against his, his head leaning down towards her ear. His mouth inches from it, his breathing tickling her neck making her tingle.

"If your whole pack wasn't on the line, I would show you just how in charge I am." Ronan whispered into her ear.

"Promise?" Mallory said moving back her bright blue eyes flashing with lust as she pulled her bottom lip into her mouth, biting the outer corner.

Ronan growled and went to pick her up. The sound of metal moving and the door creaking open stopped him. He gave her a quick look telling her later. She giggled as a man stepped out of the door.

"We've been waiting for you, Logan called, he said you would be on your way." The man with brown hair and brown eyes said judging Ronan right away.

"Mallory!" A voice behind him called out, another man came forward, he was tall and wide, his head was completely bald as he walked out with a smile.

"Hello." Mallory smiled peeking out from behind Ronan.

"Logan said you have no memories?" He asked, his voice kind of sad.

"No she doesn't. Are we going to come in and talk or just chit chat out here?" Ronan snapped, becoming even more annoyed.

Mallory giggled as she reached up and put her hand around his waist kind of hugging him from behind, trying to get him to relax.

"Who are you?" The bald man snapped back.

"Ronan, an ex-bad guy, person with the answers you need. So let's talk or we can just be on our way. We really don't have time for this bullshit." Ronan said, getting angry as he talked.

"Mallory?" The man asked her, looking past Ronan to her.

"He's ok. Temperamental but ok." Mallory smirked.

"Come in, I'm Drake and this is Phill. Mina is somewhere training recruits." Drake said to them.

"Wonderful." Ronan said sarcastically as he took Mallory's hand into his and cautiously began following Drake.

Drake walked through the door first, he stopped almost off to the side and it caught Mallory's eye. Mallory felt something in her core telling her that something was about to happen. She looked up as she was about to step through the doorway with Ronan. As she did she heard a small snap and knew something was coming down. She let go of Ronan's hand and pushed him forward. The amount of strength she put into the shove sent him forward past the doorway and into safe reach. A powder floated down over her. As she stood in the doorway waiting for something more.

Ronan let out a loud growl, his eyes set on Drake who looked surprised at Mallory's actions. She clenched her jaw looking at Drake as well. Ronan went to step towards Mallory but she backed up.

"It's powder wolfsbane." Mallory said moving away from Ronan, not having a wolf she was safe from it.

Ronan turned on his heels, he moved quicker than he should. Before Mallory could say anything Ronan had Drake by his throat and pinned up against the wall. Drake was shocked as well. He barely saw Ronan move.

"Explain!" Mallory demanded stepping in front of Ronan as Phill went to move towards him.

"We know that he's part of Shadow pack. No one is hundred percent sure that you don't remember. What if it's an act to keep everyone safe. We need to capture the enemy." Drake coughed out.

"He is not your enemy. He is my mate." Mallory said her eyes daring Phill to move.

"Mate?" Drake coughed again.

"That's right." Ronan growled as part of him felt excited that Mallory had called herself his mate.

"That's enough." A voice echoed through the room, a woman yelled as she walked towards them.

"Hey, put him down." She said to Ronan.

"Or I could kill him and finish the rest of you off." Ronan growled.

"If you're really here to help Mallory save Cross River, you will put him down and listen." The woman said her maroon hair moved slightly as she talked.

"And you are?" Ronan snapped still not letting go of Drake.

"Mina." She said quietly watching them, her muscles in her arms twitching.

Drake's eyes were starting to roll back in his head. Ronan was debating letting him just pass out but a small whimper caught his ear. He glanced over his shoulder and he watched Mallory suddenly buckle. Ronan dropped Drake and rushed to Mallory's side. Mina followed him.

"Mallory." Ronan yelled, going to her side.

"It hurts. It burns." She said moving her arms.

"Why is it hurting her?" Mina asked concerned.

"She may not have a wolf but she is half wolf." Drake coughed from the ground.

"We need to get it off of you." Ronan said going to pick her up.

"It's wolfsbane." Mina said going to stop him.

"I don't care, tell me where a shower is now." Ronan growled, grabbing Mallory in his arms.

"This way." Mina said not going to argue with him.

Chapter Twenty Six
Shifting

Mallory whimpered again as she tried to not curl into Ronan. The powder coating her skin was burning him as well but the pain was nothing compared to knowing she was in pain. Pax pushed forward, pushing strength to Ronan. It was the first time in a long time they were working together as a team. Mallory cried again as the pain started to become overwhelming. Her skin felt like it was going to peel off of her. Every small movement stung. She couldn't help but lean on Ronan.

Mina moved quickly down a hall and then took a right into a room. She pushed the door open and then moved across the room, opening another door and turning on a light. The sound of water turning on filled the room. Ronan stepped in quickly and before Mina could leave the room Ronan stepped into the shower completely clothed, hugging Mallory as the water ran over her.

"Ahh!" Mallory yelled as the water hit her.

"It's ok. Shh we just gotta get it off of you." Ronan said, placing her under the steady stream of water.

"Does it burn you like this?" Mallory said, trying to wash the powder off.

"Yes." Ronan said, letting her legs drop to the shower floor but still holding her steady.

"What? It's burning you?" Mallory asked, her voice upset that now she was hurting him.

Ronan smiled seeing her mind focus on something else other than the pain let him know the shower was working. She looked up at him through her wet hair and soaked clothing concern in her eyes.

"It's fine, love. You can make it up to me later."
Ronan smirked, leaning forward and pressing his lips
against her forehead.

"Hey girl, can we get some towels and dry clothes?"
Ronan yelled from the shower.

"It's Mina and yeah. I'll have them sent up. After
you are all set. We will meet in the study." Mina announced
to him as she left.

Ronan heard both the bathroom door shut and then
seconds later his ears picked up the bedroom door
shutting. He smirked, his eyes seeming to sparkle with
mischief as Mallory looked up at him somewhat confused.
His hands went to the bottom of her shirt as he slowly
pulled it up.

"We should get you out of these wet clothes." He
whispered, his voice dropping low as if he was telling her a
secret.

Mallory put her hands up as he slid the wet shirt up
over her head and dropped it on the floor behind him.
Mallory grabbed him by his pants and pulled him into her.
Her mouth hit him as his pelvis pushed up against her. She
kissed him feverishly. A rush of want and need racing
through her. Ronan matched her energy as he caught her
by the back of the neck. She was overwhelmed by the
taste and smell of him. The way he was intoxicated her
and she needed every part of him. A small moan escaped
her as she broke the kiss moving to kiss his neck. She
placed hungry kisses down his neck reaching his crook of
his neck she felt and heard his heart sped up. She grazed
her teeth against the spot and a small growl escaped him.
The small action sent him into a fenzy. He pinned her to
the shower wall. His mouth moving to her neck as thoughts
of marking her and claim her rattled inside of his mind,
begging for him to do it.

The sound of the shower running water began to overwhelm her, the water rushing flooded her ears. She reached over swatting at the water handle. It was too much noise, there was too much noise. She pulled back away from Ronan, his expression going from hunger to confusion as he caught his breath.

"Mallory?" Ronan said his face still inches from hers as he cupped the sides of her face.

"The water. It's too loud." Mallory said as if she was in pain.

Ronan immediately grabbed the handle and shut off the water. He waited a second. She seemed to be better. He felt her hand weaving up between them. She could feel his pulse running beneath his skin as she stopped at his heart. She could each pounding beat as if it was echoing in his ear.

"Mallory what's wrong?" Ronan worried the wolfsbane may have done something to her.

"Shh, you're too loud." Mallory whispered her voice so faint Ronan barely hurt it.

"Come on we need to get you-"

"Ahh!" Mallory yelled, her body crouching in pain.

Her skin was on fire again but this time it felt like it was going to going to fall away from her bones. The pain rushing through her was mind numbing. She grabbed on to the Ronan in front of her trying to steady herself. Her body began to shake as everything intensified. Pain everywhere. Everything hurts, it hurts to breathe. Something invisible is attacking her. She squeezed her eyes shut as she gritted her teeth. She could taste blood in her mouth. Then everything stopped. Mallory's eyes rolled back in her head. Ronan caught her trying to hold her still.

"Mallory." He panicked as he watched her go almost lifeless.

She opened her eyes slowly, in darkness. Everything was pure black, a haunting light appeared off in the distance. Then a rush of wind went whooshing by. The sound of the wind began to sped up and then as if a movie screen opened in front of the images began to flash. A haunting yellow door slowly swung open. Blood, a lake of blood. A couple with their throats slashed open, blood flowing down them. Stairs to a Batman poster room. A small boy was slaughtered in his bed. A family slaughtered in a small cabin. Wolf tracks on the floor covered in blood. A woman comes home to find her family dead. Bodies after bodies, blood after river of blood. The next flash was the same woman wearing a gray vail over her face in mourning. She stood over a candle burning something. She was mumbling words in a foreign language. Images of several women dressed in hunting gear passed through her mind, the next was one of the women in gear hunting something. She watched her chase down a large wolf and end it. As she ended it the wolf's figure turned human.

Hunting scene after hunting scene flickered in and out in front of her. Each scene where the hunters caught and slaughtered a wolf sent a thrill through her. She felt honored. Each scene where the wolves killed the hunters, mauling him sent fire into her. She felt this burning building in her.

She began to feel different, things she didn't remember or knew began to flood her mind. The knowledge was coming from these past hunters. She instantly knew everything about werewolves. She know how to hunt them, how to track them, their weakness and she felt this overwhelming feeling of duty. That she needed to honor these women and men that came and died before her. She felt all the overwhelming pain and it shook her to the core. Hate, rage and anger fueled her. She hated them all, every single one of them deserved death. She was going to make sure she eliminated them all.

"Mallory! Mallory! Breath." Ronan's voice pleaded with her.

Mallory opened her eyes and looked at Ronan. She was torn. She felt a part of her pull towards him. He was holding her face, worry was all over his face as he looked at her. She felt like maybe she loved him. Love. Something in her flipped her eyes narrowed at him. His scent invaded her nose. He…He was one of them. She gritted her teeth. His kind does nothing but kill, murder, and destroy.

"Wolf." She said to him as the words fell out of her mouth her expression turned sour.

"What?" Ronan asked, narrowing his eyebrows at her.

"Mallory what's-

Mallory threw her head forward smashing her head into his. The impact sent him backwards. He slipped on the water that had pooled at the bottom of the tub. The shower curtain caught around him as he fell. Mallory watched a small smile on his lips as Ronan's head ricochet off the tub and onto the title floor. The water from the shower pooling around him slowly being tinged with blood.

Finish him.

The words echoed in her head as she stepped out of the shower. She reached down cradling his head. One quick snap. That's all it would take. She cupped his chin in her hand ready to snap it. The tingles she got from the excitement of the that was about to happen kill sent shivers and vibrations through her. She closed her eyes about to snap his neck.

No!

The word scattered through her mind bouncing off the walls of her brain. It was like it broke through the madness, scattering the thoughts of pain, hurt and the want to kill. She dropped Ronan's head and stepped back from him. Regret and pain flooded through her as she looked down. She couldn't. She looked down at him and the rage slowly began to take over. She had to get away from him before she hurt him. She walked out of the room and into the bedroom. Clothes were laid out for her. She stripped out of her wet clothing and quickly put on the dry clothing. She put her hair into a low ponytail and exited the room.

"Mallory." Mina was waiting for her.

"The wolf is there. He needs to be taken into custody. I cannot end him. So lock him up. We need to move quickly. They are assembling at Cross River. With all four packs gathered in one location. All of them with no control except for one. We can take down four packs. We need to see your teams now." Mallory ordered.

"Mallory…what's going on? Take them down?" Mina asked her quietly.

"The wolves. You're a hunter right. Your code, the very thing you live by. Destroy all wolves. Kill before they can do any more harm." Mallory said to her looking at Mina confused.

"Mallory…We don't live by that code anymore." Mina said to her, still confused.

"I don't have time for games, take me to your weapons room." Mallory said, waving her off as she began to walk down the hall.

"Mallory, wait." Mina called after her trying to follow her down, she was moving so quickly.

There was something off about her, and the way she felt around her. Mallory was sending off some power signals. Mallory rounded a corner and walked to the vault looking door. She pulled it open and grinned. The room was lined with weapons. She began picking and choosing, crossbow, poisoned arrows, daggers, knives. She paused looking at a long thin metal string. Silver. She reached out to touch it and it burned. She frowned now wanting to have it more than ever. She looked around and found a pair of leather gloves and slipped them on. She grasped the metal in her gloved hands, it felt good. She envisioned wrapping it around a wolf's head and pulling it. The head popping off as a fountain of blood poured out of the beast. She clasped it to her belt. She then began strapping the daggers and knives to her. She put the arrows into a case and flung it across her shoulder. Lastly she grabbed the bow in her hand. She was ready.

Chapter Twenty Seven
Spiral

"*H*ey, I need help. There's something wrong with Mallory. She's talking about war and killing wolves. She all of sudden is super old school. I need someone to go check on Ronan too. She's in the weapons vault now. The power coming off her is crazy." Mina said through a walkie- talkie.

Mina turned down the volume as she got to the vault. Mallory looked ready to go to war as she began stepping out of it. She nodded to Mina.

"How many people do we have?" Mallory asked Mina.

"We have a good amount. What's the plan?" Mina asked if her body felt restless, she needed to do something to stop Mallory but she wasn't sure.

"Don't really have one. Just get to Cross River and start taking them out." Mallory shrugged.

Mallory could see the uneasiness in Mina. She knew something was up. She wasn't going to let her know she could see it.

"So we are just going in with their guns blazing?" Mina asked.

"Hmm, you right it does sound reckless. We should probably plan something." Mallory said, planning things out in her head, she couldn't let weaklings like Mina stop her.

"That might be for the best. That way we can plan accordingly." Mina said with a nod.

"So do you all have a meeting room?" Mallory asked, annoyed.

"Yeah, we have an office. It's this way," Mina said with relief.

Mallory watches Mina start walking away. If all the hunters they had here are like her then they are worthless as well. She would play along for a little bit until she saw her way out and then she was gone. She could take down the wolves without them. They were already compromised. Mallory watched Mina paused at a door waiting for Mallory to catch up. Mallory took in her surroundings and in mer seconds saw she had a way out.

"Hey can we have all high ups come to the-" Mina started to say but something hit her hard in the back of her head.

She fell to the ground like a loud thump echoing as the weight of her body hit the floor. The walky-talky getting cut off. Mallory shook her head looking down at her,

"Pathetic." Mallory muttered and then turned, beginning to walk to the exit.

"Mina." The walky-talky chirped as Mallory crossed the hall, not even stopping to check to see if Mina was hurt.

She reached the door making sure the traps were no longer in place. At least they did one thing right. The building seemed pretty secure. If Mina was in charge of training troops and upheld ridiculous ideas about wolves, then everyone here was worthless. Mallory thought reaching for the door handle. As she did the door was pushed into her. She managed to side step away from it to avoid getting hit. Mallory was ready to fight whoever was coming through it. She stood back ready.

Dark hair was the first thing she saw. He came almost rushing in. He was only wearing boxers as he stumbled through while looking around. His hazel eyes met hers and a rush of relief washed over him.

"Oh thank god you ok Mal." Adam said going to step towards her.

Mallory was hit with a rush of feelings as she recognized Adam. She was fighting herself to not react as she tried to figure out her feelings.

"Are you ok?" Adam asked, taking a step towards her and placing a hand on his shoulder.

"Adam don't!" A voice yelled from across the room.

Wolf! The word screamed through her mind as she locked eyes on Adam. Images of blood and dead bodies flooded her sight. Young children with their lives ripped away. The pain rippled through her. Wolves cause nothing but death and destruction. They need to be eliminated. Her vision cleared and she found Adam staring at her confused.

"Adam, get away from her!" Drake yelled trying to get Adam back.

"What?" Adam yelled back looking at Drake but then something hit him in the side.

"No!" Drake yelled.

A sharp pain rippled through his body as his hand went to the sight of pain. He locked eyes with Mallory. Her expression was emotionless, her eyes cold. Her hands wrapped around the handle of a dagger that was plunged into Adam's abdomen.

"Mallory." Adam winced in pain.

"You wolves need to be destroyed. You are nothing but death and destruction." Mallory said almost roboticly as she pulled the dagger out.

"Mal?" Adam choked out as he grabbed his side, trying to stop the rush of warm blood that came leaking out as the dagger was released.

Mallory shook his arm off of her shoulder and stepped back letting him curl into himself. She glanced over at Drake who was now running across the main lobby to get to Adam.

"You call yourself hunters. You are all pathetic. Your ancestors are rolling in their graves." Mallory said the words filled with so much disgust as she stepped around Adam and headed out the door.

---

*M*att knew something was going on and he felt the shift in power. He was still connected to the pack but something was missing. He needed out of this damn cell. His eyes looked across the way to see if he could see any others in the cell. He stood up the chains on his wrist feeling heavy but he had been resting this whole time. Something was telling him he needed to conserve his energy for when he needed it and now was the time. Matt walked over to the cell and leaned closely to the bars, close enough to see out but not enough to touch them. He spotted the guard and set his eyes on his victim.

"Hey." Matt called to the guard, he shifted, hearing Matt but ignoring him.

"Come let me out sweetheart." Matt said, his voice teasing.

"Hey big boy!" Matt called to him and the guard ignored him.

"Oh what princess, you too good to talk to me. That's ok I like it when they play hard to get. Always loved a good chase." Matt smirked.

"Shut up." The guard groaned, turning his back on Matt.

"Oh! Look at you showing off the goods. That is one fine ass! I could show that ass a good time." Matt said, talking louder.

"If you don't shut the fuck up. I'm going to come in there and make you." The guard said, turning around full force and stepping towards the cell.

"Don't threaten me with a good time handsome." Matt said, making a kissy face at him.

"That's fucking it." The guard growled, grabbing the keys and walking over to the cell.

"You don't scare me big boy." Matt grinned, taking a half step back.

"You should be." The guard smiled, opening the cell.

"Come get me." Matt said his voice turned deadly as the guard stepped into the cell.

That was all it took. That single step undid everything the guard had planned. Matt took one step forward and smashed the guard in the nose with his forehead. The crack echoed around the cell as the guard stumbled forward. Matt dropped his chains and stepped behind the guard throwing the chains around the guards neck as he did. He crossed his arms as the chains tightened around his throat. He then leaned forward picking the guard off his feet. The gurgles of the guard choking filled the cell. His legs kicked, swaying Matt back and forth but he held on, until there was no more movement. He waited a few more seconds and then dropped the guard. As the guard hit the ground a clunking sound brought music to Matt's ears.

"Always the ones who think they're so tough." Matt chuckled.

He had the keys. Matt grabbed them, holding them in his hands. Fumbling through them he found the key to his cuff and quickly un-did them. He then looked to the doors of his cell and walked out of them holding the keys. Time to free his pack.

Matt walked down the dark hall of the dungeon quietly. He needed to get to Jace. The old dungeons were a giant maze and he was surprised the wing he was on was mostly empty. He was almost insulted that he was cast aside like he meant nothing. He smirked a little, they underestimated him. He turned down another hall to find empty cells again. Something was wrong, there was something going on. He clenched his jaw now moving fastest down the hall.

"Matt!" A harsh whisper caught his ear.

"Sarah!" Relief flooded him as he turned to see her in the cell.

"Hold on. I got keys." Matt grinned holding them up as he walked over to the cell.

"Oh Matt! I could kiss you." Sarah smiled back.

"Flattered but I really don't feel like having my ass kicked by Lilly and then Dante." Matt smirked as he pushed the door to the cell open, ignoring the burn from the silver.

"Settle for a hug?" Sarah laughed, holding up her wrists so he could uncuff her.

Matt came over and unlocked the cuffs holding Sarah's wrists. Sarah wrapped her arms around him and squeezed.

"I'm so happy to see your goofy ass." Sarah said letting him go.

"Where is everyone?" Matt's expression changed from happy to see her to serious.

"Something's happening, they came back. Knox was angry. He pulled all the Alpha's, Beta's and Nora out of the cell. He practically had them dragged up out of the dungeon. I could hear them assembling people. I don't know what's happening." Sarah said her voice was really worried.

"We need to find out? Anyone else free?" Matt asked her, trying to think who else they could team up with.

"Wyatt and Adam. So far that's all I know. They are holding Abby and Abigail over Wyatt. So they are allowing him to go treat people." Sarah explained.

"Ok then. Let's see what else we got." Matt said, trying to process some type of plan.

"Lilly? The twins?" Sarah asked, grabbing Matt's forearm.

"They're good. Lilly was at the hunters and the twins were out recruiting." Matt winked.

"Thank god." Sarah said quietly.

"Alright let's do this rockstar." Sarah said, nudging him as she walked to the edge of the cell.

They could hear movement outside. They had to find a way around the possible guards. The presence seemed heavier in the front of the dungeons.

"Let's go back this way, there was hardly anyone deep into the dungeon." Matt said, nodding back the way he came.

"Sounds good." Sarah said starting to feel Lillian start to come back, she smiled feeling instantly better now she could feel her wolf.

"Ryker good?" Sarah asked wanting to know where Matt stood fighting wise.

"Oh he is pissed." Matt chuckled.

"Good." Sarah whispered as they found their way to the back exit.

Matt motioned for her to get behind him as he quickly peeked out. There were four guards at the back. They seemed bored and if they were waiting for some type of orders. Matt looked up making sure there was no one watching from the walls or surrounding builds.

"Ok we're good, there's only four. I can't see past the openings but we should be fine." Matt said with a shrug.

"Plan?" Sarah asked, looking past him trying to see what he saw.

"Fuck it?" Matt smirked.

"Seriously?" Sarah half laughed.

"I mean we should keep one alive so we can question them but eh…" Matt shrugged.

"I guess it's fuck it." Sarah laughed and then stepped out into the light.

"Fuck, I wasn't ready." Matt mumbled as he too stepped out.

Chapter Twenty Eight
It Begins

Mallory walked out the front exit, the sunlight hitting her in the face. She looked around quickly. She needed to move fast. She could tell any minute someone would be out trying to stop her. She spotted a motorcyclist leaning on their bike. She shrugged and began walking over to him. He saw her coming and he took the helmet, placing it on the seat. A smile rolled across his lips as he completely ignored the bow strapped across her.

"Hey beautiful." He grinned as Mallory got to him.

"Hi." She smiled brightly, eyeing the bike.

"Have you ever been on a bike before?" He said standing up straighter as if to show off his muscles.

"No. I don't believe I have." Mallory said, stepping closer to him.

"Well there's a first time for everything." He smiled, taking the helmet and offering it to her.

Mallory smiled brightly and took the helmet. She felt the weight in her hand and watched him turn around to get on the bike. She tightened her grip on the helmet in her hand, grabbing it by the straps. As he went to place his leg over the bike she swung back and brought the helmet flying forward. The helmet cracked as it hit his skull. It happened so fast that he didn't even have time to let out a sound as he fell over to the curb. Mallory reached forward, catching the bike. She shook her head as she used her foot to push him further on to the curb and away from the bike. She then swung her leg over the bike straddling it. She placed the helmet on her head, glancing over her shoulder. Her hearing and vision was so sharp now she could see and hear everything. The door to the hunters opened. She smirked, turning on the bike, throwing it in gear and taking off. Glancing over her shoulder she saw Phil running out of the front doors of the hunters layer. She laughed to herself push the bike to go faster.

Adam let out a gasp as his hands went to his wound. He was on the ground still in shock of what happened. Drake was quickly by his side, his hands going to the wound.

"Mallory, she, she stabbed me." Adam whispered in disbelief to him.

"Help!" Drake yelled, his voice echoing around the main lobby.

"Why would she stab me?" Adam asked the blood to continue to pool out of him.

"Shh, stop talking." Drake said, pulling his shirt up over his head and placing it on the deep wound that blood was leaking from.

"Drake!" Lilly's voice came from around the corner as she came running.

"Holy shit! Adam!" Lilly said, running over to them.

"What the fuck happened?" Lilly demanded as she got to them.

"Mallory. We need to get him to the medical room now." Drake said quickly.

"Ok, I'll get his shoulders." Lilly said, bending down.

"I need to apply pressure we need-"

"I'll get his legs." Ronan's voice came from behind them, cutting off Drake.

He was walking but was off, his blond hair coated in red, a trail of blood running down the side of his ear and neck. Drake blinked seeing him.

"What the hell happened to you?" Drake asked him as Ronan reached them and let out a small breath as he bent down.

"Mallory." Ronan said as he grabbed ahold of Adam's legs and nodded to Lilly.

In one motion they both lifted Adam. He groaned as they began moving him. Ronan followed Lilly's lead as they hustled down the hall, leaving a trail of dripping blood behind them. They rounded a corner and made a quick right. As they reached a large white door Lilly kicked it open and they moved into a large hospital-like room.

"Woah, woah." Some started yelling as they walked in.

"Help now. We need a medic now." Lilly ordered as she moved to the nearest bed.

She locked eyes with Ronan and nodded to him as they hoisted him up into it. Drake applied pressure to the wound while the nursing team started moving around them. Ronan took a step back and the world began to spin. He stumbled backwards into the wall. As things slowly started to become black. He was fighting with himself to not lose consciousness.

"Woah. Hey. Easy. I got you." He felt Lilly's arm on his and she steadied him.

Suddenly there was something cold on the back of his neck and he began to feel a little better. He opened his eyes looking down at the small potite blond, who was studying him.

"We need to get you to a bed as well." Lilly said, looping his arm around her neck.

"Mallory." Ronan shook his head.

"You can't go after her like this. Let's get you looked at and let your wolf start healing you before you run off." Lilly said.

Ronan went to argue but he felt the world begin to rock. He grunted his agreement and Lilly helped him over to the bed and let him lay back. He felt the darkness creeping up on him again. He reached over and grabbed Lilly's arm, he needed to tell her.

"Hey. It's ok." Lilly said as she patted his hand.

"Mallory, she's Alpha of all three packs. She has no memory and she turned." Ronan spat out as the room went to a pinpoint and the darkness overtook him.

"Shit." Lilly said his stomach turned, she snapped her fingers and two more nurses ran into the room.

"Fix him. If he's Mallory's mate. We need him." Lilly ordered as she walked across the room.

"Drake." Lilly said coming into the room where a doctor was working on sewing Adam up.

"Mhmm." Drake said as he was working on holding Adam down.

"Mallory's birthdays today." Lilly said, her stomach twisting.

"Mhmm. This is a great birthday present." Drake muttered as Adam let out a groan, the doctor digging around inside of his abdomen trying to find a bleeder.

"Her twenty-first birthday. She has no memories and it's her twenty-first birthday." Lilly said locking eyes with him.

"She turned." Drake whispered.

"Turned into what." Adam let out another growl as the doctor clamped down on the vessel.

"She's a hunter. When you first turn, you're filled with so much hate for wolf kind." Drake said, his voice faulting as he realized what Lilly was saying.

"She has no memories, Drake." Lilly said, her mind racing on what she needed to do.

"Shit, call Logan. She's going to try to kill them all. We need the packs to know." Drake said quietly.

"Adam! Adam! Hey! Can you mind link?" Drake said, shaking Adam who had slowly begun to lose consciousness.

"Drake, Ronan said that Mallory is also Alpha of all three packs. The power she has. She can command them. She is going to kill them all." Lilly said the acid was rising up in her throat.

"We need to get there now. Contact Logan. Get troops ready and head to Cross River. The wolves are not going to be able to stop her. We need to get there now." Drake said panic in his voice.

"Get Adam up and going, we need him to mind link someone who is there." Lilly said with a firm nod and began moving out of the hospital.

The world was dark. He was fighting. He didn't belong in the darkness, he didn't need to be there. There was something more. Something that needed him…Someone. He rushed around aimlessly in the dark trying to find a way out. Where was he? He was not giving in, he could not let this win.

"Ronan." The word was spoken softly, it fluttered around the darkness like a butterfly searching for the perfect flower.

Ronan narrowed his eyes. He know the voice. He had heard it once before. He was young. He had been standing by the river. The river his mother had loved. The room grew lighter and suddenly he was back at the river. He saw a young boy, six in age staring into the water. The moonlight danced about the water top as tears slipped from his face .The droplets hit the water causing ripples in the calm water. His blonde tousled hair falling over into his eyes as he hugged his knees.

"Ronan." The voice came from her as she stepped on top of the water from the moon beam.

"Hello?" A young Ronan answered as he looked up in wonder at the beautiful lighted woman.

"I am so sorry for your loss, my child." She said squatting down to talk to him.

"She's gone. He killed her." Young Ronan said, his voice breaking as his heart did.

"I know my sweet boy. He did what his father did, and his father before him and on for several generations but no more." She whispered to him.

"I am going to -

"I don't want a mate." Ronan's little eyes shot up to her.

"What is this my love?" She asked him confused.

"I don't want to hurt anyone." Ronan said, his voice breaking.

"I will grant you your plea. You will not hurt your mate." She said touching his head and a wave of light washed over him.

The scene flickered in front of him and he gritted his teeth, anger flushed through him. His younger self took it as he was not going to have a mate. Roan shut his eyes. Mallory. He needed to get to Mallory.

"Ronan." Her voice whispered in his ear and he whipped around.

"You tricked me." He said anger in his voice as he looked upon the Moon Goddess.

"No. I didn't and I would be careful with your tone." She snapped the light around her flickering as she sent out her anger.

"I need to get to Mallory." Ronan said, bowing his head at her power.

"You won't be able to save her alone, even if you got to her in time." The Goddess said to him softly.

"The hunters are going. I need out of this dark abyss. I need to get to her. I will save her." Ronan demanded.

"You will not save her. You have been denying part of yourself for years. You will not be able to save her alone. Pax is a part of you and right now you need to trust him and accept him." The Goddess started to say.

"He is not-

"He is you! You are not your father! Pax is not Hamilton! You had more love in your heart then your father had hate in his. Your mother's love and sacrifice saved you. She saw what he was and hid you. His sins never touched you. Your mother died for you and I blessed you. If you do not trust Pax and become whole, Mallory will succumb to the curse and it will over take us all." The Goddess said angrily as she stepped forward she touched his forehead pushing him back.

His head went back and he hit the ground.

Chapter Twenty Nine
Surrender

*K*nox grinned as he had them all kneel in the courtyard. Jace on his knees just in front of him. He had called for what bits and pieces of the packs that were there to be pulled out into the court yard as well. All three Alpha's kneeling in front of him. Their Beta's and the one and only Luna.

"Knox, you can't do this." Nora said, trying to stand but the guard standing behind her pushed her down to her knees.

Jace growled trying to get up and Knox grabbed a silver blade from his waistband placing it to Jace's throat. Dante growled and moved. Knox eyed him pushing the blade into Jace's skin. The blade burned and left a small droplet of blood.

"Dante." Nora whispered trying to tell him to stop.

Dante backed down, worried that Knox would slit Jace's throat.

"Good move muscle boy." Knox snickered.

"Angela, make sure the Luna doesn't speak again." He growled, Angela moved up to the front and stood behind Nora. There was a small ting noise as Angela removed her blade. She nodded to Knox as if to say she was ready.

"Ok so let's make this quick. I asked nicely in the cells but no one wanted to participate." Knox said, clearing his throat.

"I will ask one more time then." Knox snapped his fingers at the word then, and Mick began to move people forward in the crowd.

More guards with silver blades coming forward and standing behind members of each pack.

"We are going to start slaughtering people." Knox grinned.

"Knox what is it you want?" Zeke spoke up trying to delay everything.

"You didn't understand it in the cell?" Knox said letting Jace go and moving to Zeke.

"Explain." Zeke said quietly, his tone firm; being out of the silver barred cell was making him feel better by the moment.

They were all still being poisoned by the wolfsbane but away from the silver, his body wanted to heal.

"You are all going to die today." Knox announced and a hush fell over the crowd.

"You all will, slowly, section by section." Knox snickered, his guards now moving about the crowd.

"Unless…Your Alpha's surrender their titles to me." Knox smiled big.

"If they don't …well then why should there be packs if I am not the Alpha." Knox said, shrugging his shoulders.

"Knox- " Zeke went to say but was sliced by a sharp pain in his shoulder.

Zeke looked down at his shoulder, his eyes were so fixated on the members of his pack now forced to the ground in front of him, blades dangling behind them that he didn't even see Knox step forward and plunge the silver dagger into his shoulder. Knox stepped back, ripping it out a low painful growl escaped Zeke. The wound burned as it leaked blood down the front of his chest. His pack members let out a small yell.

"If you speak again, there will be one less Alpha I have to worry about " Knox hissed.

"You know…I don't know why I didn't think about this before. I could actually just do this the old school way. It will take longer than everyone surrendering but I could just kill them one by one. If you kill an Alpha you get their title." Knox said, summarizing for himself.

"Yeah that actually makes everything all the more easier. Seeing how your bleeding Alpha Zeke…you can go first." Knox snapped his fingers and the guard behind him bent down and picked Zeke up by his shoulders.

"Knox!" Jace yelled going to get up but a silver rod was shoved into his back pinning him down against the ground.

"Coward!" Jace yelled grass and mud rubbing against his cheek as he tried his hardest to fight back.

Knox's eyes glowed gray as he began to make his way over to Jace, his eyes fixated on him. Reaching him he took the heel of his boot and placed it on Jace's face. He began pressing down.

"You! I can't stand you the most!" Knox growled.

He lifted his foot up and slammed it down. As the heel of Knox's boot hit Jace's face, his skin split right where his cheek bone was.

"Knox, you are scum. Just like your father! Worthless! Pathetic!" Asher yelled trying to get his attention.

The guard behind Asher knocked him forward and pinned him to the ground with another silver rod. Knox didn't even hear Asher, he was fixated on crushing Jace. Knox slammed his foot again, a crack being heard, blood shooting out of Jace's mouth. Again his foot came down and another crack as the skin split away at his brow bone, blood now leaking into his eye.

"No!" Nora screamed trying to get up and do something.

Angela went to grab her but Nora was up on her feet Angela held her dagger in her hand fiercely going to attack Nora. Nora dodged her first blow and went forward with both her fists, her hands still bound together. She hit Angela in the stomach, sending her back. As Angela stumbled not expecting that type of strength from Nora, Angela landed on her back. Knox raised his foot to stomp Jace's face again. Nora hit him with such force, throwing her whole body into him. She fell backwards on top of him. Knox didn't even see it coming. He hit the ground, his back pressed into it as Nora lunged on top of him. She trapped him to the ground with her wolfsbane drenched handcuffs. She pressed them deep in his throat. He began to try to struggle underneath her. The more she pressed the more he began to choke and gag.

Angela was up and moving. She reached Nora wrapping her hand around her hair and pulling her back, dragging her off of Knox. She held her dagger at her throat, holding her in place. Nora's eyes locked on Jace who was still face down on the ground not moving. Her heart was panicking in her chest. She could still see him breathing but the sight made her want to vomit.

"You fucking bitch. I will gut you!" Angela screamed, yanking Nora up by her hair and bringing back the dagger.

"No!" Knox yelled as he got up, his hand on his throat, trying to get the words to form and rub the pain away.

"No?" Angela asked, confused and frustrated.

"I want her to see. I want her to see him. I want them to slowly die, watching each other die." Knox said sinisterly.

"How?" Angela asked, now even more confused.

"We'll burn them." Knox grinned.

The crowd began to move and the urge to fight came over them. The guards began trying to push the crowds back. Angela glanced at the pack members, it was taking too long. They needed to do this quickly. The more they drew this out the more they had time to process and resist. They were loyal to their Alpha's and not Knox. Knox could not control them.

"Bring me supplies to make a fire." Knox laughed.

"Alpha, the pack members." Angela whispered.

"What, fear based loyalty is the best." Knox laughed.

"Alpha, you can't control them, they are not loyal to you…yet." Angela said worriedly.

"They will be." Knox shrugged eagerly waiting for his supplies, he did not even get what Angela was hinting at.

"Where is Ronan?" Angela whispered for once wishing he was here, he made everything go smoothly, he could always take Knox's chaos and insanity and make it work out reasonably.

"Hmm. He is taking a long time at Red Wood. I get too overwhelmed with all this to even think about this. Kai as well." Knox muttered.

"Do we have the hose hooked up?" Knox asked Mick.

"Yes Alpha." Mick suddenly was grinning as he said yes.

"Give the loyal pack members a good dosing." Knox grinned.

"Alpha hoses?" Angela asked as she watched the guard roll out the hoses.

She traced the hoses back to large water containers and was confused. Knox winked at her and nodded. Water began to spray the pack members. They began to scream and yell as they hit the ground. Then Angela smelt it. It was water mixed with wolfsbane. She grinned.

"That is amazing." Angela laughed.

"Mhmm." Knox said, winking to her.

"When did you think of that Alpha? I am impressed." Angela smiled relieved that they had some more ammunition.

"Actually it was one of Ronan's ideas. Speaking off Ronan. He needs to be here." Knox said quietly.

"Ronan needs to be here." Angela muttered as if she was some sulking toddler who was just told she was not the favorite.

"Watch it. He is still your Beta." Knox snapped at her and she immediately bowed her head.

"Fire supplies now. I want a barn fire. Huge, enormous. We will tie them facing each other and set them ablaze." Knox laughed, as they all began to scramble to fulfill his twisted vision.

"Ronan!" Knox's eyes glossed over as he sent out the mind link.

Roan shot up as his head felt like he had been hit with a rock. He was shaking and his body felt charged. His hand went to the back of his head. The wound Mallory had caused him was healed. He quickly swung his legs off the hospital bed and began moving. He needed to got to Mallory. Coming out into the opening he was looking for anyone. He didn't know how long he was out for. The urgency eating away at him. Pax was whimpering relentlessly in his mind from the minute he opened his eyes. Adam was still out in the bed, monitors strapped to him. Ronan clenched his jaw. He disliked Adam but it was because he could feel the closeness Mallory and him had.

Even if Mallory didn't remember him. Mallory was going to be crushed when she finally did come back. He made a face as he walked over to Adam. The dumbass needed to live.

"Hey." Ronan shook him, Adam didn't respond.

"Damn it! Hey!" Ronan yelled louder and shook him harder.

"Mallory!" Adam said, jumping up, his eyes locked with Ronan.

Ronan clenched his jaw, hearing his mate's name come out of his mouth. The jealousy coursing through him made him want to rip Adam apart.

Adam will help Mallory. We need him to get to her, to help her. Pax said quietly as if he was trying to talk Ronan down.

Ronan was taken back by hearing Pax speaking rationally and he was the one wanting to murder Adam for saying Mallory's name. Ronan clenched his jaw and narrowed his eyes at Adam.

"I need you up and moving. If you care about her as much as you act like you do, we have to go stop her before she makes mistakes she can never come back from." Ronan said annoyed to him.

"Fine." Adam muttered not wanting to work with Ronan but was willing to join under the same cause.

"Let's move." Ronan snapped as he didn't even give Adam time to get up and get moving.

"Can you mind link anymore there? See what the status of your pack, warn someone what's coming?" Ronan said, still talking harshly to Adam.

"I can try. What about you? Can you fucking do something to stop any of this? You know you caused this?" Adam snapped.

"I fucking-

"Ronan!" The mind link shattered his brian as Knox summoned him.

"Alpha." Ronan sent back quickly trying to make the pain subside.

"You are my Beta. My right hand! Here we are about to make history and you're still not back with Red Wood!" Knox screamed.

"There were some issues. History? Knox what are you doing?" Ronan said, regaining himself.

"About to have an old fashion burning at the stakes. Things are about to get real. Get here now!" Knox summoned him and cut the mind link off.

"What the hell was that?" Adam asked, watching Ronan try to recover from being summoned.

"Knox, he's summoning me. I need to leave now. I am still linked to him. He is doing something big and about to start burning people at the stake. I need you to get intouch with the hunters and Red Wood. We need everyone we have." Ronan said and without choice he began slowly walking out the door, Adam was watching him fight with himself about leaving.

"What are you going to do?" Adam snapped.

"Try to delay the chaos. I had planned to do what I just said to you but now Knox, I can't disobey his order." Ronan growled as he grabbed a hold of the doorway trying to stop himself from going out of it, the pain surging through him from trying to move against it rushing through him.

"Fucking go. I'll bring back up. Try to get to Mallory if you can. Stop her. Stop Knox, be something useful. If anything happens to my pack, anyone I love or Mallory I'm killing you the slowest way possible." Adam vowed.

"Keep your end of this bargain or the same to you." Ronan said letting go of the door jam and moving out.

Out. Pax said quickly as Ronan got outside.

No. Ronan growled back.

Out. Pax demanded.

No." Ronan said a growl coming through.

We will be faster in wolf form. I can get you there quicker, we could even out run her. Please. Pax whimpered.

It was nagging and wearing on him. The sentence the Moon Goddess told him. He didn't want to risk but something deep down inside was telling him for once to trust Pax. He took a deep breath and listened to Pax push for control. He let himself slowly slip away. It was slow and painful, the pain annoying and stinging as Pax pushed forward. The fear behind it makes the transition slow. Ronan's scream soon turned to a howl and in his place stood an all white snow wolf. It shook off the feeling as if it was a pesky bug.

I'm trusting you. You fail and Mallory dies. Ronan said to him.

I won't fail her. Pax vowed and took off.

Chapter Thirty
Chaos

The sound of stacking wood echoed around the courtyard. Nora wincing each time the wood was dropped, her eyes locked on Jace who was still slumped over on the ground. She shut her eyes and tried to fixate on him and see if she could hear his heart. Her heart pounding in her chest was the only sound she could hear as she fought back tears. It couldn't end like this. She looked out over the courtyard, her heart sinking even more, her pack members struggling to not fight. Every time one of them moved so much an inch, the guards fired the wolfsbane poisoned water onto them. The moon starts to peek out against the sunset. She squeezed her eyes shut and begged the Moon Goddess for help.

Large stakes went up on either side of the platform. Knox nodded to the guard standing next to Jace. He bent down, picking him up from under his arms. Knox grinned as he watched as the guard dragged Jace up the platform. Another guard came behind Nora and pulled her to her feet. She gritted her jaw as she began being led to the second stake. She watched as they could barely get a rope around Jace, he kept slouching over.

"Stop!" A cry from the crowd.

"You can't do this!" another desperate as they began to push toward the platform, everyone wanting to fight.

Knox grinned and snapped his fingers as a wave of wolfsbane poured down on them. Each member sank into the ground screaming as it burned their flesh.

"It will be all over soon. Once the Alphas are dead then I will be your Alpha and you will no longer suffer. You can look at me as your savior." Knox chuckled.

Nora watched as women hunched over their children trying to block them from the water. Husbands leaning over their families taking the brunt of the poison. Each member yelled out in pain. Children screaming and crying.

"Please. Make it stop." Nora whispered in a plea.

"Oh we will, sweet heart. It's gonna hurt like hell…or should I say burn." The guard laughed, strapping her to the stake.

"All right, hurry up! I want everyone to be able to see. We wait any longer and the sun will be down." Knox grumbled.

Nora watched the guards scramble off the platform as another began making a torch. She bit her lip trying to think of something, anything she could possibly do. She needed to save them, she had to save them. She looked over at Jace. They had placed him directly across from her so she could watch him die slowly. He was still out of it. The head injury was much more severe than what she first thought. She pulled on the ropes with everything she had. The ropes only became tighter as they cut into her wrists. She could feel her skin splitting as she struggled. The guard stepped forward raising the torch as he went to put it to the stack of wood.

"I love you." She whispered to Jace as she took a deep breath in, failure filling her heart as she looked up at the sky, a one last plea for help from the Moon Goddess leaving her mind.

The guard looked to Knox who seemed to be enjoying the show, waiting for him to give the nod to set the platform on fire.

A low, guttural growl caught Nora's ear, her head wiping to the front of the courtyard. The noise was becoming increasingly louder. Knox's face filled with confusion not knowing what the sound could be. The noise began to change as it came closer. The low growl turned into a vroom noise as it broke through the courtyard. A bright red motorcycle came charging through. The rider was small in frame, the helmet matching the red apple color of the motorcycle as people dodge to get out of the way of it. It zoomed by the platforms. The rider was heading straight towards where Knox was standing.

"Stop it!" Knox commanded as the guards blinked, not sure what was happening.

They began to move at the motorcycle. The person cranked back on the throttle twice before popping a wheelie. As the bike revved midair, the rider let go and stepped off the motorcycle sending it flying towards the guards moving towards the bike. They tried to duck and dodge the bike but it skidded towards them taking three of them out. The bike bounced towards Knox he let out a low growl as the bike skidded to a stop in front of him.

"Who the fuck do you think you are?" Knox growled his eyes glowing as he bowed up.

The guards were on their feet in no time. They were coming towards the biker. The biker pulled a crossbow from their back and began firing it at the guards coming. The arrows hit each of their targets making them buckle and fall down. Some succumb to the arrow wounds. The tip of the arrows were silver and then they were also dipped in wolfsbane. Running out of arrows the biker tossed the crossbow down. The biker reached up and pulled off the candy apple red helmet. Holding it in her hand it became a weapon.

Her long raven hair flowed down her back as she readied herself. A smirk on her face. The guard lunged at her and she took a step back and swung, her helmet smashed against his skull, a large crack splitting down the helmet. The guard fell over to the ground on impact. Two guards attempted to corner her. She smirked, her eyes still focused on Knox. She hummed the helmet towards Knox. He jumped back when the helmet hit the ground right in front him. The ground cracking from the impact.

"Mallory!" A voice yelled distracting her for a minute.

Her eyes looking over at the stakes and the people tied to them. Something tugged at her heart. She knew them. She felt something push forward something below the surface wanting her to run to them. Her hand on the dagger as she felt herself fighting that part of her. The world suddenly began to slow down. She narrowed her eyes, not sure what was happening. She looked to her right and one of the guards was coming towards her, his hand holding a knife as he charged her. Mallory stepped back, she was shocked that she could still move as if nothing was happening. The guard still moved slowly from her. Mallory stepped out of the way at the same time she plunged her dagger into his back. The world snapped back in time as the guard screamed.

Mallory yanked the dagger out, kicking his knees out from behind him. The men fell over screaming. The poison settled into him. She locked eyes with Knox again beginning to advance forward.

"Stop her!" Knox yelled commanding the rest of the guards to start fighting her.

She was soon surrounded. She stretched, rolling her head to the side. She grabbed her other dagger and adjusted them. She was ready for whatever they thought they could do. She locked eyes with Knox. A subtle glow started to form around hers. Knox narrowed his eyes…what was she? The glow coming off of her was amber. He had never seen that color before. He pushed further back into the courtyard putting distance between them. His eyes narrowed as he watched her fight. It seemed like seconds had past and five of the seven men that had surrounded her were down on the ground. Some were injured, others were dead. Three of them had their throat cut and were leaking a river of blood around her as she prepared herself for the last remaining two. The two guards exchanged looks and stepped towards her. Before Knox could blink, they were on their knees holding their throats.

Fear built up in Knox. He had never seen anything like this. The fear was growing and panic was setting in. The thought of possibly running off entered his mind. Then something caught his eyes out of the corner of the courtyard. A white wolf appeared from the entrance to the left charging towards Knox. Knox grinned seeing the wolf. His secret weapon. Ronan had actually shifted to Pax to get here. Relief and excitement quickly replaced fear and panic. This girl would meet her end with Pax.

"Kill her." Knox commanded him, a gin coming across his face.

Pax stopped in his tracks, his body shaking as he moved and locked eyes with Mallory. Mallory stepped forward wiping the blood off her dagger. She then began moving towards Pax.

Shift. I need to break the bond with Knox. We will not kill or hurt. Ronan ordered.

Pax grunted and allowed Ronan to shift back. Mallory paused in her tracks as she saw Ronan. Confusion flashing in her eyes as she looked stunned.

"Why did you shift? You should have let Pax rip her throat out." Knox growled looking past Roan to Mallory.

"Kill her!" Knox screamed seeing Ronan turn away from Mallory and square up with him.

"No!" Ronan yelled at him.

"I am your Alpha! You will do as I say! I command you to kill her!" Knox screamed.

"No!" Ronan yelled as his body began to shake.

"You cannot disobey me!" Knox growled.

"I Ronan Anderson renounce you as my Alpha." Ronan said his body shaking as pain ripped through him from severing the ties to Knox.

Knox yelled and grabbed his chest as the bound was broken. He glared at Ronan, his face filled with anger.

"You renounce me for what? This girl?" Knox yelled.

"You will not hurt her." Ronan growled, stepping towards .him

"You, you are betraying me after everything! This! This was your plan. This was what you wanted! You owe me everything. If it wasn't for me you would have been left in that woods alone." Knox growled.

"I! I was the one who pulled you away from that river! The one to drag you out of your pity party after your mother died! Me!" Knox shouted.

Images of a young Knox leading a very young Ronan away from the river, his arm draped across his shoulders. Ronan could still hear Knox telling him that everything was going to be ok. That there were bigger, better things out there. Ronan shook his head trying to chase the memories away.

"It's different now. This is what you wanted. I just made the plan, but this needs to stop now." Ronan said to him firmly.

"You wanted this too! Do you hear yourself! You wanted to burn Dark Waters to the ground. Revenge for your mother. What about that? What about the revenge you needed!" Knox screamed at him, his body shaking with rage at the betrayal.

Ronan clenched his jaw, trying to not let the things Knox was screaming get to him.

"You can die right along with them, traitor." Knox said as his claws emerged from his fingertips and he swung at Ronan going for his throat.

Mallory walked through the crowd of poisoned pack members, ignoring their pleads for help. Walking by the poisoned water she paused. All these strong, ruthless wolves laying on the ground, covered in wolfsbane, pleading for her help. She gritted her teeth, pain and anger ripping through her. She cut the hose so the hose would not move around and turned the water on. Now they will be in a lake of wolfsbane and they can drown in it. Mallory thought as she continued to walk towards Knox.

The words kill, destroy every wolf. Repeated in her head. Her eyes glowing brighter with each step she took. Energy poured into her as she walked. It was like she was drawing it from somewhere. She was tapping into a source that was making her stronger, faster, and unstoppable.

"I need everyone! Someone stop her!" Knox screamed, as his strike missed Ronan's throat and slashed his cheek.

Ronan let out a roar and lunged forward hitting Knox in the gut. The two hit the ground. Knox brought his knee up as they fell and kicked Ronan away from him.

The guard holding the torch near Nora and Jace dropped it as he took off running to assist. The torch rolled towards the pile of stacked wood. As it rested against the outer wood pile, smoke began to rise. The pile turned ablaze.

Men began moving forward trying to reach her before she reached Knox. Mallory was too quick. She was by his side in no time. He knocked Asher over and into her as he tried to get away from her. There was something about this woman. The power flowing from her was almost terrifying.

Ronan tackled Knox again and they tumbled on the ground each taking blows at each other. Knox buried his claws into Ronan's side and Ronan pierced his shoulder. Mallory moving towards them caught Knox's eye. Knox slammed his fist into Ronan's face. He grabbed a handful of mud and rubbed into Ronan's eyes as he stood up getting off the ground.

Knox waved at Angela who was already moving towards them. He was frantically looking for a way out of this. He was too slow. As Mallory stepped towards him the world slowed down. She grabbed her dagger in her hand and stepped into him slamming the dagger into his throat. As the blade pierced the back of his neck, time sped back up. She pulled and the blade went clean through the other side. A fountain of blood exploded out of Knox's neck as he slumped over. Angela skidded to a halt seeing Knox decapitated.

"No!" Angela yelled, looking down at the puddle of blood quickly forming around Knox.

She turned to try to run but Mallory was too fast. Angela found herself in pain as she went to move forward. Looking down over the front of her chest there was a blade piercing through it. The front of her shirt slowly turned red as she dropped. Mallory turned her eyes on the crowd, the wolfsbane was creeping around the remaining pack members. The Alpha's were still bound and gagged in front of her. She was hit with a surge, a strange rush of power; her eyes glowed gray. She felt confused, like she was now in control of something else. Mick came running towards her, she didn't see him coming but the world slowed down telling her something was intended to harm her. She turned slowly to him, she had a blade out and was ready to run him through.

"Stop." Mallory commanded.

Mick stopped in his tracks, almost frozen. Mallory tilted her head to the side. Was he listening to her? He didn't move. She walked slowly over to him, her eyes studying him.

"Stand on one leg." Mallory said and smirked as Mick followed her instructions.

Mallory's smirk grew into a grin as she walked over to him. She wondered how far this could go.

"Stab yourself." Mallory ordered him.

"What!" Mick yelled his hand shaking as he fought the command.

"Why are you listening to me?" Mallory asked, watching him struggle.

"You killed Knox. He was our Alpha. Now you are by default we have to listen to you" Mick answered with sweat beading across his forehead, as the knife he was holding began turning towards him, his own hand turning against him.

"Hmmm. Interesting. Stab yourself somewhere fatal." Mallory laughed as she turned walking away from him.

"No. You can't make me do this." Mick yelled as Mallory tilted her head at him, watching

"Hmm…looks like I can." Mallory grinned as the knife Mick was held pressed into his chest.

"I Mick Reno-" Mick started to say but the blade pierced his chest, he could no longer hold out and his own hands plunged the knife into his heart.

Mick dropped to his knees, blood pouring out of his mouth. Mallory looked at the scene indifferent and shrugged slightly before going to turn. Mick's body fell forward, the blade pushing completely through his chest as face planted into the ground.

"Mallory!" Nora screamed trying to get her attention, there was something wrong, she would fight for her pack but Mallory was being ruthless.

Mallory looked at her and narrowed her eyes, hate flashing through them. The smoke turned black as the flame slowly began burning through the wood getting closer and closer to Nora and Jace.

Chapter Thirty One
Tragedy

Matt and Sarah raced out into the courtyard, their eyes wide seeing the destruction. Blood scattered around from the dead bodies of Knox and his pack. Matt looked out over the lake in which Cross River, Red Woods, and Moonlight pack's members were laying groaning in pain.

"Matt." Sarah whispered her eyes locked on Mallory walking to the platform.

"We need to help the packs. Free the Alpha's. Mallory will save her parents. We need to get the pack members out of that water. It's poison." Matt spit out the instructions as he shoved the keys into Sarah's hands.

"Go." He said to Sarah as he made the choice to brave the poison.

"How is she that strong?" Sarah said to him, something still not feeling right.

"I don't know but right now the packs are suffering. We need to take care of them." Matt said with his eyes locked on the hose, he needed to get the poison off of them.

Sarah rushed to the Alphas and Betas beginning to as quickly as possible unlock them from their handcuffs and chains. Once the wolfsbane was away from them they should start feeling better.

"Sarah?" Dante groaned the poison had made him so weak he was hunched over.

"It's me." Sarah smiled, taking his face in her hands after she undid his cuffs.

He grabbed her in a hug squeezing her tightly. His face then flashed with concern.

"Sarah, we need to stop Mallory. She is hell bent on killing all wolves." Dante said letting her go and going to stand.

"What?" Sarah said, her eyes scanning the courtyard as she watched Mallory get to the burning pile of wood.

Nora could tell her daughter wasn't there anymore. The hate in her eyes. She knew what it was like, how it could eat away at you. It was so hard not to give. If her pull to Jace wasn't so strong she would have gone down the same path. She looked up at the sky night had fallen and the dark over casted predicted their pending doom. The moonlight shimmered down and Nora found herself begging for help. She prayed, pleaded, and begged for the Moon Goddess's help. Mallory sat there watching the flames creep higher up the wood pile.

"You know you are the worst kind and deserve to burn." She muttered to Nora.

"You a hunter, with a wolf. You turned your back on your own kind to let them kill and destroy everything. They are nothing but dangerous animals." Mallory spat.

"Mallory, you know you are both. If you can just see past the hate. We have lived in peace for years. Not every wolf is a bloodthirsty killer." Nora said moving her foot to the outer part of the stake, the heat from the fire burning her skin.

"Our ancestors would be rolling in their graves. I am glad I do not remember you or anyone." Mallory said and she spit on the ground in disgust.

"Mallory you need to remember. This is your home." Nora begged.

"I have no home." Mallory growled.

Something wet hit her cheek. She reached up and touched the small wet droplet. Another one hit her cheek. Mallory looked up at the sky and a large raindrop hit her in the forehead. The fire began to hiss as buckets poured out of the sky. The fire was quickly being put out. She looked back at the pack members laying on the ground. The wolfsbane poisoned water had finally run out, they were laying in a lake of wolfsbane but now the rain water was washing it away. She narrowed her eyes watching a red headed man pulling people out of the poison. Mallory let out a loud sigh as anger flooded her. She locked eyes with Nora. The amount of hate coming off of Mallory made Nora's stomach twist.

"You! This is all your fault!" Mallory yelled and began climbing the pile of wood.

"Mallory baby, please listen." Nora begged her daughter.

"Stop talking to me!" Mallory yelled, drawing a sword out in front of her, pointing the blade at Nora.

"You will die with your precious wolves and I will find a way to kill the rest of them. They will all pay for what their ancestors did." Mallory vowed.

"Mallory Renee Lynn!" Jace's voice boomed from the opposite side of the pile.

"Jace." Nora whispered, she was slightly relieved seeing him up.

"Jace, it's her birthday. She's twenty one, it's the hunter curse." Nora yelled to him.

"You." Mallory tilted her head looking at him as if she recognized him.

"Mallory, we are your mother and father. You are our everything. Baby, don't you remember. You used to run through this courtyard laughing like a wild thing. Adam or Dad chasing after you. We have healed that part of the past." Nora whispered, trying to get her to see or feel something.

"You are from the wolf's blood line that started it all." Mallory said, turning from Nora ignoring everything she was saying and walking to Jace.

"Your great grandfather's father lined the streets with innocent blood. Your own father had massacres of not only his own kind but innocents." Mallory said, stopping in front of him.

"Mallory we come from a very dark past but your mother and I have stopped it all and rose above it. Mallory you are a product of that love." Jace said, trying to reach her.

"Love." Mallory said taking a step back as a memory tried to break through.

"Mallory look around. You think this is what's going to bring peace." Jace said, trying to get her to see what she was doing.

"There will be peace when there are no more wolves." Mallory said bitterly.

"Mallory, just try to remember." Jace pleaded with her.

She drew back the sword and went to lunge forward to pierce her father through the chest. She had blocked out everything and was set on one thing and one thing only. Death to all wolves.

"Mallory! No!" Nora screamed tears fell down her face as she tugged on the chains holding her to the stake.

Nora's voice echoing around the courtyard. Her pain rippled through the silence. Dante and Sarah rushed the platform trying to get there in time. Ronan stood up seeing the scene in front of him as he cleared the mud out of his eyes. He needed to get to that platform and fast. He shifted effortlessly to Pax. The white wolf ran full speed towards the platform. A white blur was all that could be seen as he leaped up on to stage.

Pax shift! Pax shift! Ronan yelled inside of their mind as his paws hit the platform.

In a blink of an eye Ronan was standing on the platform. Moving like no one had ever before. The shift takes a toll on a wolf but Ronan was moving as if nothing happened.

Mallory lunged the blade forward and Ronan jumped, blocking Jace. A pain ripped through him as the blade pierced his skin. A loud nose breaking the silence as Ronan inhaled sharply from the pain.

"What?" Mallory whispered as she saw Ronan impaled.

The fog of hate that had been clouding her eyes is lifted. Pain courses through her as tears begin to fill her eyes. Her body physically begins to react before her mind can comprehend. The world began to slowly start to flicker around her. The flickering turned into flashing and the world around her shifted. She was kneeling in a lake of blood. Her blood stained hand held tightly to a blade that she didn't recognize. She looked around her and there were dead bodies everywhere. People she didn't recognize. Their blank wide eyes staring at her. She went to move back but her hand was still attached to her blade. Her eyes followed the blade down and widened as she saw it impaled into a chest. The chest did not belong to Ronan. A man with long dark curly hair and ice blue eyes looked at her as the life faded out of his eyes She looked around, this was not her home. She was not in the courtyard. Where was she? Who was he? She felt a deep sadness wash through her as her body tried to resist it wanting to give into the rage bubbling below the surface. She shoved it down.

He looked like her father, she thought looking at the man and then as if everything snapped into place she realized the scene in front of her was something from the past. She looked down at her blood stained hands and forearms, they were not her hands. A sick feeling pitted in her stomach. This hunter finished her assignment.

"Cursed until the past is undone." A voice whispered around her as the world began to rapidly flicker around her.

In a bright flash she was back on the platform. Her eyes locked with Ronan's painful but forgiving ones.

"Ronan." Mallory whimpered as the pain of what she did washed her, her chest felt like it was going to collapse.

"It's ok, love." Ronan whispered blood starting to seep out of the corner of his mouth.

"Why?" Mallory whispered as her eyes began searching for some way to undo what she did.

"It was the only way." He smiled, the pain started to leave him as his knees got weak, he touched the blade, wrapping his hand around it and pulling it out of his chest.

As the blade left his chest a river of blood began to flow out and he crashed to his knees. Mallory crashed to her knees, her hands going to his shoulders.

"No. No. No. No." Mallory begged as tears began to slip down her cheeks.

A loud roar of an engine from the entrance of the courtyard. Headlights beaming out over the dark courtyard as Adam and the hunters began to unload out of cars. They were too late.

Images flooded her mind. Her father chased her through the courtyard from the garden. Her mother scooped her up and threw her into the air. Adam throwing rocks at her window, begging her to come out and play.

Wyatt fixing all of her scrapes and boo-boos. Images of Matt coming to her defense as she was covered in mud head to toe, he was always getting her out of trouble. Logan teaching her how to fight. Ronan, he made her feel whole…Her chest felt like it was going to crack.

"Mallory, it's ok." Ronan said his hand going to the side of her cheek as it was getting hard to hold himself up right.

"Can't you heal. Please heal. Heal, you're a wolf. Please." Mallory said, her voice cracking as she spoke.

Ronan went to say something but he could no longer hold himself up on his knees and collapsed forward. Mallory caught him in her arms and lowered him to the floor. The blood is now pooling out around him.

"No! No! I'm sorry!" Mallory screamed, her hand going to put pressure on the wound.

Ronan placed his hand on top of hers as if trying to comfort her as he closed his eyes slowly. The pain seemed to vanish.

"Hey it's ok. I didn't hurt you. Pax, didn't hurt you." Ronan said, realizing in his last moments that he had broken his own curse.

"Please!" Mallory screamed out.

Adam raced towards the platform hearing Mallory's screams and pleas. Logan not too far behind.

The world seemed to pause, everything stopped moving except Mallory. A small light began to emerge as it got closer to Mallory it got brighter. Mallory kept her hand over Ronan's wound.

"Well I am certain that if you were born back when the wars first started it would have ended quickly and there would be no wolves." The Goddess said, looking around.

"Please. Help him." Mallory whispered.

"You help him." The Goddess said with a small shrug.

"Me! He's dying! Please." Mallory demanded her eyes looking up at her.

"Yes he's bleeding out through the wound you caused him. The wound that was meant for your father. Look around Mallory. Look at the destruction you caused." The Moon Goddess snapped.

"I know!" Mallory cried out, the weight of it all crushing her.

"Well, do something about it." The Goddess sighed heavily.

"Like what!" Mallory screamed at her, anger pushing through.

"Mallory, you are the daughter of Nora and Jace. Their power runs through your blood. You are half hunter, half wolf. Dig deep and figure this out." The Goddess yelled back frustrated.

The Goddess reached forward and with the palm of her hand hit Mallory in the middle of her forehead. An image of her mother in wolf form healing her father's wounds flashed through her head. She could heal? Mallory thought as her vision cleared.

"Be careful, everything comes with a price." The Goddess said as she faded away.

The world snapped into place as she watched Ronan's eyes flutter closed. Her mind went into a panic.

"She could have freaking stayed long enough for me to figure this shit out." Mallory gritted her teeth.

Feel the energy in our core. A voice bounced around in her brain.

What? Who? Mallory whispered in surprise.

Introduction later. I will push strength to you. Use the energy to help him heal. Hurry he's dying. The voice snapped.

She could hear his heartbeat slowing, the soft beating getting further and further apart. She took a deep breath in and shut her eyes. She began to draw on something in the pit of her stomach. This energy was building and building as she focused on his wound. She then imagined the energy flowing through her hands and helping his body heal. The wound slowly began closing but his heart beat still shallow.

"Mallory, you can kill yourself if you do too much." Nora said, pulling on the chains again.

Mallory ignored her as she tried to push the energy faster into him. Hearing his heartbeat staying the same and not improving, she began to panic. She felt strength flood through her as if something inside of her had kicked into overdrive. Her body started shaking as she felt weakness settling.

Dante and Sarah had made it to the platform. Sarah rushed towards Nora, going to set her free. Nora struggled against the chains, trying desperately to get free.

"Stop her!" Nora yelled looking at Sarah, her eyes going to Mallory.

"Dante, she will kill herself trying to heal him!" Jace yelled trying to break his own chains.

Adam reached the stage and raced towards Mallory, going to pry her from Ronan. His hands grabbed her shoulders. He began to pull her back.

"No!" Mallory screamed trying to keep her hand on Ronan.

A force projected out of her sending Adam from her and everyone else flying off the stage. The force also went into Ronan. All the energy she had flew into him. As the force left her she felt herself go weak and start to feel like she would lose consciousness. Mallory looked down at Ronan as she began to get woosy. The wound was healed, she smiled faintly.

A loud gasp went through Ronan as he jolted up right. His hand went to his chest. He was shocked to see the hole gone.

"Good." Mallory said seeing him sit up and then she fell back.

"Mallory." Ronan said, turning to his side and scoping her into his arms.

"What happened? Mallory what's wrong!" He said, trying to get her to open her eyes.

"Tired." She muttered curling into him, he could hear her heartbeat slowing.

"Mallory, hey no! Stay with me." Ronan said, shaking her lightly.

"Mallory!" Nora yelled her eyes looking at her daughter going lifeless and her eyes flickered to Jace.

"Wyatt!" Jace yelled pulling on the chains, they began to break but still held him.

Logan was on the stage in no time. He rushed over to Ronan and looked at Mallory in his arms.

"Mallory!" Ronan yelled at her, shaking her again.

"I'm sorry, sorry for all of this." Mallory muttered, her lips starting to lose color.

"It's ok. Hey Rebel, stay with us ok. Wyatt's coming." Logan said looking at Jace, he was masking the worry on it.

"Mallory, stay with me!" Ronan shouted loudly.

"Hmm, you were worried about Pax hurting me." She laughed a little, her hand going to his face.

"Damn it. You. You will not leave me." Ronan said firmly.

"Be nice to him ok." Mallory said quietly as her hand fell down.

"Lay her down!" Logan yelled as Mallory's heart stopped.

Ronan laid her down on the wood platform. Adam was at the platform now.

"Adam Compressions! Ronan you're going to need to breathe for her." Logan commanded as he stood up looking to see where Wyatt was.

Ronan scooted to her face and locked eyes with Adam, his face pale white as he started to press on Mallory's chest.

"Jace." Nora yelled as Sarah began unlocking her cuffs.

"Ronan, if you are her mate, mark her!" Jace yelled, his eyes locking with Nora, the same scene playing out in front of him as it did years ago, when Nora saved them from the Lobos. Only this time instead of it being Jace and Nora it was his daughter. Jace's stomach sank watching.

Ronan went to shake his head no. Years of telling himself he did not have a mate or deserve one flashing through his mind. He looked down at a lifeless Mallory; he could feel part of himself dying with her. A low growl came from the other side of Mallory. Adam pulled Mallory up off the ground and thrusted her into Ronan. Moonlight floated down over them as the rain turned to a trickle and then stopped. The Moonlight reflected on Mallory as if lighting the spot Ronan was to mark her. Ronan felt his fangs come down.

Mark her and save her. A voice said, it seemed to float around him in the moonlight.

"*H*ello again." Her voice was as musical as it was the first time.

"I'm dead?" Mallory asked the Goddess with a small shrug as she walked to her.

"Almost." The Goddess answered with a small smile.

"Are they ok?" Mallory said with pain in her voice.

"They will be. You may have hurt a lot of them but the only ones that were fatal were the ones that needed to be." The Moon Goddess said, beginning to walk away.

"Hey wait!" Mallory said and followed after her

As she walked the room became more and more filled with light. She followed the Goddess over to a stone area and in the center was a large fountain that flowed down into a pound. She looked down at the water.

"You are nothing like your mother or father." The Goddess said her tone even with no emotions in it.

"I know." Mallory said her voice full of disappointment.

"You were unstoppable when your memories were gone. When you had no attachment to anything. A ruthless killing machine." The Goddess said again mono toned.

"I hurt a lot of people." Mallory admitted her voice ashamed.

"You can't help the curse. It was meant to do what it did. You can help your actions now. " The Goddess said, putting her hand down into the water.

"I'm dead." Mallory said, unsure of what she was talking about.

"You saved him." The Goddess said quietly.

"I know it's the reason I am here." Mallory said, confused.

"No, you broke his curse, the one that plagued his family. For generations his bloodline killed their mates. He locked his wolf away in hopes he would never have to deal with him. No connection, no bond. Pax is not like the wolves in his family history. He did not deserve that. Ronan had to give in to him and trust him to get to you in time. That was unlike anything I had seen before. The shift, the communication. For a wolf that had been locked away for so long not be feral and stay in control. Truly remarkable." The Goddess said impress.

Mallory was silent. She didn't know what to say. She felt like an absolute failure all the way around. Her mother resisted the hunter's curse. Saved the world twice. She just almost ruined an entire race in a few hours.

"Your mother was too perfect." The Goddess chuckled as if she heard Mallorys thoughts.

"She may have prolonged the curses but it was waiting for you. The unbroken part. You see, no one knew about Ronan's family line. It was not Jace's family that caused the massacres that led to the humans cursing wolf kind. Ronan's family was the pack that was set to marry your mothers. The young man was infatuated with your great great great grandmother. Her beauty overwhelmed him and the anger, lust, and hate consumed him. He took his revenge on the humans. He then laid blame on Jace's great great great grandfather hoping the humans would take his pack out. The curse touched his line as well, cursing their wolves to hate anything that they love. You see this had to happen this way. Your mother fought fate so hard and if Lance would have shown up sooner we may have not had to wait till you to fix everything. You not having a wolf or hunter side made you vulnerable. You had to go with fate. The odds were against you." The Goddess explained.

"So this was one whole big game! You let all of this happen! You're a Goddess for fuck sake you could just wave your hand and undo it." Mallory yelled at her.

"Curses need to be broken, not undone." The Goddess snapback.

"Well I did nothing but play your game. Congratulations." Mallory said, going to turn and walk away.

"You did something. You broke Ronan's curse effortlessly and you fought at the end. Your sacrifice broke the remaining pieces of the curse. Blood for blood. There is just one last piece." The Goddess said and moved her hand.

"I am not doing-" Mallory started to say but then something moved out of the shadows.

"Mallory." It spoke walking out.

A bright silver wolf that seemed to shimmer walked out. Mallory instantly felt the pull and connection. Her wolf. She had waited years feeling useless and defected all this time. She walked over to her and placed her head against her hand.

"Aurora." Aurora said her name as she pressed further into Mallory's hand.

"She is mine?" Mallory asked, running her hand over Aurora.

"Yes, the last piece, the wolf locked away, freed. The Goddess smiled.

The wolf shimmered and seemed to melt into Mallory. Mallory looked confused but could still feel her there. She went to ask the Goddess what good this was if she was dead when a pain went through her, her hand shot up to her neck. She looked to the Goddess.

"About time. Your mate is saving you." The Goddess motioned for her to come here.

"Saving me?" Mallory asked, walking over to the fountain.

"When you mark your mate it's not just saying you belong to one another. Your hearts are bound. It's why a wolf can die of a broken heart when their mate dies." The Goddess said with a wink.

"I don't think I should go back." Mallory whispered, she had caused so much chaos and hurt to so many how could they ever forgive her.

"So I'm-" Mallory started to say.

"You have a big mess to clean up." The Goddess laughed and then shoved her into the fountain.

Chapter Thirty Two
Full Circle

Ronan sunk his teeth down into her flesh, the taste of her blood flooded his mouth as he pulled back. As he pulled back letting his canines out of her, a light burst through the courtyard coming from out of Mallory. The white light was blinding. Ronan held on to her tightly as he shut his eyes. A surge of energy flies through everyone in the courtyard. The force healing anyone hurt or poisoned. As the light dimmed the pack member once in horrible pain and laying on the ground began to stand as if nothing had ever happened. The packs began to move towards the platform.

Ronan opened his eyes slowly and looked down at Mallory. His arms held her tightly to him. He clenched his jaw as nothing happened.

"No, you do not get to leave." Ronan said, looking down at her.

"You! You come back now." Ronan demanded as he looked down at her perfect face.

He heard movement around him and he let out a low growl. Wyatt made his way up to the platform with his heart in his stomach. Sarah quickly unchained Jace and he moved towards them. Ronan backed away with Mallory growling, his eyes glowing bright white.

"That is my daughter!" Jace bellowed.

"My mate." Ronan growled back.

"My mate." Ronan repeated, his chest shaking as the words leaked from his soul.

She was his mate. She died because she was his mate. No Pax didn't kill her and he didn't hurt her but she died saving him.

"Enough!" Nora yelled, they both stopped and looked at her.

"Wyatt. Ronan, let Wyatt check her." Nora begged her voice broke as she spoke.

Ronan shook his head no. He didn't want to know. If he held on to her then no could confirm what the pain in his chest was telling him. Wyatt moved towards him and Pax pushed forward, sending him strength. Wyatt put his hands up as if to say he didn't mean any harm.

"No. No. No one is going to tell me she's-" Ronan stopped talking and then locked eyes with Nora.

"No one is taking her from me." Ronan growled.

"I will pry her from your dead body." Jace growled, stepping forward, Nora reached out to stop him.

"That is the only way you will get her." Ronan vowed, getting ready to fight Jace.

"I've caused enough damage." Mallory whimpered as she curled into Ronan.

"Mallory?" Ronan whispered his arms going around her.

"Mallory." Jace whispered, kneeling down just by Ronan.

"I'm so sorry. I am so, so sorry." Mallory whispered into Ronan's chest.

"It's ok. Everyone is ok." Ronan said quickly his eyes flickering around to each person daring someone to save differently.

"Ronan, I killed you. I almost killed my father. I was going to let the pack drown and my mother burn." Mallory said, pulling back from him.

"Mallory, that wasn't you." Nora said, coming to stand next to Jace.

"I thought I mended the hunter curse all those years ago when my love for your father won." Nora said her tone disappointed in herself.

"The Goddess said you're too perfect. She needed someone less perfect to mend all curse." Mallory said, shaking her head.

"Less perfect." Mallory laughed angrily at herself, thinking about how much she messed up.

"There were more?" Nora asked, looking at Jace.

"Cursed until the past could be undone." Mallory said out loud, clicking in place.

"The past?" Nora whispered.

Mallory nodded finally understanding and put her hand to Ronan's face and a small smile on her lips.

"You broke your family's curse when you trusted Pax." Mallory said to him.

"I didn't break anything. You still died." Ronan said, his voice filling with anger.

"That wasn't you. That was me, breaking the rest of the hunter's curse. I couldn't let you die. We had to go through what our families before caused." Mallory whispered.

"Who's your father?" Jace said his tone was still very firm and filled with fight.

"Lance from Dark Water." Ronan spat out.

"Lance!" Jace growled, going forward.

"Jace no!" Nora said, grabbing him by his arm.

"He is Lance's son!" Jace yelled, looking at Nora like she was crazy.

"He is our daughter's mate. He saved her life. He brought her out of the hunter's curse." Nora yelled at Jace.

"He is still-

"Are you your father's son?" Nora said, narrowing her eyes.

"Yes but-" Jace started and Nora cut him off.

"Are you like your father?" Nora said, stopping in his tracks.

"I didn't know my father. I was left with a pack of rogues before he slaughtered my mother." Ronan said quietly.

"Lance's bloodline was cursed to kill their mates as punishment for starting the war. It was not Dad's family that slaughtered the village. It was Lance's family. It was meant to be blamed on Dad's. Lance's side was betrothed to Mom's side. The jealousy and anger is what was passed on. The original hunter did kill her mate and wipe out a large portion of wolves. I had to live through that and chose to do it differently." Mallory explained.

"She didn't tell me." Nora said, looking at the moon, almost angry.

"We need to start tending to the injured and I have a lot of apologies and forgiveness to beg from the packs." Mallory said shift in Ronan's arms.

"Mallory when you crossed realms. You healed everyone." Nora whispered to her as if it hurt to say.

"I. What? How?" Mallory said, now really looking at her father's face, the cracked jaw, broken nose, were all lined and straight.

The burns on her mothers wrists and feet were gone. She looked over Ronan's shoulder and the pack members were no longer where the lake of poison was. She looked around confused.

"You are your mother's daughter." Jace whispered quietly.

"So now what." Mallory asked quietly.

Ronan kept his grip on her afraid to let her go. His eyes glanced at Jace who seemed to have relaxed. If he needed to, he would do whatever it took to make Mallory ok.

"Home?" Nora whispered, holding her hand out to Mallory.

Mallory wrapped her hand around Ronan's and with the other took her mother's as she stood. A glow began to radiate around Mallory more brightly than anyone had witnessed before. The packs around her began to glow with amber eyes. They all bowed their heads to her as they did. Mallory locked eyes with her father, a small smile on his lips as he bent his head slightly. Aurora pushed forward in her, her eyes glowing bright amber. Ronan felt Pax move forward as he sensed Aurora, excitement coursing through him as he now could meet his other half.

"Wait." Mallory whispered, she looked up at the sky waiting for a sign that what she was about to do was right.

A shooting star whipped across the sky as if telling her to go for it.

"I Mallory Renee Lynn Knight give the titles back. I name Jace Knight as Alpha of Cross River. Asher Cross as Alpha of Red Wood, and Zeke Warren Alpha of Moonlight. We will resume the council working as one." Mallory said and she caught her father raising an eyebrow.

"We do not need one all powerful person. That leaves too much to chance. We need to be united. Powerful together. Safety in numbers." Mallory told him.

"That's my girl." Jace said moving forward and kissing the top of her head.

"Home." Mallory said and pulled Ronan towards her, as if saying he was coming too.

"I-" Jace said, eyeing him, Nora slipped her arm through Jace's small giggle escaping her.

"He is her mate." Nora continued.

"I didn't agree to it." Jace mumbled letting Nora lead him down the platform.

Mallory watched her parents move across the courtyard. She squeezed Ronan's hand.

"This could be your home." She said quietly.

"Charming." Ronan smirked looking around at the destruction.

"It's ok to be scared." Mallory smirked.

"Seeing the destruction you caused. You're lucky I am still here." Ronan jokes.

"Come on." Mallory said going to tug him but Ronan stayed put.

There was more commotion coming from the south entrance to the courtyard. Ronan stepped in front of Mallory protectively. He watched Kai walking in with some of the rogues and the rest of moonlight.

"Damn it." Ronan said moving forward away from Mallory and across the platform.

Kai stand down. Ronan mind link him.

Kai looked at him and shrugged as if he wasn't sure what he meant. The packs in the courtyard began to surround them.

"Ronan, I'm sorry I couldn't do it." Kai announced.

Jessica from Moonlight came out from behind him putting her hand on his shoulder and letting everyone know it was ok.

"Thank god." Ronan muttered, Mallory came up behind him and wove her fingers into his.

Mallory watched everyone reunite as she looked around her eyes and fell on Adam. Her chest hurt for him. They had always planned for them to be each others mates.

"Hey, I need to go talk to Adam." Mallory said to Ronan going to unlock her fingers from Ronan's.

"But do you?" Ronan grumbled looking over at Adam.

"Yeah, he's my best friend." Mallory said tugging on his hand.

"Fine." Ronan muttered and kissed her on the forehead.

Mallory took a deep breath and walked over to him, she was nervously playing with her fingers as she got to him.

"Hey." Mallory said quietly.

"Don't have a knife on you do you?" Adam smirked a little.

Ronan let out a growl from where he was standing. Mallory already felt bad enough. Adam made a face at Ronan to tell him to shut up. Ronan began to move towards him but Mallory shot him a look telling him to stop.

"I am so sorry." Mallory flinched at his comment but Adam waved her off.

"I know. I'm just…just." Adam let out a long sigh.

"I'm glad you're ok." Adam whispered.

"I know and I am so sorry." Mallory said again.

"You can't change what the Moon Goddess decides. I just wish I would have been the one." Adam said with a shrug.

"I know. You will find your one." Mallory said, stepping forward and placing her hand on his shoulder.

Ronan growled behind them and began to step forward towards them.

"Your naked mate is irritating but although annoying, I can see why he is your mate." Adam sighed, rolling his eyes at Ronan.

"Listen pretty boy you're not going to win me over with your words. Hurry up and find your own damn mate." Ronan said, coming over and pulling Mallory into him.

"Um he's right about you being naked." Mallory said in her voice trying to hide embarrassment.

"Well I had other things to worry about other than clothing." Ronan shrugged, he was not embarrassed at all.

"Kai clothes." Ronan yelled over his shoulder.

"You're not his Beta anymore." Mallory laughed.

"Actually I am. Knox is dead but I renounced my loyalty to him, not Shadow Pack." Ronan smirked.

"Yeah but there's no Alpha." Mallory said confused as Kai ran up the platform a strawberry blond hair girl following behind him.

Roan went quiet for a second thinking, she really didn't know. All the power she was giving off. He needed to know what her intentions were before he told her.

"The rogues. I…I have been a rogue my whole life. What is to happen to them? They were just following orders." Ronan asked cautiously.

"You know, you didn't seem to care so much about others when I first met you." Mallory said, studying him.

Ronan shrugged, not really answering. It was honestly her fault. He was so shut down and closed off before her.

"They will be given the option of becoming part of a pack or staying in rogue life. Anyone threatening or dangerous will be threatened or taken care of. My father is…protective." Mallory said quietly.

"Ok. Do I have those options?" Ronan said quietly.

"Yes." Mallory said the word, hurting her as she spoke it, afraid of what he would say.

"There is an Alpha of Shadow pack." Ronan chuckled as he looked at Mallory.

"Who?" Mallory asked him confused.

Ronan stepped into her, his hand caught her wrist as he pulled her towards him. Mallory became flushed as she went towards his naked self.

"You." Ronan whispered in her ear, his breath tickling her ear lobe.

"Me!" Mallory said her embarrassment disappeared from her face and field with concern.

"Yes Alpha, you." Ronan whispered quietly into her, loving the shades of red crossing her face.

"No…I can't." Mallory began looking around her as if she would find an answer.

"You killed Knox, you inherited the role." Ronan smirked and paused thinking.

"So what are you going to be my Luna?" Mallory smirked.

"I'll be anything you want." Ronan winked at her, the smirk made him want to throw her over his shoulder and take her away.

"Excuse me…Beta. Your clothes." Kai said, interrupting them.

"Thanks and explain." Ronan said shortly, letting go of Mallory and began getting dressed.

"I couldn't do it. Kill the Luna of Moonlight. All the blood shed. I just wanted a way out. I joined Shadow Pack before I didn't fit in anywhere. I thought it was a place I could belong to but I didn't sign up for this." Kai said quietly.

Mallory tilted her head at Kai's state. It hit her in her chest. The statement resonated deep within her. She had felt that all her life. From not having a wolf to no super powers. She had such shoes to fill and didn't even come close. The night sky seemed to flicker.

"Ok." Mallory whispered out loud as she understood the sign.

"Kai Shadow Pack might be a place where you could still belong. Let's get everyone situated. Kai you are now Gamma of Shadow Pack. We will figure out everything else, later." Mallory said firmly.

Kai's eyes glowed as the title became his, he felt a wave go through him and he looked at her confused.

"Me?" Kai asked quietly.

"Yes you. You're not afraid to say what's right from wrong." Mallory smiled.

Ronan smiled proudly as he held Mallory. She let out a small sigh. He felt safe, he made her feel like she belonged.

"Thank you Alpha." Kai said, bowing his head.

"You're welcome." Mallory smiled.

"Who are you?" Adam came up behind Ronan asking the question.

Ronan tensed up ready to fight Adam if needed. Pax growled inside of him thinking he was questioning Mallory.

"Me?" The small voice came out from behind Kai.

Haley had followed him across the way. She was the first person at Moonlight that sized him up. She then began guarding him. Kai thought it was funny and almost cute. She was on his tail since they left Moonlight.

"Yes." Adam said his whole body language changed as the girl became flushed in the cheeks.

"Haley." She said quietly, trying to look away from him but couldn't.

Kai looked behind him, he didn't realize the girl had followed me. He moved completely out of the way.

"Mate." Haley said her flying over her mouth as the words came out.

"Mate." Adam confirmed back, taking a step towards.

Mallory's face lit up as she moved backwards into Ronan making Ronan push away, so Adam could be closer to Haley.

"What pack are you with?" Adam asked, stepping closer to her.

"Moonlight." She whispered her big green eyes looking up from the ground shyly.

"How have we not crossed paths?" Adam whispered.

"Alpha Zeke is my uncle, I was away, my mother left the pack several years ago to be with a human and she got sick." Haley explained.

"Ok well, we will leave you to get to know your mate. Adam, maybe check in with Zeke, see how everyone from his pack is doing. Let him know his niece is your mate?" Mallory smiled big.

"That actually sounds good." Adam nodded and offered his arm to Haley.

Haley blushed and wrapped her arm around his as they began walking off. Mallory felt an instant relief as Adam found his mates. She let out a sigh as she watched them walk.

"So you're going to stay Alpha?" Ronan asked, studying her.

"I think so. Something tells me this is what I'm supposed to do." Mallory said quietly, looking out over the now empty courtyard.

"Well you've kind of weeded out the bad eggs already." Ronan smirked and nodded to Knox, Angela's and Mick's bodies.

"Funny." Mallory said as she took his hand into hers and began walking.

"Where are we going?" Ronan asked, confused.

"It's late, I can't repair any more damage tonight. I want a shower and bed." Mallory said, leading Ronan out of the courtyard.

Chapter Thirty Three
End

*T*he night faded quickly into day. Mallory was up looking out the window watching the sunrise. She had been waiting for what seemed hours. As if the sunshine could erase the nightmare she caused the night before. She saw her parents briefly before turning in. Her father grumbled about Ronan following her up to the room but right now Ronan was the only thing that felt stable. The only thing she felt sure of. She still had to face the pack, her parents, and sort through Shadow pack. She let out the breath she was holding as the sunlight scattered across the floor. She was thankful she only killed Knox, Angela, and Mick. Images of her mother tied to a stake while she watched fire creep towards her. All of the emotions she didn't feel in the moment were rushing into her. Her chest tightened, her stomach twisted inside of her. She felt all of it now. The blinded hate buried her and blocked everything. The weight of it all was now crushing her. The image of her father begging her to think about what she was doing and fight. The sword, she could feel the weight of it in her hand.

She could feel the weight of the blade she was holding as she pushed it through Ronan's skin, she felt it all. Her insides flopping and wiggling inside of her, making her feel sick. She understood it was something that had to be done but it still made her guts twist and wrench as if she was going to vomit them all up. She felt the back of her neck get hot and she could feel her hands shake. She shut her eyes trying to breathe.

How was she going to face all this? How was she going to be an Alpha? She felt like a failure for so long and now her chance to prove herself was happening and she wanted to disappear. Could she do this? She felt like she couldn't breathe. The inside of her head was filled with own screams. Her body was vibrating. Then peace wrapped around her. Her chest began to feel like it could move again. Her breathing began to regulate and the noise in her head slowly started to become quiet. She leaned into him as his presence grounded her.

"You're ok." His voice whispered in her ear, his voice chasing the rest of the feelings away.

She shut her eyes, the words you're ok making her body actually believe them. She took a deep breath in. He felt her relax in his arms, the tension leaving her body. He suddenly turned her around, her eyes opening as she spun in his arms. His right hand caught her hip and steading her, his left hand going to her chin. His eyes looked into her eyes.

"It's gonna be ok." Ronan said to her firmly.

"Just because you've said it twice doesn't mean that I can do all this." Mallory said her voice shaking a little as the feelings started to come rushing back.

"You can do this. I will be with you every step of the way if this is something you want." Ronan said as if there was no doubt.

"Something Is telling me this is what I have to do." Mallory sighed.

"Then you'll do it and I'll kill anyone that gets in your way." Ronan swore.

Mallory laughed instantly, feeling better. Ronan's eyes darkened as he stepped into her more. Her laughter turned into a small smile.

"You say kill like you mean it." She said trying to avoid how flushed her body was feeling from his gaze.

"I mean it. One hundred percent of the time." He growled his hand moving to the back of her neck as he pulled her in for a kiss.

The kiss melted her and set her on fire all at once. His hand moved down over her ass squeezing it as he deepened the kiss, a small moan escaped her mouth as it vibrated against his mouth. He growled back in response, breaking the kiss and his mouth began moving down her neck. Seeing her mark made him want her even more. His lips brushed over her fresh mark and she felt her knees wobbly. She inhaled sharply as she clung to him.

Three knocks came from the bedroom door and Ronan growled, the vibration of the noise buzzed across her skin causing her to shiver, her body wanting her to ignore the knocking.

"Mallory." Nora's voice came through the door as she knocked again.

"Shit, it's my mom." Mallory said, pushing Ronan lightly.

"So.." Ronan grumbled and buried his face in her neck.

"No..really." Mallory responded breathlessly.

"Fine but you sound like a teenager." Ronan smirked, stepping back.

"Shut up." Mallory said, making a face at him.

"Come in." Mallory yelled to the door.

"Mallory we need to…to..talk." Nora said, taken back by Ronan standing so close to Mallory.

"I know…I really don't know what to say. I-" Mallory started to say.

"No, it's fine. We need to meet about Shadow Pack and your new title." Nora said quietly.

"Yeah I know, we should call a meeting, is Asher and Zeke still here?" Mallory asked for processing.

"Yes, the hunters are here too. Logan apologies for his crew showing up late… for once. We're going to be in the hall. I figure you could come down with..Ronan..right?" Nora said his eyes went from Mallory to Ronan.

"Ronan." He answered by holding his hand out to her.

"Nora." Nora smiled, shaking his hand back.

"Ok well get dressed and we will see you in the conference room." Nora smiled at them as she nodded to her daughter and stepped out of the room as quickly as she came in.

Nora took a deep breath walking out the door. The world felt like it was spinning. Everything happened so quickly, the takeover, Mallory shifting, the destruction, and now her daughter was an Alpha to a group of rogues that tried to undo everything they had built. Her mate was their Beta and the mastermind of the plan. She knew that he had saved her and saved them but Zara grumbled inside of her. She made her way to the conference room where Jace was waiting at the door for her. He could feel every emotion rolling off of her. Without saying a word he scooped her into a hug, trying to drain it all away from her.

"It's a lot." Nora whispered, still trying to remain strong.

"It will be ok." Jace said, placing his lips to her forehead.

"I know." Nora whispered back, shutting her eyes as he kissed her.

"She's coming down in a second…with Ronan. Behave." Nora said, touching his cheek lightly.

"Mmm." Jace grunted as he tensed up.

"Seriously, come on." She said, shaking her head as her hand grabbed his hand. She took a breath in as she turned the door open to the conference room.

Asher and Zeke were talking amongst themself, Logan had a very angry look on his face. Nora shot him a weird look when she walked in and he frowned deeper. Nora raised an eyebrow at him worried now that he looked upset. Jace eyed Zeke and Asher as they sat up when he walked into the room.

"What's going on?" Jace asked flat out.

"Jace…Nora…you know we have the utmost respect for you and everything you and your family have sacrificed over the years." Zeke started.

"Cut through the bullshit and say what you have to say Zeke." Jace said, stepping up to the table, his eyes glowing.

"Mallory." Zeke started to say but the growl that came from Jace shook the table.

"Jace, he's just trying to say-" Asher started to talk.

"You're just trying to tell them that their daughter being Alpha of Shadow pack is a problem." Logan said now also up on his feet, eyes glaring at Zeke and Asher.

"Logan, that's not what we were saying." Asher said quickly.

"Then you better fucking clarify quickly." Jace growled his hands pressed into the table.

"We are just saying that Shadow pack is dangerous." Zeke said quietly.

"Well then I guess it's a good thing their Alpha is my daughter." Jace growled.

"Your daughter-" Zeke started to say when the door to the room opened and a loud angry growl bursted through it.

All three Alphas bowed up ready to fight. Nora reached over and grabbed Jace's hand, stopping him. Her eyes scanning the room as a very angry Ronan stood in the doorway blocking Mallory from them. Mallory stepped in front of Ronan, blocking his way as her hand touched his wrist.

"His daughter almost killed you all. Wanted to kill you all. Almost succeeded. I didn't. I was sucked into a curse, which none of you can imagine what that feels like. Something I had to go through because of a past that linked my family. I broke that curse and others. I don't expect you to completely forget what I did but I can't undo it either. All I can say is that yes Shadow pack was deadly and so was I. But aren't we all? My mother single handedly took down a super race of mutants. My father's rage and strength is deadly. Asher I've seen you fight and Zeke your well spoken mannerism do not cover up your reputation. Logan you have a name for yourself as well." Mallory said, looking at each of them.

"Mallory, we are not saying you are to blame. There are others though that we need-" Zeke started to say eyeing Ronan.

"Without him you would all be dead. He is the only reason any of you are alive. Not only did he break the hunter's curse but he had arranged an undoing of all his plans. Jessica and Hannah both would be dead. He made sure they lived." Mallory growled her eyes glowing bright white as she stepped towards Zeke.

The power rolling off of her was felt in waves as Zeke tried his best not to lower his head, since he was the main target of the blow. Ronan stepped up to Mallory and touched her shoulder lightly.

"Mallory, tell us what you intend to do? What's the plan for Shadow pack and you being Alpha?" Asher asked quietly, he could feel Jace being just as angry as Ronan and Nora was surprisingly suppressing her emotions.

"I am going to stay Alpha." Mallory said firmly, glancing at her father.

"Are you sure that is something you want to do?" Jace asked, trying to hide his own feelings.

"Yes. The Shadow pack needs someone who understands. They are all misfits and need guidance. They are not all bad. The few that were leading were bad and are now gone. Red Woods should understand that." Mallory said, looking at Asher.

"Damn." Logan smirked looking at all of them, proud of Mallory for calling Asher out.

A small smile went across Nora's face and a proud one on Jace's. Mallory had a point and everyone in the room had a past.

"I will meet with the members of Shadow pack. The ones that wish to remain with me will stay until we find land and a pack area. The ones who don't will be asked to leave or worse. They can choose to stay rogues but they will not be permitted to be a threat." Mallory continued.

"Hunters back, you Rebel." Logan smiled, throwing a wink at her.

"As does Cross River, you may stay here until you have your pack and land sorted." Jace said, squeezing her shoulder lightly.

"Red Woods came from a bad place, your family brought it out of it and saved it. You will do the same for

Shadow pack, Red Woods is behind you." Asher said with a small nod.

"Moonlight will back this decision as well but we will not hesitate to step in if this goes south…even if you are Jace and Nora's daughter." Zeke said calmly.

"That is the expectation of all of the packs is to uphold the others and make sure we are not a harm to each other or other kinds." Mallory said with a nod.

"Well then it settled and you will also have a seat on the council. We will need to inform the other packs and let them know." Nora said quietly, looking at everyone.

"We have land." Ronan spoke up behind Mallory.

"You have land? Where?" Jace asked curiously.

"Between Red Woods and Silver Mountain." Ronan said quietly, he had been trained for years not to tell a soul.

"In the Dark Woods?" Jace asked, his eyebrows frowning.

"In the place where the forest is so thick there is no sunlight?" Asher asked, looking at Ronan like it was unbelievable.

"Perfect place to never be found." Ronan said smugly.

"Is it set up for pack lands?" Zeke asked, a little amazed that they had been surviving in the Dark Woods.

"Mhmm." Ronan said annoyed with the questioning.

"Ok great, we have pack lands and now we need to meet the pack. Making progress." Mallory said before the questioning turned ugly.

"Let's go meet the pack, we can use Cross River's hall. I am sure Zeke and Asher would like to get home." Mallory said quietly.

She grabbed ahold of Ronan's hand and went to set forward. Jace and Nora both reached forward and touched Mallory to stop her from leaving. The world flickered around her as she stopped. The sound was sucked out of the air and she was left in a blurred state. Then the fog disappeared.

She was no longer in the conference room. She was surrounded by trees that seemed to go on forever as they reached up to the sky. She immediately knew they were in the Dark Woods. It was true that it was so dark you could not see the sunlight. Ronan had her by the hand leading her through it. Finally light came sparkling down from the tree tops and they were in a clearing. They walked into the pack lands and it was like walking into an enchanted village. The sun made all of the tops of the house sparkle, the roof tops were made out of copper. The pack greeted them happy to see them, they all bowing to her at her arrival. She felt like she belonged. Ronan squeezed her hand and began to show her around.

The world flickered once more and faded to a new scene. She was in Cross River's garden. Laughter filled the air as she walked around remembering the garden she used to play in.

"Has Ronan built you one yet?" Her mother's voice came from behind her.

"He says he has a surprise for…the baby." Mallory said, pausing and placing her hand on her growing belly.

"I bet that's what it is. You loved this garden." Nora smiled, squeezing her arm.

"All the kids loved it and still do." Mallory laughed and nodded to her father chasing a dark-haired boy around the fountain.

"He's gonna fall in." Malllory smirked.

"Jace!" Nora yelled and the two stopped running and looked at her.

"What?" They both yelled.

"Jace, do not push Dad-

There was a loud shriek as the dark-haired boy shoved Jace into the fountain.

"Into the fountain." Nora laughed, shaking her head.

"Told you. Dad never learns." Mallory joined in laughing.

"Mallory." Ronan's concerned voice broke through to her and she blinked.

She was back in current time, she shook her head lightly. She felt a strong sense of calmness rush over her and she knew she was doing the right thing.

"Sorry, I guess I'm still tired." She smiled at him.

"You ok?" Ronan asked, touching her cheek, his eyes filled with concern.

"Perfect now." Mallory smiled brightly.

"Let's go meet our pack." Mallory smiled with a nod.

"Ok." Ronan said looking at her funny but mimicked her smile.

"Jace, are you ok?" Zeke asked, walking up to him as he watched Mallory start walking to the door.

"Yeah. I had some doubts but hearing her and seeing her just now. This is what she is meant for." Jace said firmly.

"What about Cross River? Who will be the next Alpha if it isn't Mallory?" Zeke asked quietly.

"My brother will be." Mallory said from the doorway looking at her mother.

Nora smiled softly and put her hand to her belly. Jace looked at her confused and Nora nodded yes. Jace stepped quickly around Zeke and rushed to Nora. His hand went to her belly.

"We're kind of old to be doing this again." Jace laughed.

"You'll be just fine Dad…don't play too close to the fountain." Mallory laughed

Author's note:

This is the last book in The Alpha's War Series. Follow me on FaceBook S.E Dymek for updates on upcoming books. As well as instagram and Tik Tok sedymek. My website which also has events listed is Sedymek.com.

Upcoming novel: Falling in Love with Death

What if you were a beacon for death? You could always feel it around you and on some weird level it was comforting. I mean aren't we all just one wrong turn, wrong step, one close call from meeting death? But what if death didn't want you? What if he did but couldn't have you?